The Arcane Chronicles: Volume 3

CW01080646

A role-playing game support book, containing the lands of Em

Welcome to the third tome of the Arcane Chronicles, where y[...] [...]yers on incredible adventures filled with danger, intrigue, and excitement! In this book, you will find details of the lands of Emberfrost, from Frostfall to Sunfire Dominion.

This volume details the lands, the key residents, histories, economics, demographics, all to immerse your players further in to the world your campaigns. There are over 50 adventure hooks for your players continued adventures.

As with the first two volumes of The Arcane Chronicles, these details are non-system specific, therefore you should easily be able to fit the information contained herein to support any fantasy role playing game campaign.

Are you ready to embark on an epic journey? Gather your fellow adventurers, sharpen your weapons, and ready your spells, for the world of fantasy awaits. Let the adventure begin!

The Guardian of the Chronicles

Contents

Preface

Welcome to this volume of The Arcane Chronicles fantasy role playing game supplement, where we explore the lands of Emberfrost. While the focus of this book revolves around the dynamics of a human-centric and quasi-medieval feudal society, it is important to note that the content within is versatile and adaptable to various fantasy role-playing game systems.

The lands depicted in these pages draws inspiration from a medieval framework, where the social, political, and cultural aspects of human civilization take centre stage. We delve into a realm of knights, lords, ladies, and peasants, exploring the intricate web of relationships, hierarchies, and obligations that shape this quasi-feudal society.

However, it is crucial to emphasize that the contents of this volume are not limited solely to the human-centric setting presented. The concepts, rules, and lore provided herein can be readily customized and transplanted into any fantasy role-playing game of your choice.

Whether your game system embodies a different culture, era, or species, the principles outlined within this book serve as a foundation to build upon. You have the freedom to adapt and modify the material to suit your desired setting, seamlessly integrating the concepts of land rights, trial by combat, or other aspects of 'feudal' life into your unique gaming experience.

Consider this volume as a toolkit, a repository of ideas, rules, and guidelines that can be employed to enrich your fantasy role-playing adventures. It provides a starting point from which you can mould and shape your own unique world, injecting it with the desired flavour and atmosphere that suits your gaming group's preferences.

Embark upon this journey with an open mind and a creative spirit. Unleash your imagination, customize these concepts to your liking, and let the rich tapestry of your own fantasy realm unfold before you. May the adventures that await within these pages inspire and ignite your gaming sessions with excitement, intrigue, and endless possibilities.

Now, let us venture forth into the realms of fantasy and forge unforgettable tales that will be cherished for generations to come.

The Guardian of the Chronicles

Introduction

As a games master, weaving the intricate web of relationships, hierarchies, and obligations in the realm of Emberfrost can add depth and realism to the players' experience. Here are some suggestions on how to accomplish this:

1. **Quests and Missions:** Design quests and missions that require players to interact with various NPCs from different social classes. They might be tasked with helping a noble resolve a dispute with a neighbouring lord, or assisting a peasant village with a threat from a wild creature. This will expose the players to different perspectives and social dynamics.

2. **Social Events:** Arrange social gatherings, feasts, and tournaments where players can interact with knights, lords, and ladies in a more relaxed setting. This provides an opportunity for players to build alliances, make enemies, and forge friendships within the noble circles.

3. **Feudal Obligations:** Emphasize the feudal system's obligations and responsibilities. Lords might request their knights to perform specific tasks, and knights, in turn, may call upon their vassals for support. This creates a sense of duty and loyalty within the hierarchy.

4. **Class Conflicts:** Introduce conflicts between different social classes, such as tensions between the nobles and the commoners or rivalries between knights of different lieges. These conflicts can drive plotlines and character development.

5. **Intrigue and Politics:** Incorporate political intrigue and power struggles within the noble courts. Players can be drawn into conspiracies, secret alliances, and machinations that affect the balance of power in Emberfrost.

6. **Peasant Life:** Allow players to experience the life of the commoners. They might have to navigate challenges faced by peasants, such as harsh living conditions, bandit raids, or unfair treatment by local lords.

7. **Chivalric Code:** Explore the concept of chivalry and how it impacts the knights' behaviour and interactions with others. Players might be put in situations where they must choose between upholding their honour and following their liege's orders.

8. **Interconnected Stories:** Create storylines that interconnect characters of different social classes. Players from various backgrounds can find common goals and motivations, encouraging collaboration and camaraderie.

9. **Rising through the Ranks:** Allow players to advance in social status. A peasant might have the chance to become a squire, then a knight, earning the respect of nobles or even being granted a title.

10. **Consequences of Actions:** Emphasize that the characters' choices and actions have consequences within the social structure. Honourable deeds might gain them favour, while dishonourable acts could lead to ostracism or even open conflict.

By integrating these elements into the gameplay, the games master can create a rich and immersive world of Emberfrost, where players can explore the complexities of its society, forge alliances, and leave a lasting impact on the realm's future.

Volumes 1 and 2 of The Arcane Chronicles, which detail plotlines, play upon some of these features.

Weaving in historical events and allowing for a changing world can significantly enhance the realism and immersion in the players' experience. Ways you might achieve this are:

1. **Context and Depth:** Historical events provide context and depth to the game world. By referencing past conflicts, wars, and significant moments, players can better understand the current state of Emberfrost and the motivations of its inhabitants. Within this volume are many events you might use as hooks for adventure plots.

2. **Dynamic Setting:** Allowing the world to change over time makes it feel more alive and dynamic. Players can witness the consequences of their actions, see how the realm evolves, and understand that their choices matter.

3. **Realistic Consequences:** Historical events can have lasting effects on the setting. Players might encounter remnants of past conflicts, meet characters who have been influenced by historical figures, or witness regions still recovering from wars.

4. **Cultural Significance:** Historical events can shape the beliefs and customs of different cultures within Emberfrost. Players can interact with various groups, each with their traditions and values influenced by their unique history.

5. **Unpredictable Plot Twists:** Historical events can serve as a foundation for unexpected plot twists and surprises. Players might uncover forgotten relics or secret societies tied to the realm's history, adding depth and mystery to the story.

6. **Roleplaying Opportunities:** Historical events provide opportunities for roleplaying, allowing players to step into the shoes of legendary figures or take part in momentous events, contributing to a sense of grandeur and significance.

7. **Relevance of Lore:** Lore and backstory become more meaningful when they are connected to historical events. Players may feel more invested in learning about the world's history, as it directly impacts their current adventures.

8. **Long-Term Campaigns:** For long-term campaigns, allowing for a changing world ensures that the story remains fresh and engaging. Players won't feel like they are stuck in a static environment, and their actions will shape the direction of the narrative.

9. **Emotional Investment:** Historical events can evoke emotions in players. They might feel sorrow for tragic events, pride in overcoming challenges, or awe at the scale of epic battles, leading to a more immersive experience.

By incorporating historical events and embracing a changing world, the games master can create a living, breathing realm in Emberfrost that captures the players' imagination and offers a deeply rewarding and realistic roleplaying experience.

MAPS

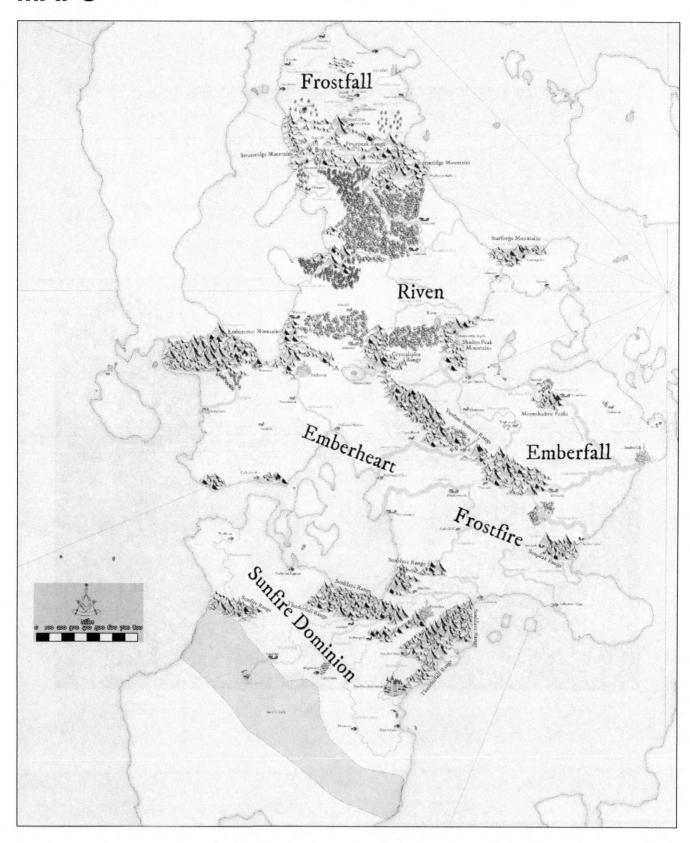

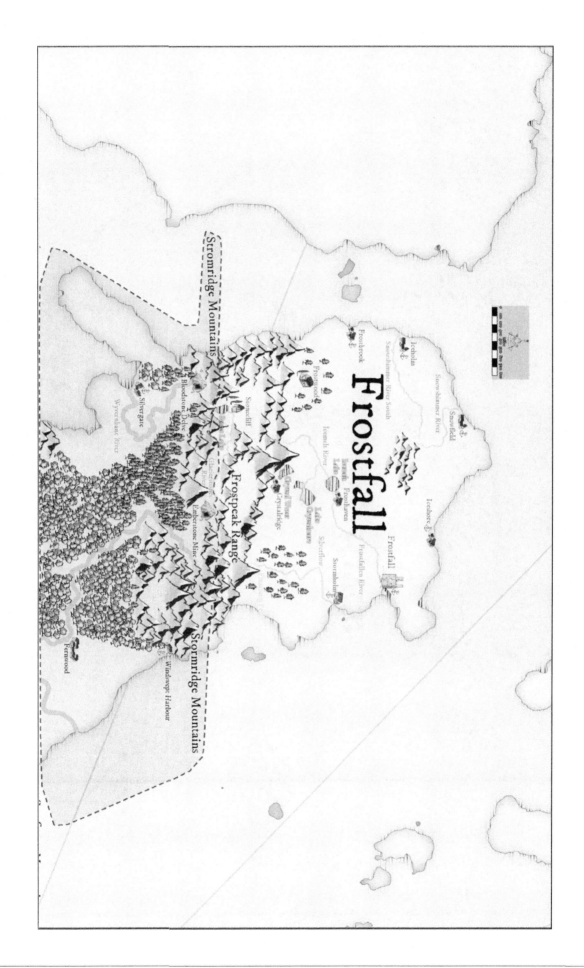

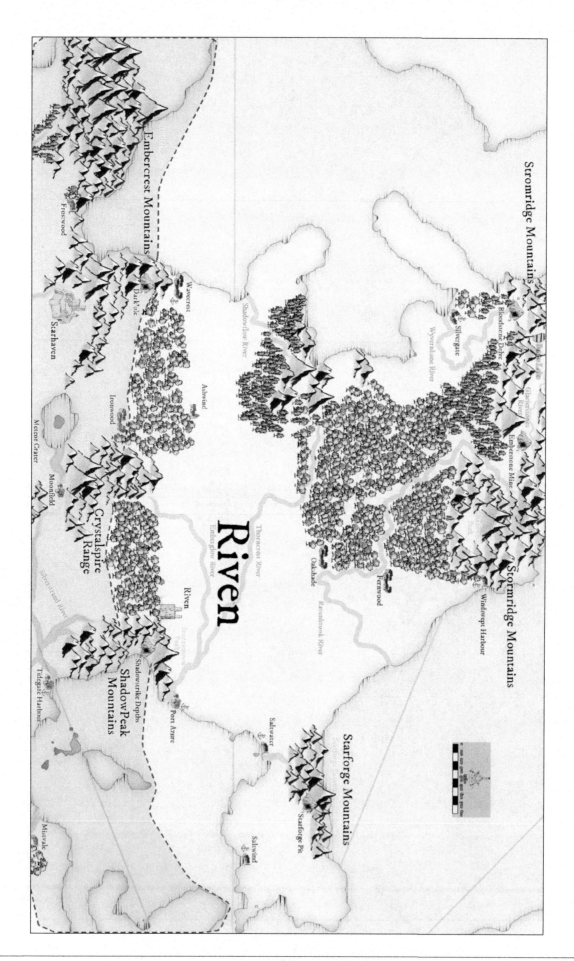

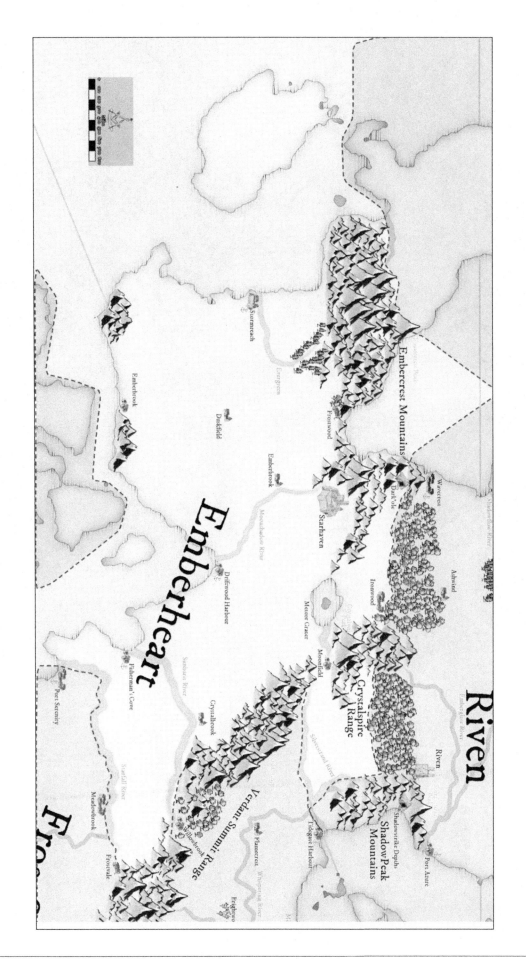

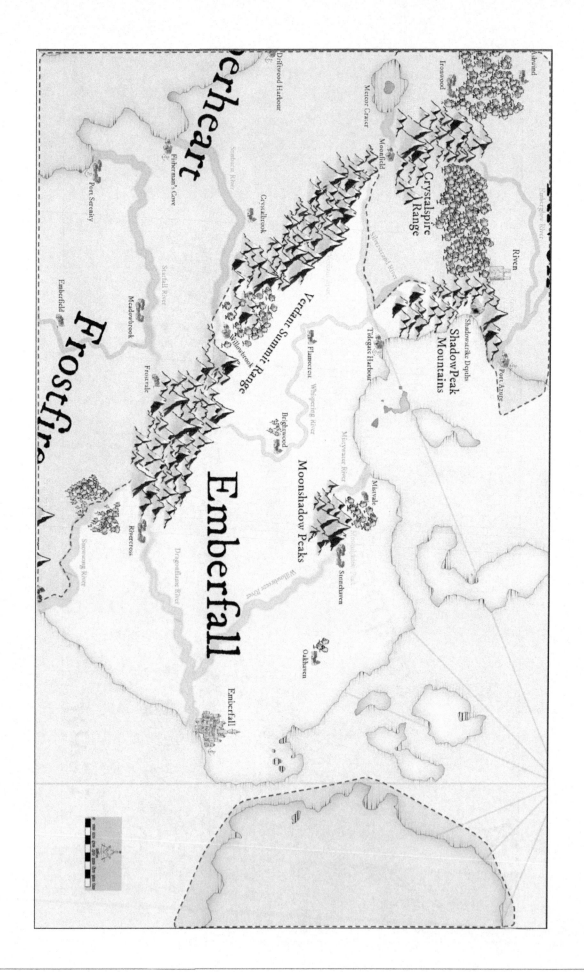

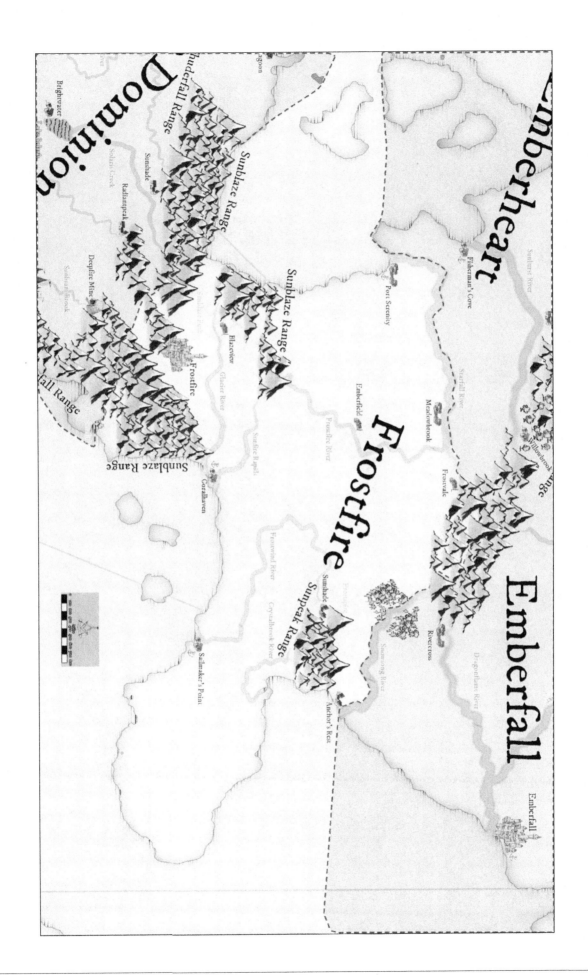

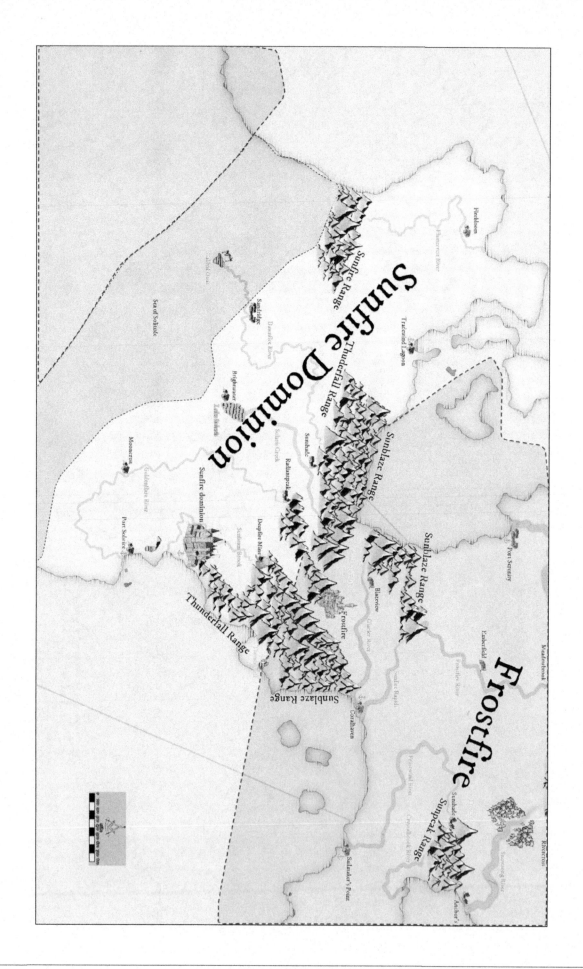

The lands of Emberfrost

Key Facts

Average dimensions of the city states of Emberfrost in miles:

	Frostfall	Riven	Emberheart	Emberfall	Frostfire	Sunfire Dominion
North - South	660	1250	500	830	1020	2050
West - East	870	900	800	1120	1240	740

Emberfrost:

4950 miles north - south, and 3360 miles west - east, as the Wyvern flies;

Approximately 6, 210,000 miles^2

For comparison this makes Emberfrost 1.6 times bigger than the United States of America.

The lands of Emberfrost are ruled by King Magnus Flameheart and Queen Imara. King Magnus formerly of Frostfall, Queen Imara, formerly of Sunfire Dominion.

Titles

Across the lands of Emberfrost the following official titles are used:

- High King or, Ardree and Queen or Ardroe

- Lord or Ealdorman, Lady or Ealdormannesse - Ealdormen are regional rulers or governors who exercise authority over a specific territory or land

- Maorm or Thayn, Maormess or Thayn-yet - A noble or landowner who holds a position of importance and influence in the kingdom. They are often the city, town or village leader.

Emberfrost operates under a quasi-feudal system, where authority and power are distributed among various titles and roles. At the apex of the hierarchy are the High King or Ardree and Queen or Ardroe, who hold the highest authority over the entire realm. They act as the central governing figures and set the overall direction for the kingdom.

Beneath the High King and Queen are the Ealdormen and Ealdormannesses. These regional rulers or governors exercise authority over specific territories or lands, ensuring the implementation of the High King's policies and maintaining law and order in their respective domains.

Further down the chain of command are the Maorms and Maormesses, also known as Thayns and Thayn-yets. These nobles and landowners hold positions of importance and influence within Emberfrost, and they often serve as leaders in cities, towns, or villages. They oversee local governance, address the needs of their communities, and represent their regions at the regional level.

This quasi-feudal system establishes a hierarchical structure that allows for governance and administration across Emberfrost. While the High King and Queen hold supreme power, the delegation of authority to Ealdormen, Maorms, and other officials ensures efficient management and local representation. However, like any system of governance, it may be subject to tensions, rivalries, and struggles for power between the different noble factions, as they each strive to protect their interests and assert their influence over the realm.

Major Rivers

Frostfall	Information
Silverflow River	The Silverflow River in Frostfall is a vital waterway that serves as a key transportation route for both trade and travel. Its strategic location connects several major cities and towns, making it a bustling hub of commercial activities. Merchants use barges and boats to transport goods, such as weaponry, armour, textiles, and enchanted artifacts, along its sparkling waters. Travelers often use the river as a safer and quicker alternative to overland routes, especially during harsh winter conditions. The Silverflow River is also known for its shimmering silver hue, which is caused by minerals and sediments in the water. Along its banks, you might spot otters, water birds, and fish, such as trout and salmon, thriving in the icy currents.
Glacierstones River	The Glacierstones River, as its name suggests, originates from the glaciers high up in the Frostfall mountains. Its icy waters cut through rocky gorges and boulders, creating a breathtaking sight as it flows down the slopes. The river's powerful currents have been harnessed for various purposes, providing the watermills their power in towns and villages along its flow. The Glacierstones River is not only a source of energy but also a treacherous obstacle for those who dare to explore its untouched and untamed areas. Due to the river's pristine nature, it is a haven for wildlife. You might encounter wild goats, foxes, and a variety of birds along its course, while the more elusive snow leopards and wolves prowl the surrounding territories
Frostfallen River	The Frostfallen River meanders through the heart of Frostfall, providing both a lifeline and a scenic attraction for the city's residents. The river's banks are lined with quaint bridges, gardens, and recreational areas, where locals and visitors gather to enjoy leisurely strolls and picnics. The Frostfallen River's calm and tranquil waters also serve as a source of freshwater, essential for the city's residents and industries. Although fishing is a popular pastime along its shores, the river is not teeming with aquatic life due to its cold temperatures. However, you may spot swans gracefully gliding on its surface, adding to the river's charm.
Icemelt River	The Icemelt River flows from the snow-capped peaks of Frostfall and plays a crucial role in irrigating the fertile plains below. As the name suggests, the river carries the melted ice and snow from the mountains, ensuring a constant water supply for agriculture and livestock. The Icemelt River serves as a lifeline for farmers, providing the water needed for their crops to flourish. As it meanders through the plains, it creates lush green oases amidst the icy surroundings, attracting a diverse range of wildlife. You might find herds of reindeer, hares, and various bird species, such as pheasants and quails, thriving in the fertile regions surrounding the river.
Snowshimmer River	The Snowshimmer River runs through the northernmost territories of Frostfall, where the landscapes are reminiscent of a winter wonderland. The river's unique name comes from the way its surface sparkles and shimmers like crushed diamonds, reflecting the sunlight and moonlight in an enchanting display. This natural phenomenon has inspired various myths and legends among the locals. The Snowshimmer River is a source of inspiration for artists and poets who seek to capture its ethereal beauty. The river is home to a variety of cold-water fish, such as tundra char and whitefish. Additionally, you might encounter herons and eagles hunting for fish along its shores.

Riven	
Ravenbrook River	The Ravenbrook River in Riven serves as a crucial water source for both agricultural and industrial purposes. Its waters flow through the verdant valleys and glens, nourishing the fertile farmlands that border its banks. Farmers grow crops like barley, oats, and potatoes, while also tending to herds of sheep and cattle. The Ravenbrook River is teeming with life, offering excellent fishing opportunities for anglers seeking trout and salmon. Otters and water voles are common sights along its shores, adding to the river's natural charm.
Thorncrest River	The Thorncrest River winds its way through the dramatic landscapes of Riven, cutting through imposing hills and rocky gorges. The river's swift currents and cascading waterfalls have made it an essential source of hydropower for the watermills.
Shadowflow River	The Shadowflow River is an enigmatic watercourse that meanders through dense forests and mist-shrouded glades in Riven. The river is a sanctuary for various bird species, such as nightjars, owls, and woodpeckers. Along its banks, elusive creatures like red squirrels and badgers find refuge, creating a haven of biodiversity.
Emberglow River	The Emberglow River lives up to its name with a unique natural phenomenon that occurs during the twilight hours. The river's waters reflect the hues of the setting sun, giving it a mesmerizing and fiery appearance. People from all over Riven come to witness this beautiful spectacle. The Emberglow River's warm waters are favoured by certain fish species like perch, pike, and eels. Local legends also speak of magical creatures, like the elusive selkies, who are said to inhabit its depths.
Wyvernbane River	The Wyvernbane River boasts breathtaking vistas as it traverses the breathtaking highlands of Riven. Its deep gorges and rugged cliffs attract adventurous explorers and thrill-seekers seeking to challenge themselves against its rapids. The river's waters support a diverse ecosystem, home to salmon, brown trout, and migratory birds like herons and dippers. The nearby woodlands provide shelter to elusive creatures like red deer and wild cats, adding an air of mystery to the Wyvernbane River's surroundings.

Emberheart	
Moonshadow River	The Moonshadow River in Emberheart serves as a vital waterway for transportation and trade. Its calm and steady flow makes it ideal for both cargo boats and passenger vessels, facilitating the movement of goods and people between towns and cities. The riverbanks are adorned with lush vegetation, providing a habitat for various wildlife. Along its shores, you can find graceful swans, colourful kingfishers, and playful otters, creating a picturesque scene for nature lovers.
Silverstrand River	The Silverstrand River is renowned for its sparkling and crystal-clear waters that reflect the sunlight, giving it an ethereal appearance. The river is a popular destination for recreational activities like swimming, canoeing, and picnicking. Fishermen frequent the river in search of trout and grayling, while the surrounding forests provide shelter for deer, foxes, and wild boars.
Evergreen River	The Evergreen River flows through the enchanting forests and verdant meadows of Emberheart. It sustains the fertile farmlands that line its course, providing irrigation for crops like wheat, vineyards, and orchards. The river's name is apt, as the evergreen trees along its banks maintain their lush foliage throughout the year. This, in turn, attracts an abundance of birdlife, including thrushes, warblers, and woodpeckers, who find sanctuary among the branches.
Sunburst River	The Sunburst River is a picturesque waterway, renowned for its breathtaking sunrises and sunsets that paint the sky with vibrant hues. The river's banks are home to charming villages and towns, where fishing and agriculture are central to the local economy. Fishermen cast their nets for pike, perch, and bream. The river also attracts majestic herons, ducks, and migrating storks during certain seasons.
Starfall River	The Starfall River gets its name from the stunning meteor showers that often grace the night sky over Emberheart. The river serves as a natural boundary between Emberheart and Frostfire, creating a strategic position for trade and defence. The Starfall River's flowing waters support a variety of aquatic life, including crayfish, freshwater mussels, and various fish species.

Emberfall	
Willowbreeze River	The Willowbreeze River meanders gracefully through the picturesque landscapes of Emberfall, providing a serene and calming atmosphere. Along its banks, you can find willow trees swaying in the breeze, and the area is frequented by a variety of birdlife, including songbirds, ducks, and herons.
Dragonflame River	The Dragonflame River is a majestic and powerful waterway that carves its way through rugged terrains and mountainous regions of Emberfall. Named after the legendary dragons of old folklore, the river is often adorned with hot springs and geysers that give rise to the mystical aura of the area. The river's currents are strong and fast, making it ideal for adventurers seeking thrilling rafting experiences. The surrounding cliffs and forests provide a habitat for eagles, falcons, and elusive mountain goats.
Snowsong River	The Snowsong River originates in the snowy peaks of Emberfall and flows through lush valleys and meadows. It's cold and pristine waters are a vital resource for irrigation and agriculture, supporting the growth of fruits, vegetables, and vineyards in the region. The river is teeming with trout and salmon, attracting fishing enthusiasts from nearby towns and villages. In the winter months, the riverbanks become a haven for graceful swans and migrating birds.
Whispering River	The Whispering River meanders through dense forests and mystical landscapes, its name derived from the soft, soothing sounds of its flowing waters. The area is home to a variety of wildlife, including deer, foxes, and rabbits, while the tranquil waters offer a sanctuary for otters and beavers.
Mistywater River	The Mistywater River is shrouded in an ethereal mist that rises from its cool and foggy waters. The river passes through enchanting woodlands and marshy wetlands, sustaining a rich diversity of flora and fauna. The area is a haven for birds, with a wide range of waterfowl and migratory species making their home here. The river's mystical ambiance attracts folklore and tales of hidden treasures and ancient spirits, making it a source of inspiration for local myths and legends.

Frostfire	Information
Glacier River	The Glacier River, as the name suggests, originates from the icy peaks of Sunblaze Peaks (mountains). It flows gracefully through the fertile plains of Frostfire, providing a vital source of water for agriculture and supporting the growth of various crops. The river's calm waters are also utilized for irrigation, allowing farmers to cultivate an abundance of fruits, grains, and olives. Along the riverbanks, you can find a variety of water-loving creatures, such as ducks, swans, and otters.
Frostfire River	The Frostfire River is a prominent waterway that runs through the heart of the Frostfire plains. Its currents are swift and powerful, making it ideal for transportation and trade. Merchants and traders utilize the river to transport goods to and from the various settlements of Frostfire, facilitating the exchange of commodities and cultural influences. The river is teeming with fish, particularly trout and salmon, attracting fishermen from nearby villages.
Crystalbrook River	The Crystalbrook River is a breathtaking sight, with its clear and pristine waters winding through the picturesque landscapes of Frostfire. Locals believe that the waters of Crystalbrook possess healing properties, and many come to bathe in its refreshing streams. The river is home to a variety of aquatic life, including colourful fish and rare freshwater turtles.
Frostwind River	The Frostwind River originates in the highest peaks of the Sunpeak Range (mountains), carrying cold and invigorating waters through the valleys and plains. The river is harnessed for its hydropower potential, providing energy to the watermills that lie along its course. It also plays a vital role in cooling down the warmer plains during scorching summers.
Sunfire Rapids	The Sunfire Rapids are a striking contrast to the placid rivers of Frostfire. Originating from the mountainous regions, this river gains momentum as it cascades down the steep slopes, creating powerful rapids and waterfalls. The fast-flowing waters are ideal for adventurous souls seeking whitewater rafting experiences.

Sunfire Dominion	Information
Goldenflare River	The Goldenflare River is the lifeblood of the Sunfire Dominion's expansive plains. Its waters are utilized for irrigation to support the cultivation of crops such as wheat, barley, and dates. The river's fertile banks are home to sprawling farmlands and orchards, creating a rich agricultural landscape. Farmers also raise livestock near its waters, including cattle, goats, and sheep. The river attracts a diverse array of wildlife, including water birds, crocodiles, and gazelles that come to drink and find food.
Solaris Creek	Solaris Creek is a smaller river that winds its way through the arid landscapes of the Sunfire Dominion. While not as substantial as the Goldenflare River, Solaris Creek still plays a crucial role in providing water for local communities and their livestock. The riverbanks are dotted with palm trees and other desert flora. Desert foxes, desert hares, and various reptiles can be spotted in the vicinity. The river ends at Lake Solaris.
Dawnfire River	The Dawnfire River runs through the heart of the Sunfire Dominion, connecting various settlements and towns, it ends at Calihal Oasis. Its waters are essential for the region's economy, supporting fishing industries that provide sustenance and trade opportunities. Fish like Dawnfire perch and catfish are abundant in the river. Additionally, the river's gentle currents allow for leisurely boat rides and water-based transportation.
Sunbeam Brook	Sunbeam Brook is a small, sparkling waterway that meanders through the sunlit meadows of the city of Sunfire Dominion. Though not navigable, the brook provides clean and refreshing water for nearby villages and travellers passing through. Its presence also attracts a diverse range of butterflies, colourful songbirds, and small mammals that flourish in the idyllic grasslands.
Flamecrest River	The Flamecrest River flows gracefully through the northern regions of Sunfire Dominion. It is a focal point of trade and cultural exchange between the two regions of Sunfire Dominion. The riverbanks are inhabited by desert monitor lizards, scarab beetles, and other desert fauna.

Key Cities and towns

Frostfall

City / Town / Village	Population
1. Frostfall (City)	40,000
2. Stormholm (Town)	18,500
3. Frostwood (Town)	12,800
4. Stonecliff (Town)	9,200
5. Iceholm (Town)	7,500
6. Frostbrook (Village)	4,600
7. Iceshore (Village)	3,700
8. Snowfield (Village)	2,900
9. Frosthaven (Village)	2,200
10. Crystalridge (Village)	1,800
Total Population	103,200

Riven

City / Town / Village	Population
1. Riven (City)	55,000
2. Fernwood (Town)	22,500
3. Oakshade (Town)	18,200
4. Ashwind (Town)	15,800
5. Wavecrest (Town)	12,700
6. Port Azure (Village)	8,300
7. Saltwater (Village)	6,900
8. Saltwind (Village)	5,500
9. Windswept Harbour (Village)	4,200
10. Silvergate (Village)	3,800
Total Population	152,900

Emberheart

City / Town / Village	Population
1. Starhaven (City)	180,000
2. Stormreach (Town)	82,500
3. Driftwood Harbour (Town)	78,200
4. Ironwood (Town)	65,800
5. Moonfield (Town)	51,700
6. Fisherman's Cove (Village)	19,500
7. Frostwood (Village)	12,900
8. Crystalbrook (Village)	9,700
9. Duskfield (Village)	8,300
10. Emberbrook (Village)	6,800
Total Population	515,400

Emberfall

City / Town / Village	Population
1. Emberfall (City	95,000
2. Stonehaven (Town)	41,500
3. Rivercross (Town)	37,200
4. Willowbrook (Town)	30,800
5. Tidegate Harbour (Town	27,500
6. Mistvale (Village	18,700
7. Brightwood (Village	15,900
8. Flamecrest (Village	11,300
9. Frostgate (Village) - Population: 9,800	9,800
10. Oakhaven (Village)	8,600
Total Population	296,300

Frostfire   **Sunfire Dominion**

City / Town / Village	Population		City / Town / Village	Population
1. Frostfire (City)	88,000		1. Sunfire Dominion (City)	85,000
2. Meadowbrook (Town)	58,500		2. Port Solstice (City)	73,500
3. Port Serenity(Town)	45,200		3. Sandridge (Town)	62,800
4. Sunshade (Town)	38,700		4. Radiantpeak (Town)	57,800
5. Coralhaven(Town)	32,800		5. Sunshade (Town)	54,700
6. Anchor's Rest (Village)	22,300		6. Tradewind Lagoon (Village)	32,500
7. Sailmakers Point (Village)	18,900		7. Mooncrest (Village)	26,500
8. Emberfield (Village)	14,500		8. Emberbrook (Village)	21,900
9. Blazeview (Village)	11,700		9. Brightwater (Village)	18,400
10. Frostvale (Village)	9,800		10. Firebloom (Village)	15,700
Total Population	340,400		Total Population	448,800

Mountains

The definition of a mountain is any peak, over 1,000 ft, approximately 300 metres.

Name of Range	Location	Tallest peak, feet	Additional information
Frostpeak Range	South **Frostfall**, border with Riven	Frostfang Peak - 27,542 feet	Borders with Stormridge mountains
Stormridge Mountains	North **Riven**, border with Frostfall	Shadowfall Peak - 25,712 feet	Contains Bloodstone Delve (mine) on the western edge of the range. While Emberstone mine is located on the southern edge of the range, at about midpoint of the range.
Starforge Mountains	Eastern **Riven**, on the Saltwind pernisula	Starforge Summit - 18,285 feet	Contains Starforge pit (mine) to the south-west of the range
Embercrest Mountains	North-west **Emberheart**	Embercrest Peak - 16,801 feet	Contains Dark'ole (mine) to the south-west of the range
Crystalspire Range	North-east **Emberheart**, on the border with Riven and Emberfall	Crystalveil Peak - 18,940 feet	The source of Starfall River, which feeds Meteor Crater Lake. Also, where the crystal peak is located.
Verdant Summit Range	North-east **Emberheart**, on the border with Emberfall and Frostfire	Verdant Apex - 14,742 feet	Runs from the south of Meteor Crater town, south-eastwards towards Rivercross town. There is a shallow hills section with a pass through the mountains at Willowbrook.

Mountains continued…

Name of Range	Location	Tallest peak, feet	Additional information
Shadowpeak Mountains	North-east **Emberfall**, on the border with Riven	Stormcrown Peak - 14,976 feet	Contains Shadowstrike Depths (mine) to the south-west of the range
Moonshadow Peaks	North **Emberfall**, near Stonehaven	Moonshadow Peak - 4,502 feet	There are deep and dangerous shafts, which are rumoured to be haunted. No mining has ever been done here.
Sunpeak Range:	East **Frostfire**	Frostspire Peak - 18,212 feet	Near the border of Frostfire and Emberfall. The port of Anchor's Rest is located at the north edge of the mountains
Sunblaze Peaks	South-west **Frostfire**	Sunblaze Summit - 26,271 feet	On the border of Frostfire and Sunfire Dominion
Thunderfall Range	North-east **Sunfire Dominion**	Thundercliff Summit - 25,390 feet	Contains Deepfire mine to the south-west of the range
Sunfire Range	West **Sunfire Dominion**	Sunfire Summit - 17,810 feet	On the southern edge of the mountain range is the Sea of Solitude desert

Mines and mining

Various valuable and sought-after materials would be found together in mines due to the geological composition of the regions. Some of the commonly found materials include:

1. **Gold and Silver**: Both gold and silver are highly prized and frequently found together in mines. They are used for currency, jewellery, and various luxury goods.

2. **Iron and Coal**: Iron ores are abundant and are used in the production of various tools, weapons, and building materials. Coal is a vital source of energy for smelting iron and other metals.

3. **Copper and Tin**: These metals are essential for the production of bronze, a widely used material for weapons, tools, and decorative items.

4. **Lead and Zinc**: Lead and zinc deposits are are found together and are crucial for producing brass, pewter, and other alloys.

5. **Gemstones**: Various gemstones like diamonds, emeralds, rubies, sapphires, and garnets are used for jewellery and ornaments.

6. **Quartz and Granite**: These quarried minerals are used for construction purposes, including buildings and statues.

7. **Marble**: Quarried marble is valued for its use in sculptures, architecture, and decorative arts.

8. **Cobalt and Nickel**: These metals are used in the production of coloured glass and ceramics.

9. **Sulphur**: Sulphur is essential for the production of gunpowder, used for weaponry and mining explosives.

10. **Salt and Saltpeter**: Saltpeter is significant for producing gunpowder, while salt was used for various purposes, including food preservation and tanning.

It's important to note that the specific resources found in mines vary from region to region, and the availability of these materials plays a crucial role in the economic and technological development of the lands. Mining operations and trade of these materials are vital for sustaining various industries and fostering cultural exchange between lands.

The mines in Emberfrost:

Mine Name	Located in	Produces
Bloodstone Delve	Riven	Coal and Iron
Emberstone Mine	Riven	Copper, Lead, Tin, and Zinc
Starforge Pit	Riven	Lesser Gemstones, small traces of rare metals
Dark'ole	Emberheart	Gold and Silver. Smaller amounts of rare metals and rare Gemstones.
Shadowstrike Depths	Emberfall	Salt and small quantities of Saltpeter and Sulphur
Deepfire Mine	Sunfire Dominion	Granite, Marble and Quartz

Language and dialects

In Emberfrost, the following dialects are spoken across the lands:

1. Northern Frostspeak: Spoken in the northern areas, including Frostfall and northern Riven. This dialect is influenced by the rugged and cold terrain of the mountains.

2. Trade speech: Found across all parts of Frostfall. This dialect incorporates maritime influences and trade-related terminology.

3. Central Heartland: Spoken in the central heartland of Emberfall, this dialect is considered the standard form of speech in all the lands, used in official communications and among the nobility.

4. Eastern Plains: Found in the eastern plains of Emberfall, this dialect has a warm and welcoming tone, reflecting the fertile and prosperous nature of the lands.

5. Southern Sunfire: Spoken in the southern territories, near the borders of Sunfire Dominion and Frostfire. This dialect has been influenced by the interactions between the two regions, blending elements of both cultures.

6. D'tish: Spoken only by the tribes that live along Sunfire Dominion's southern border and those who venture into the Sea of Solitude desert. This dialect has been influenced by desert life.

In Emberfall, the mix of dialects brings about various difficulties and nuances in communication and understanding among the different regions:

1. **Divergent Vocabulary**: Each dialect may have specific words and expressions that are unique to their region's culture and environment. This can lead to confusion and misunderstandings when people from different areas converse.

2. **Pronunciation Variations**: Different dialects may pronounce certain words or sounds differently. This can make it challenging for speakers of one dialect to comprehend speakers of another, especially when unfamiliar sounds are involved.

3. **Cultural Sensitivities**: Some dialects may use certain phrases or idioms that are considered offensive or disrespectful in other regions. This lack of awareness can inadvertently cause friction between individuals from different areas.

4. **Formality Levels**: The level of formality in speech can vary between dialects. For example, the Central Heartland dialect might be more formal and rigid in its structure, while the Eastern Plains dialect may have a more relaxed and casual approach. This discrepancy in formality can create social dynamics during interactions.

5. **Regional Pride and Identity**: People from different regions may take great pride in their dialect and see it as an essential part of their identity. This pride can sometimes lead to bias or stereotypes about others who speak differently.

6. **Misinterpretation of Intent**: Nuances in phrasing and intonation can lead to misunderstandings regarding the speaker's intentions or emotions behind their words. What might be a friendly jest in one dialect could be perceived as an insult in another.

7. **Difficulty in Diplomacy**: When officials and representatives from different regions need to collaborate or negotiate, the differences in dialects can create challenges in establishing clear communication and reaching agreements.

8. **Language Barriers**: The D'tish dialect, spoken by the tribes near Sunfire Dominion's southern border and in the Sea of Solitude desert, may be entirely unfamiliar to speakers of other dialects. This can hinder communication and create a sense of isolation for these communities.

To address these difficulties, the people of Emberfall might employ translators, use the Central Heartland dialect as a common language for official communication, or develop cultural exchange programs to foster understanding between regions. Nevertheless, the diverse mix of dialects also enriches the cultural tapestry of Emberfall, celebrating the unique identities of each region while challenging its inhabitants to build bridges of understanding.

Players may find themselves navigating linguistic nuances, deciphering regional dialects, and adapting to the unique customs of each area. Whether it's bartering with the Desert Traders in Sunfire Dominion, negotiating trade agreements with the merchants of Frostfall, or unravelling the enigmatic language of ancient scrolls in Emberheart, the need for effective communication and cultural sensitivity can greatly impact their success. Misunderstandings can lead to intriguing plot twists, alliances, or conflicts, offering players a dynamic and immersive experience where every conversation and interaction holds the potential for discovery and adventure.

Emberfrost Calendar

Emberfrost has 300 days in a year.

The 10 months of the year are all 30 days long.

Each day is 20 hours long.

The names of the months are:

Snowdeep, Snowmelt, Frostmorn, Firstbud, Suncrest, Naturebloom, Naturefade, Longshadows, Frostfingers, Firstsnow

Winter month: Firstsnow and Snowdeep

Spring: Snowmelt, Frostmorn & Firstbud

Summer: Suncrest and Naturebloom

Autumn: Naturefade, Longshadows and Frostfingers

Hours of daylight

The hours of daylight vary across Emberfrost and the range of daylight from winter to summer varies, from almost a static 10 hours in southern Sunfire Dominion, to a much greater variation in Frostfall, 4 - 16 hours.

Hours of Daylight table: hours at month start – hours at month end

Month	Frostfall	Riven	Emberheart & Emberfall	Frostfire & North Sunfire Dominion	South Sunfire Dominion
Snowdeep	4 - 6	7 - 8	8 - 9	9 - 9	9 - 10
Snowmelt	6 - 8	8 - 9	9 - 9	9 - 10	10 - 10
Frostmorn	8 - 10	9 - 10	9 - 10	10 - 10	10 - 10
Firstbud	10 - 13	10 - 11	10 - 11	10 - 10	10 - 10
Suncrest	13 - 16	11 - 13	11 - 12	10 - 11	10 - 10
Naturebloom	16 - 13	13 - 11	12 - 11	11 - 10	10 - 10
Naturefade	13 - 10	11 - 10	11 - 10	10 - 10	10 - 10
Longshadows	10 - 8	10 - 9	10 - 9	10 - 10	10 - 10
Frostfingers	8 - 6	9 - 8	9 - 9	10 - 9	10 - 10
Firstsnow	6 - 4	8 - 7	9 -8	9 - 9	10 - 9

Tracking the passage of time

The daytime is split into hours with each hour tracked, on either sundials, or water clocks in the larger towns and cities. The day is typically split in to 5 parts:

Emberfrost terminology	English version
Sun up to first heat	Early morning
First heat to heat rising	Mid-morning / late morning
Heat rising to full heat	Midday / noon
Full heat to suns setting	Afternoon
Suns setting to days end	Early evening / sunset / twilight

In Sunfire Dominion where the days are pretty close to 10 hours long all year, these daylight parts, equate to be roughly 2 hours long each. But in far north of Frostfall, in the depths of winter where, only 4 hours of daylight occur, the 5 parts of the day are under an hour each.

The passage of the night hours is tracked by marked by candles, with each hour passing marked upon the candle. The night time is marked in watches, every two hours, so in the depths of winter there can be as many as 8 watches in the far north of Frostfall. Sunfire Dominion has only 5 watches at night all year.

The night watches are referred to as first watch, second watch, third watch, etc.

Events in the calendar of Emberfrost:

Date	Event	Description
1st Snowmelt	Emberfire Carnival	The first day of the year, marking the end of the winter season and the awakening of the land. The lively carnivals mark the end of winter and the beginning of warmer days. The carnivals often feature street performances, games, and festivities, bringing the community together in a spirit of joy and anticipation.
15th Frostmorn	Emberfrost Unity Day	This holiday commemorates the unification of the Emberfrost Kingdom. It is a day of national pride, with parades, ceremonies, and speeches honouring the history, culture, and achievements of the realm.
30th Firstbud	Spring Blossom Festival	This joyous festival marks the end of spring and the awakening of nature. It features colourful parades, flower displays, and various outdoor activities, symbolizing new beginnings and growth.
1st Naturebloom	Suncrest festival	The midpoint of the year, when the sun reaches its highest point in the sky, bringing warmth and light to the land. This festival honours the power of the sun and its life-giving energy. People gather to witness the sunset and offer prayers and thanks for the abundance and vitality it brings to the land.
30th Naturebloom	Harvestmoon Feast	This festival pays tribute to the bountiful harvest and the hard work of farmers. It is a time of feasting, sharing the harvest's abundance, and expressing gratitude for the sustenance it provides.

Date	Event	Description
10th Longshadows	Starfall Spectacle	This magical event celebrates the mesmerizing display of shooting stars. People gather under the night sky, making wishes upon the falling stars and enjoying performances of stargazers and astrologers.
30th Frostfingers	Frostfall	The last day of the autumn, marking the transition from autumn to winter and a time for reflection on the passing year.
15th Firstsnow	Hearthfire Festival	This holiday marks the gathering of families and communities around hearth fires. It is a time of storytelling, feasting, and sharing warmth and companionship.
1st Snowdeep	Embernight	The longest night of the year, where bonfires are lit to ward off the cold and darkness, symbolizing the resilience of the people of Emberfrost.

Non-Date related events in the calendar of Emberfrost

These events celebrate the wonders and unique aspects of Emberfrost's natural world, creating a rich tapestry of traditions and celebrations across the lands. Celebrating various happenings and natural occurrences:

1. Aurora's Embrace: During certain nights in winter, the night sky comes alive with breathtaking auroras that dance across the heavens. People gather in open fields to witness this celestial spectacle, rejoicing in the mesmerizing display of colours.

2. Ice Blossom Revelry: As the first rays of sunlight touch the frozen landscape in early spring, tiny ice blossoms bloom across the land. Communities come together for a joyous celebration, decorating their homes and streets with these delicate ice flowers.

3. Emberfall Migration: Each year, a grand migration of magical creatures takes place in Emberfall. As thousands of winged creatures soar across the skies, the residents marvel at this enchanting display, hosting festivities to honour and protect these creatures during their journey.

4. Enchanted Forest Gala: In the heart of the Emberfrost forest, a mystical event occurs once a year, where the trees emit a soft, enchanting glow. People don exquisite costumes and celebrate in the woods, believing that the spirits of the forest are among them.

5. Moonlit Masquerade: On nights of the full moon, the Moonlit Coven hosts a grand masquerade ball, where attendees wear masks to invoke the moon's power. The dance floor shimmers with moonlight as guests perform elegant dances and enjoy magical delights.

6. Frostfire Crystal Festival: In the depths of winter, when the sun sets, the Frostfire Crystal Caves come alive with radiant luminescent crystals. The caves become a stunning spectacle, and the locals hold an annual festival to celebrate their awe-inspiring beauty.

7. Sunfire Dominion Oasis Day: In the arid desert of Sunfire Dominion, an oasis springs to life for a brief period each year. People journey to this precious source of water, setting up vibrant markets and jubilant gatherings in the midst of the desert.

8. Emberheart Vineyard Harvest: In the fertile vineyards of Emberheart, the autumn harvest brings abundant grapes and festivities. People join in grape-stomping contests, sample the finest wines, and enjoy the camaraderie of the harvest season.

9. Beneath the Frozen Waves: In the heart of winter, when the frozen lakes and rivers of Emberfrost are at their coldest, an extraordinary event unfolds. Skilled ice mages and enchanters perform an ancient ritual, infusing the frozen lakes with mystical energies. Participants, guided by the enchanters, descend into the enchanted waters, protected by magical barriers that maintain a comfortable temperature. As they venture deeper, they encounter astonishing sights, such as ethereal underwater gardens, glowing sea creatures, and luminescent crystals. This mesmerizing underwater realm is believed to hold ancient secrets and hidden treasures. Those who dare to explore might discover artifacts of great power or gain profound insights.

10. Emberfall's Night of Echoes: During the darkest night of autumn, when the veil between the realms is said to be thinnest, Emberfall's Night of Echoes commences. In this mystical event, people light candles and lanterns in remembrance of loved ones who have passed away. It is believed that on this night, the spirits of the departed return to offer guidance and comfort. Participants share stories, leave offerings, and engage in acts of kindness to honour the memories of those who came before. The night is both solemn and heartwarming, fostering a deep connection between the living and the spirits of Emberfrost.

Climate

Climate temperature ranges for Emberfrost, taking into account the daylight hours and seasonal variations:

Table of average temperature °C:

average temperature °C	Frostfall	Riven	Emberheart & Emberfall	Frostfire & North Sunfire Dominion	South Sunfire Dominion
Winter months					
day	-10 to -5	0 to 5	5 to 10	10 to 20	25 to 35
night	-20 to -15	-5 to -10	0 to 5	0 to 10	15 to 25
Spring months					
day	-5 to 5	5 to 10	10 to 15	20 to 30	35 to 45
night	-15 to -5	0 to 5	5 to 10	10 to 20	25 to 35
Summer months					
day	5 to 15	10 to 20	20 to 30	30 to 40	40 to 50
night	-5 to 5	5 to 10	10 to 20	20 to 30	30 to 40
Autumn months					
day	5 to -5	10 to 5	15 to 10	30 to 20	45 to 35
night	-5 to -15	5 to 0	10 to 5	20 to 10	35 to 25

Please note that these are approximate temperature ranges and can vary depending on specific geographical features, elevation, and other factors. The temperatures provided give a general sense of the climate in Emberfrost.

Table showing the average rainfall in millimetres (mm) for the different regions of Emberfrost:

Season	Frostfall	Riven	Emberfall	Emberheart	Frostfire & North Sunfire Dominion	South Sunfire Dominion
Winter Months	100-150	80-120	60-100	40-80	20-60	10-40
Spring Months	80-120	60-100	40-80	20-60	10-40	5-20
Summer Months	60-100	40-80	20-60	10-40	5-20	2-10
Autumn Months	80-120	60-100	40-80	20-60	10-40	5-20

Please note that these average rainfall values are estimates and can vary from year to year. The given ranges provide a general indication of the expected rainfall in each season for the respective regions. Other factors such as local topography and climate patterns can also influence the actual rainfall patterns in these areas.

Average snowfall in millimetres (mm) by season for the different regions of Emberfrost:

Season	Frostfall	Riven	Emberfall	Emberheart	Frostfire & North Sunfire Dominion	South Sunfire Dominion
Winter Months	500 - 1500	150-250	100-200	50-100	None	None
Spring Months	100 - 300	None	None	None	None	None
Summer Months	None	None	None	None	None	None
Autumn Months	100 - 300	50 - 250	None	None	None	None

Please note that the suggested snowfall amounts provided are approximate and can vary depending on local conditions and specific weather patterns. In some regions, snowfall may be minimal or non-existent during certain seasons.

The actual impact of specific mountains will be discussed in the weather variations sections in the individual City states.

In a general sense, as altitude increases by approximately 300 meters (or about 1,000 feet), the following effects on snowfall can be observed:

1. Increased Snowfall: Higher elevations often experience colder temperatures, allowing for snowfall even when lower-lying areas may receive rain. As a result, higher-altitude regions may generally receive more snowfall compared to lower-altitude areas.

2. Enhanced Snow Accumulation: Steeper slopes and mountainous terrain at higher altitudes can enhance the accumulation of snow. The terrain can act as a barrier to prevailing winds, causing uplift and condensation, which leads to increased snowfall and accumulation.

3. Longer Snow Season: Higher-altitude regions tend to have longer snow seasons due to lower average temperatures. Snow may persist on the ground for extended periods, making it possible for multiple snowfall events to occur throughout the winter season.

4. Increased Snowfall Variability: Snowfall at higher altitudes can be more variable compared to lower-altitude areas due to localized weather systems, microclimates, and orographic effects caused by mountains. These factors can lead to significant variations in snowfall amounts over relatively short distances.

5. Effect on Precipitation Type: At very high altitudes, where temperatures remain consistently below freezing, precipitation is more likely to fall as snow rather than rain. This is particularly true in colder climates.

In general terms, the drop in temperature per 300 meters of elevation, also known as the lapse rate, can vary depending on several factors such as atmospheric conditions, local topography, and regional climate patterns.

As a general rule, the average temperature tends to decrease by around 1 degree Celsius (or approximately 1.8 degrees Fahrenheit) for every 300 meters of upward elevation gain.

This relationship between elevation and temperature is known as the environmental lapse rate. It is influenced by the adiabatic cooling effect, which occurs as air rises and expands, leading to a decrease in temperature. This lapse rate can vary due to factors like moisture content, prevailing wind patterns, and atmospheric stability, among others. Therefore, the actual temperature change with elevation may deviate from the average lapse rate in specific locations.

It's important to note that the lapse rate is an average estimate and can vary significantly in different regions and under different weather conditions. Local factors such as mountain ranges, bodies of water, and wind patterns can influence temperature changes with elevation. Additionally, weather systems and localized effects can also impact temperature variations, leading to deviations from the average lapse rate.

The effect of the sea on the lapse rate is known as a maritime or coastal influence. When a mountain range is close to the sea, it can modify the lapse rate and lead to specific weather patterns.

The maritime influence tends to moderate the temperature changes with elevation, resulting in a smaller lapse rate compared to inland areas. The presence of the sea provides a source of moisture and heat, which can contribute to more stable atmospheric conditions. As a result, the temperature decrease with elevation may be less pronounced near coastal regions compared to inland areas.

As a general rule for mountains near to the seas, the average temperature tends to decrease by around 0.5 degrees Celsius (or approximately 0.9 degrees Fahrenheit) for every 300 meters of upward elevation gain.

Wind

Frostfall:

- Winter: Moderate to strong winds from the west and east due to the influence of the nearby seas.
- Spring: Generally moderate winds with a mix of directions.
- Summer: Light to moderate breezes from the west and east coasts.
- Autumn: Moderate to strong winds from the west and east coasts.

Riven:

- Winter: Moderate to strong winds from the west and east coasts.
- Spring: Moderate winds with a mix of directions.
- Summer: Light to moderate breezes from the west and east coasts.
- Autumn: Moderate to strong winds from the west and east coasts.

Emberheart:

- Winter: Moderate winds from the west coast and light winds from the east coast.
- Spring: Generally light to moderate breezes with a mix of directions.
- Summer: Light to moderate winds from the west coast.
- Autumn: Moderate to strong winds from the west coast and light winds from the east coast.

Emberfall:

- Winter: Moderate winds from the east coast and light winds from the west coast.
- Spring: Generally light to moderate breezes with a mix of directions.
- Summer: Light to moderate winds from the east coast.
- Autumn: Moderate to strong winds from the east coast and light winds from the west coast.

Frostfire:

- Winter: Moderate to strong winds from the west and east coasts.
- Spring: Generally moderate winds with a mix of directions.
- Summer: Light to moderate breezes from the west and east coasts.
- Autumn: Moderate to strong winds from the west and east coasts.

Sunfire Dominion:

- Winter: Light to moderate winds from the west and east coasts.
- Spring: Generally light winds with a mix of directions.
- Summer: Light to moderate breezes from the west and east coasts.
- Autumn: Light to moderate winds from the west and east coasts.

Average wind speeds (mph)

	Winter	Spring	Summer	Autumn
Frostfall	10-25 mph	5-15 mph	5-15 mph	10-25 mph
Riven	10-25 mph	5-15 mph	5-15 mph	10-25 mph
Emberheart	5-15 mph	5-15 mph	5-15 mph	10-20 mph
Emberfall	5-15 mph	5-15 mph	5-15 mph	10-20 mph
Frostfire	10-25 mph	5-15 mph	5-15 mph	10-25 mph
Sunfire Dominion	5-15 mph	5-15 mph	5-15 mph	5-15 mph

Prevailing wind directions for each season and region

	Winter	Spring	Summer	Autumn
Frostfall	North	Northeast	East	Northeast
Riven	Northeast	Northeast	East	Northeast
Emberheart	West	West	Southwest	West
Emberfall	Northeast	East	Southeast	East
Frostfire	East	Southeast	South	Southeast
Sunfire Dominion	Northeast	East	Southeast	East

Law and Crime

The crimes committed in Emberfrost can be categorised into crimes against the person, against property and against authority.

Crimes against the person included:

- murder
- assault
- insulting a neighbour
- public disorder

The most common crimes are typically against property. These included:

- petty theft
- ploughing someone else's land
- poaching
- counterfeiting coins
- arson

Poaching is considered a social crime and many villages do not punish people who carry out poaching, if they are poor and just trying to feed their families.

Crimes against authority included:

- betraying your lord
- treason

Resolving offences committed:

Moot Court: The Moot Court, or assembly, serves as a gathering of the community to discuss matters of law, resolve disputes, and make decisions.

- It is presided over by the ruler, or their representative, and involves participation from free-folk and vassals in the larger towns and cities. The court will be scheduled on the last day of every holiday festival. Whilst waiting for trial, any serious offender would have to pay a small sum per day, to be detained in the town hold, or prison.
- In the smaller towns and villages, the town village leader would preside and the 'jury' will be made up of villagers who know the accuser and the accused. The jury would listen to accounts from both, and possibly witnesses, before deciding who is telling the truth. Because the jury will know both the accuser and the accused, they can use their knowledge of both people's characters to make their decision.
- There are usually two types of punishment: outlawing and fines. The most common form of justice is the fine, or wergild. The amount of wergild will vary, depending on the circumstances and the severity of the offence.

Wergild:

The principle of wergild is where compensation must be paid for any harm caused to another person, or to their property. The amount of wergild varies depending on the social status and injury inflicted.

Scale of Wergild:

- Serf/Peasant: 1-5 wergild units

- Minor injuries or damages caused to a serf or peasant.

- Commoner: 11-15 wergild units

- Moderate injuries or damages caused to a commoner.

- Craftsman/Merchant: 25-30 wergild units

- Significant injuries or damages caused to a skilled craftsman or merchant.

- Free-folk/Nobleman: 35-60 wergild units

- Grave injuries or damages caused to a freeman or minor noble.

- High Noble/Ruling Class: 80-100 wergild units

- Severe injuries or damages caused to a high noble or ruler of the land.

Note this scale is a general guideline and should be adjusted based on the specific context and cultural norms of your fantasy world. The exact values and range of the wergild units can be modified to suit the dynamics and hierarchy within your quasi-feudal society. As a general rule the killing of a high noble should pretty much bankrupt a minor noble, they would lose all their money, lands and belongings. The killing of a serf should likewise pretty much bankrupt the average commoner or merchant. This should allow you to adjust the actual values according your system and campaign.

Wergild units table: Injuries or damages

	Minor	Moderate	Major / total loss
Serf/Peasant	1 - 5	6 - 8	8 - 10
Commoner	5 - 10	11 - 15	16 - 20
Craftsman/Merchant	10 - 15	16 - 24	25 - 30
Free-folk/minor noble	15 - 24	25 - 34	35 - 60
High noble / Ruler	50 - 65	65 -80	80 - 100

Trial by Combat

Disputes and accusations can be resolved through trial by combat, where the accused and the accuser engage in a battle to determine guilt or innocence. The victor is seen as favoured by the gods and their claims are upheld. In the realm of Emberfrost, certain rules and guidelines are followed to ensure a fair and honourable resolution to disputes and accusations. These customs are seen as outdated and antiquated in the heart of Emberfrost, the Moot courts rather impose Wergild fines. But in the outer edges of Emberfrost, both across Frostfall and Sunfire Dominion, trial by combat is still seen as a reasonable option for dispute resolution. It is also practiced in some of the more remote villages.

a. Challenge and Acceptance: The accuser must formally challenge the accused to trial by combat, stating the nature of the dispute or accusation. The accused has the option to accept the challenge or decline, though refusal may be seen as an admission of guilt.

b. Selection of Champions: Both the accuser and the accused may choose a champion to fight on their behalf. Champions are skilled warriors who represent the interests of their respective parties. The accused may also choose to fight personally if capable.

c. Venue and Time: A designated venue is chosen for the trial by combat, often a neutral ground agreed upon by both parties. The time and date of the battle are determined, allowing for adequate preparation and training.

d. Weapons and Armor: The type of weapons and armour used in the combat are agreed upon by both parties or prescribed by tradition. The combatants are typically allowed to use their preferred weapons and wear protective armour.

e. Combat Rules: The combat follows established rules, such as no strikes to vital areas or no use of magic, depending on the specific customs of the land. The combatants engage in single combat until one surrenders, is rendered unable to continue, or is killed.

f. Divine Intervention: It is believed that the gods favour the just and righteous in trial by combat. Some cultures allow combatants to seek divine assistance or blessings before the battle, while others believe the outcome itself is a sign of divine favour or judgment.

g. Outcome and Verdict: The outcome of the trial by combat determines the verdict. If the accuser's champion wins, the accused is found guilty and must face the consequences. If the accused's champion wins, they are deemed innocent, and the accuser's claims are dismissed. In some cases, a draw or inconclusive outcome may lead to alternative resolutions or further trials.

h. Honor and Conduct: Both combatants are expected to fight with honour and abide by the rules of combat. Cheating, treachery, or dishonourable conduct may result in severe penalties and loss of reputation.

Blood Feuds

In cases of severe offenses, blood feuds may be initiated between families or clans. This allows them to seek vengeance for crimes committed against them until a resolution is reached, or compensation is paid. Blood feuds are sanctioned conflicts between two families or clans that have been wronged by each other, typically resulting in a cycle of revenge and retribution.

a. The feud can only be initiated by the affected party or their immediate family members. Blood feuds must be declared publicly, either through a formal declaration or by word of mouth, to make it known to all parties involved.

b. The feuding parties are expected to settle their disputes through combat or other forms of physical confrontation. Negotiation or legal arbitration is generally not accepted in blood feuds.

c. Blood feuds are governed by a code of honour and must be fought according to agreed-upon rules, such as restricting the conflict to certain locations or specific weapons.

d. The feud continues until one side is defeated or until both parties agree to a formal reconciliation and the exchange of reparations.

e. The killing of non-combatants, or children is generally forbidden in blood feuds, although there may be exceptions in extreme circumstances.

f. Outsiders are not allowed to interfere in blood feuds unless they have a direct personal stake in the conflict or have been explicitly invited by one of the involved parties.

g. The feuding parties are expected to respect temporary truces or safe zones, such as religious sites or neutral territories, where violence is prohibited.

h. Blood feuds can only be resolved through a final act of vengeance, surrender, or a negotiated settlement that is mutually agreed upon by both parties.

Outlawry

Those who commit heinous crimes, or repeatedly break the laws, may be declared outlaws. Outlaws are considered outside the protection of the law and can be hunted down by anyone without repercussions.

Land Rights

There are two tiers of Land ownership in Emberfrost. Those at the Emberfrost and City State ruler level, then all other land ownership. Each of the City State rulers pay a yearly tribute to the King and Queen of Emberfrost. This tribute takes the form of a percentage tax of all produce within their lands, and at the Kings request provision of a fighting force. This custom came about from the uneasy truce, between the rival city states to end the long years of warfare that were a constant drain on the lands.

All other land ownership is taxed by the city state ruler, who grants protection throughout their lands, in exchange for service and loyalty. The major vassals (lords and ladies) , in turn, provide protection and support to the commoners living within their lands. A tax is collected by the governing vassal, or ruler, each year at taxing day and 10% is sent to the King and Queen.

a. City State Hierarchy: The ruler (lord or lady) holds ultimate protection of all the land within their domain. They have the authority to grant parcels of land, known as fiefdoms, to vassals who swear fealty and pledge their service and loyalty.

b. Feudal Obligations: Vassals, upon receiving land, are obligated to provide military service, financial support, and counsel to the ruler. These obligations ensure the vassals' loyalty and contribution to the overall governance and defence of the realm.

c. Fief Tenure: Vassals hold their fiefdoms as long as they fulfil their obligations and maintain the trust of the ruler. Failure to meet obligations or betrayal of loyalty may result in the revocation of the fief and its redistribution.

d. Land Use and Productivity: Vassals have the right to govern and administer the land granted to them. They are responsible for managing and utilizing the land, ensuring its productivity through agriculture, resource extraction, or other means suitable to the region.

e. Protection and Justice: Vassals are expected to provide protection and maintain order within their fiefdoms. They enforce the law, settle disputes among their subjects, and ensure justice is served, also see **Moot Courts** above. They may establish local courts or appoint representatives to handle legal matters.

f. Commoner Rights: Commoners, who live and work on the land, have certain rights and responsibilities. They owe allegiance and support to their respective vassals in exchange for protection and access to resources. Commoners may have limited rights to own land themselves or engage in certain trades and crafts.

g. Hereditary Succession: In most cases, land and titles are passed down through hereditary succession within noble families. The ruler or lord designates the successor, typically a direct descendant or a chosen heir, to inherit the land and responsibilities associated with the fief.

h. Feudal Dues: Vassals may owe various dues to the ruler or lord, such as taxes, tribute, or a portion of the produce and income generated from their fiefs. These dues contribute to the overall wealth and power of the ruling authority.

Note: It's important to remember that the specific rules and customs around land rights can vary in different regions and cultures within Emberfrost, check the relevant city state specific section to see if any local changes are relevant to your campaign, or specific adventure.

Hospitality

The practice of hospitality is highly valued, where individuals are expected to provide food, shelter, and protection to guests. Breaking the laws of hospitality is seen as a grave offense.

Kinship and Family Honor

Family ties and honour play a significant role in society. Crimes committed against a family member can result in severe consequences, as they are seen as attacks on the family's honour. See also blood fueds.

Oathbinding

Oaths and promises are considered sacred, and breaking an oath is seen as a betrayal. Those who break their oaths may face severe penalties or be subjected to blood feuds.

Sanctuary

Certain places, such as temples or sacred groves, provide sanctuary for those seeking refuge. Once inside, individuals are protected from harm and cannot be harmed or arrested.

In the realm of Emberfrost, the concept of sanctuary holds immense significance, for it is a sacred vow honoured by temples, sacred groves, and certain revered locations. These sanctuaries are hallowed grounds, regarded as havens where those in need of respite and protection can find solace. Once someone steps within the boundaries of these sanctuaries, they are granted an inviolable shield, ensuring their safety and immunity from harm or arrest.

1. Temples of Tranquility: Scattered throughout Emberfrost are temples dedicated to the gods and goddesses of peace and protection. These serene places serve as sanctuaries for the weary and troubled, offering them a haven where they can seek refuge from the tumultuous outside world. Within the sacred walls, priests and priestesses maintain the sanctity of the place, ensuring that no harm comes to those who have sought solace.

2. The Sacred Grove of Eldermyst: Deep within the heart of Emberfrost's ancient forests, lies the Sacred Grove of Eldermyst. Surrounded by towering trees and lush foliage, this ethereal sanctuary is protected by druids who have sworn to safeguard all who seek refuge within its enchanting embrace. The ancient trees are said to be imbued with mystical energies, creating an impenetrable barrier to shield those within from harm.

3. The Hidden Sanctuary of the Sapphire Falls: Disguised amidst the breathtaking beauty of cascading waterfalls and glistening sapphire waters, the Hidden Sanctuary of the Sapphire Falls provides a place of safety for the desperate and vulnerable. Protected by a group of mysterious guardians, this sanctuary remains a well-kept secret, known only to those who truly need its protection.

4. The Sanctum of the Everlasting Flame: Within the heart of a dormant volcano, the Sanctum of the Everlasting Flame stands as a testament to the devotion of Emberfrost's fire-worshipping cult. Here, flames dance eternally, fuelled by the belief that the fires hold a divine power to shield and shelter those who seek sanctuary from the world's strife.

5. The Celestial Observatory: High atop the snow-capped peaks of Emberfrost's tallest mountains, the Celestial Observatory serves as a sanctuary of knowledge and enlightenment. Under the guidance of wise sages, this sanctuary welcomes seekers of wisdom, offering them protection as they delve into the mysteries of the cosmos and the secrets of ancient texts.

The concept of sanctuary is deeply ingrained in the cultural fabric of Emberfrost, and the sanctuaries themselves are revered and protected by those who believe in the inherent value of compassion and refuge. These sacred places serve as beacons of hope and compassion, embodying the core values of the realm and offering a glimmer of peace amidst the tumultuous challenges of life.

Note: It's important to remember that these laws are inspired by historical practices and should be adapted and modified to fit the specific needs and context of your fantasy world.

Cults, Societies and Guilds

In the diverse and enchanting realm of Emberfrost, a tapestry of cults, secret societies, and guilds weaves through the fabric of society, each with its own mysteries, agendas, and traditions. These clandestine organizations range from ancient orders that protect long-forgotten knowledge to exclusive guilds of artisans and mages who craft extraordinary wonders. As the land's natural wonders and magical phenomena continue to captivate its inhabitants, the cults, societies, and guilds of Emberfrost flourish, offering a myriad of opportunities for intrigue, adventure, and deeper exploration into the realm's hidden truths.

Cults

1. **The Cult of the Frost Mother:** This ancient cult worships the Frost Mother, a powerful deity believed to be the personification of the icy tundra. They perform rituals to appease her and seek her blessings for bountiful winters and protection from harsh elements.

2. **The Order of the Obsidian Eclipse:** A secretive and malevolent cult that worships dark and mysterious entities from the depths of Emberfrost's underworld. They seek to bring chaos and destruction to the land, believing it will grant them power and dominion.

3. **The Moonlit Coven:** A mysterious cult of witches and warlocks who draw power from the phases of the moon. They practice ancient rituals and magic, often involving illusions and divinations.

4. **The Cult of Eternal Sun:** Devotees of the Eternal Sun, a mythical celestial body said to bring warmth and prosperity to the land. They hold elaborate ceremonies during solstices and equinoxes to honour and invoke the blessings of the Eternal Sun.

5. **The Cult of the White Wolf:** A nomadic cult that venerates the elusive and mythical White Wolf, believed to be a spirit guardian of the tundra. They revere the wolf's cunning and prowess and invoke its protection in their travels.

6. **The Fire Heart Cult:** A cult that started in Sunfire Dominion and worships the magical heart of a long-extinct dragon. They believe the dragon's heart possesses immense power and seek to tap into its magic for personal gain.

7. **The Cult of the Crystal Spire:** Followers of an enigmatic crystal spire that rises from a remote mountain peak, in the Crystalspire mountain range. They believe the spire is a conduit to the realm of spirits and seek its guidance in their spiritual quests.

8. **The Order of the Revenants:** A cult of necromancers who can manipulate the powers of dark magic to raise the dead. They believe in the cycle of life and death, and they view their necromantic arts as a means of preserving ancestral wisdom.

9. **The Wailing Sisters:** The Wailing Sisters: A dark cult of mourning women who are said to have the power to communicate with the spirits of the deceased. They seek revenge, for the slaying of their kin.

10. **The Cult of the Eternal Shadow**: A malicious cult, who work deep in the underworld. Intent on installing a new order over the lands. Many have 'disappeared' at the hands of this cult.

The Cult of the Frost Mother:

Chief People in the Cult:

1. **High Frost Priest/Priestess:** The highest-ranking leader of the Cult of the Frost Mother, serving as the primary intermediary between the cultists and their deity. They are believed to have direct communion with the Frost Mother and are responsible for guiding the cult's rituals and practices. Eira Frostglade is the current High Priestess, she took over from Sigrun Iceheart upon his death in mysterious circumstances.

2. **Icebound Oracles:** Gifted individuals chosen by the Frost Mother herself, the Oracles possess the ability to receive visions and prophecies from the deity. They play a crucial role in interpreting signs and guiding the cult's decisions.

3. **Frostweavers:** Skilled ice mages who dedicate themselves to mastering the ancient magic of ice and frost. They are the enforcers of the cult, wielding their powers to protect their fellow cultists and strike fear into their enemies.

4. **Temple Wardens:** Devoted guardians responsible for protecting the sacred temples and shrines dedicated to the Frost Mother. They ensure the sanctity of these places and safeguard the cult's artifacts.

Cult's Motives: The cultists' primary motive is to honour and appease the Frost Mother, ensuring her favour and blessings upon the land. They believe that by performing rituals and offerings, they can gain her protection during harsh winters and ensure abundant resources from the icy tundra.

Cult's Objectives:

1. **Harsh Winter Rituals:** The cult performs elaborate rituals to invoke the Frost Mother's power, seeking her assistance in ensuring harsh but bearable winters that are crucial for their way of life.

2. **Safeguarding the Tundra:** The cult sees itself as the custodian of the icy tundra, protecting it from those who would exploit its resources recklessly. They believe in maintaining a delicate balance with nature.

3. **Expanding Their Influence:** The cult aims to grow its influence over the people of Emberfrost, attracting new members who share their reverence for the Frost Mother.

Cult's Enemies:

1. **Worshipers of the Emberflame:** The Cult of the Frost Mother considers the followers of the Emberflame, a rival deity representing fire and warmth, as their adversaries. The two cults often clash over their opposing beliefs about the balance of nature.

2. **Warmongering Tribes:** Certain warrior tribes in Emberfrost, who thrive on the concept of strength through harsh conditions, see the Frost Mother's cult as a threat to their dominance and seek to eliminate them.

3. **Ice Hunters:** While not inherently an enemy, the cult often finds itself at odds with the ice hunters, as they hunt wildlife on the tundra, which the cult views as sacred creatures.

The Cult of the Frost Mother is an enigmatic and powerful force in Emberfrost, holding deep reverence for the icy tundra and the deity they believe governs its fate. Their rituals, practices, and devotion to the Frost Mother set them apart, and they remain steadfast in their mission to ensure the harmony and survival of their frigid homeland.

The Order of the Obsidian Eclipse

The Order of the Obsidian Eclipse is a sinister and dangerous cult that operates in the shadows of Emberfrost. Led by powerful and enigmatic figures, the cult's motives are shrouded in darkness, and their ultimate goal is to plunge the land into chaos and destruction.

Chief Figures in the Cult:

1. High Priestess Seraphina Shadowbane: Seraphina is a charismatic and malevolent sorceress who wields dark magic with ease. She is the mastermind behind the cult's activities, and her icy demeanour and cunning intellect make her a formidable leader.

2. Lord Malachai Darkthorn: Malachai is a formidable warrior and a ruthless tactician. He commands the cult's enforcers and leads their military operations with precision and brutality.

3. Lady Isadora Nightshade: Isadora is the cult's chief manipulator and infiltrator. She excels at deception and uses her charm to bend others to the cult's will.

Cult's Motives: The Order of the Obsidian Eclipse seeks to unleash chaos and destruction upon Emberfrost, believing that by doing so, they will gain favour from the dark and mysterious entities they worship. They are driven by a thirst for power and dominion, and they revel in the suffering and fear that their actions sow among the populace.

Cult's Objectives: The cult's main objective is to create widespread chaos and destabilize the established order in Emberfrost. They aim to weaken the influence of existing authorities and plunge the land into darkness. They are known to conduct dark rituals and seek to open gateways to otherworldly realms, where they believe they can harness unimaginable power.

Cult's Enemies: The Order of the Obsidian Eclipse has many enemies, as their malevolent actions and dark deeds have earned them the ire of various factions. These include:

1. The Cult of the Frost Mother: The followers of the Frost Mother view the Order as a despicable force seeking to desecrate the natural balance of the land.

2. The Knights of the Silver Sun: An order of noble and righteous knights dedicated to protecting Emberfrost from all forms of evil. They are sworn enemies of the cult and seek to bring them to justice.

3. The Circle of Elders: A council of wise and ancient wizards who are aware of the cult's dangerous activities and are actively working to thwart their plans.

4. The Blades of Dawn: A skilled group of elite mercenaries who have taken it upon themselves to eliminate the Order of the Obsidian Eclipse, viewing them as a threat to peace and stability.

5. The Guardians of the Forgotten Ruins: An ancient order of scholars and protectors of sacred sites who oppose the cult's efforts to disturb ancient relics and unleash malevolent forces.

The Order of the Obsidian Eclipse remains a malevolent force lurking in the shadows, spreading fear and uncertainty throughout Emberfrost. Their dark influence must be rooted out and stopped to ensure the safety and well-being of the land and its inhabitants.

The Moonlit Coven

The Moonlit Coven is a secretive and enigmatic cult of witches and warlocks, harnessing the mystical energies of the moon to shape their magic. Their ceremonies often take place under the moonlight, and they are known for their proficiency in illusions, divinations, and other esoteric arts.

Chief Figures in the Cult:

1. High Enchantress Selene Darkthorn: Selene is the enigmatic and charismatic leader of the Moonlit Coven. She possesses an uncanny ability to commune with the moon's celestial energies, granting her powerful insights and foresight into the future.

2. Warlock Orion Shadowweaver: Orion is a skilled and ambitious warlock, highly skilled in the dark arts. He serves as Selene's second-in-command and is often entrusted with leading covert missions and safeguarding the cult's secrets.

3. Witch Astrid Moonshadow: Astrid is a master of illusion magic, known for her ability to manipulate perception and deceive even the most discerning of minds. Her talents are crucial to the cult's clandestine activities.

Cult's Motives: The Moonlit Coven's motives are deeply intertwined with their reverence for the moon's mystical influence. They seek to unravel the hidden knowledge of the cosmos, the secrets of the past, and the future's unfolding. Their primary aim is to attain a deeper understanding of the universe and to unlock the potential of their magical abilities.

Cult's Objectives: The cult is driven by a desire to access the moon's power during its various phases, believing that each phase grants them unique magical insights and strengths. They often conduct sacred rituals under specific moon phases to enhance their abilities, and they strive to accumulate arcane artifacts related to celestial bodies.

The Moonlit Coven also values the preservation of ancient knowledge and seeks to safeguard ancient tomes and scrolls from falling into the wrong hands. They see themselves as guardians of forgotten wisdom and work to maintain the balance between the magical and natural worlds.

Cult's Enemies: While the Moonlit Coven does not actively seek conflicts, they do have adversaries due to their secretive nature and association with mystical arts. Some of their potential enemies include:

1. The Temple of the Radiant Sun: A religious order devoted to the worship of the sun, they see the Moonlit Coven's practices as a perversion of the divine order and view them with suspicion.

2. The Arcane Council: A governing body of esteemed spellcasters and scholars who are cautious of the Moonlit Coven's esoteric practices and keep a watchful eye on their activities.

3. Witch Hunters and Vigilantes: Groups of individuals who are prejudiced against practitioners of magic and often perceive the Moonlit Coven as a threat to societal order.

4. The Cult of the Frost Mother: The Moonlit Coven's fascination with celestial forces and ancient wisdom often clashes with the nature-based beliefs of the Frost Mother's cult.

5. The Order of the Obsidian Eclipse: The dark and malevolent nature of the Order is a stark contrast to the Moonlit Coven's pursuits, and conflicts may arise due to opposing ideologies.

The Moonlit Coven remains a mysterious force, guided by the phases of the moon and seeking enlightenment through the secrets of the cosmos. Their magical practices and devotion to lunar energy make them a captivating yet enigmatic presence in Emberfrost.

The Cult of Eternal Sun

The Cult of Eternal Sun is a devout group of worshippers who venerate the Eternal Sun, a mythical celestial body believed to radiate boundless warmth and prosperity to the land of Emberfrost. Their rituals and ceremonies revolve around the solstices and equinoxes, during which they seek to honour and invoke the blessings of the Eternal Sun.

Chief Figures in the Cult:

1. High Priestess Aria Sunweaver: Aria is the wise and compassionate leader of the Cult of Eternal Sun. She is deeply attuned to the rhythms of the celestial bodies and possesses the ability to interpret the signs of the heavens.

2. Sunscribe Lucian Dawnflare: Lucian serves as the cult's primary historian and keeper of sacred texts. He is a meticulous scholar who dedicates his life to preserving the ancient teachings and prophecies related to the Eternal Sun.

3. Solar Guardian Elara Firebloom: Elara is a skilled warrior who acts as the protector of the cult and its followers. She is said to be gifted with extraordinary strength and agility, which she attributes to the blessings of the Eternal Sun.

Cult's Motives: The Cult of Eternal Sun is motivated by their unwavering belief in the Eternal Sun's benevolent power and its ability to bring prosperity and abundance to Emberfrost. They see themselves as the chosen custodians of the sun's blessings, charged with spreading its warmth, light, and prosperity to all corners of the land.

They are driven by a deep sense of spiritual fulfilment and devotion to the celestial forces they worship. The cult views their rituals and ceremonies as essential in maintaining a harmonious connection with the Eternal Sun, ensuring its continued favour upon the land and its inhabitants.

Cult's Objectives: The cult's main objective is to preserve and propagate their sacred knowledge of the Eternal Sun. They strive to deepen their understanding of celestial phenomena and how they influence the natural world. Through their rituals during solstices and equinoxes, they aim to enhance the sun's influence, prolonging the days of warmth and prosperity.

Moreover, the Cult of Eternal Sun seeks to act as ambassadors of goodwill, promoting unity and cooperation among the people of Emberfrost. They offer their blessings and aid to those in need, believing that their acts of kindness and compassion will further fortify the blessings of the Eternal Sun.

Cult's Enemies: Despite their benevolent intentions, the Cult of Eternal Sun faces opposition from various factions in Emberfrost, often due to religious and ideological differences:

1. The Temple of the Radiant Sun: This religious order worships the physical sun and views the Cult of Eternal Sun's reverence for the Eternal Sun as an affront to their beliefs. Tensions may arise due to conflicting interpretations of the sun's divine nature.

2. The Moonlit Coven: The Moonlit Coven's esoteric practices and association with lunar forces stand in stark contrast to the Cult of Eternal Sun's devotion to the sun. They may view each other's practices with curiosity and occasional mistrust.

3. The Order of the Obsidian Eclipse: The dark and malevolent nature of this cult directly opposes the light and benevolence espoused by the Cult of Eternal Sun. They may find themselves engaged in conflicts over their conflicting ideologies.

4. The Cult of the Frost Mother: The nature-based beliefs of the Frost Mother's cult may differ significantly from the sun-centred worship of the Cult of Eternal Sun, leading to potential misunderstandings or disputes.

The Cult of Eternal Sun remains steadfast in their devotion to the mythical Eternal Sun, spreading its warmth and blessings to those who embrace its light. Their dedication to harmony and prosperity makes them a beacon of hope in Emberfrost, even amidst the challenges presented by their enemies.

The Cult of the White Wolf

The Cult of the White Wolf is a nomadic and enigmatic group that worships the elusive and mythical White Wolf, a legendary spirit guardian believed to roam the tundra.

Chief Figures in the Cult

1. High Shamaness Lyana Iceclaw: Lyana is the revered leader of the cult, believed to have a special connection with the spirit of the White Wolf. She is wise and mysterious, guiding the cult's rituals and teachings. Her ice-blue eyes are said to possess an uncanny ability to see into the hearts of those who seek the cult's protection.

2. Runewolf Thrain Wolfsbane: Thrain is a skilled warrior and hunter who leads the cult's hunting parties and protects the group during their nomadic journeys. He is known for his keen tracking abilities and his unwavering loyalty to the White Wolf.

3. Moon Priestess Selene Snowpaws: Selene is a master of lunar magic and divination, using the phases of the moon to guide the cult's decisions and ceremonies. She is believed to receive visions and messages from the White Wolf in her dreams.

Cult's Motives: The cult's primary motive is to honour and revere the spirit of the White Wolf, which they see as a guardian and protector of the tundra and its inhabitants. They seek to maintain a harmonious relationship with nature and draw strength from the wolf's cunning and prowess.

Cult's Objectives:

1. Preserve the Ancient Traditions: The cult aims to uphold and pass down the ancient traditions and knowledge related to the White Wolf from one generation to another. They believe that in doing so, they can maintain the balance between humanity and the wild.

2. Protect the Tundra: The cult sees itself as the guardians of the tundra and its creatures. They strive to protect the delicate ecosystem from harm, including defending against external threats like poachers or invaders.

3. Seek the White Wolf's Blessings: The cult conducts ceremonies and rituals during significant celestial events, such as lunar eclipses and solstices, to invoke the blessings and protection of the White Wolf. They believe that the spirit of the White Wolf watches over them and guides them in their journey.

Cult's Enemies: The Cult of the White Wolf faces various challenges and adversaries:

1. Tundra Raiders: Nomadic tribes or groups seeking to exploit the resources of the tundra are often in conflict with the cult's mission to preserve and protect the land.

2. Superstitious Villagers: Some settled communities in the region view the cult with suspicion and fear due to their mystical practices and connection to the mythical White Wolf.

3. Rival Cults: There may be other cults or religious groups in the region vying for influence or territory, leading to occasional conflicts or tensions.

The cult remains steadfast in its devotion to the White Wolf, believing that their unique relationship with this mythical creature brings harmony and strength to their nomadic way of life in the tundra.

The Fire Heart Cult

The Fire Heart Cult is a secretive and ambitious group that originated in Sunfire Dominion, and their worship centres around the magical heart of a long-extinct dragon.

Chief Figures in the Cult

1. High Arch mage Ignatius Emberflare: Ignatius is the enigmatic and charismatic leader of the Fire Heart Cult. He is a master of fire magic and is said to have discovered the ancient dragon's heart deep within a hidden cavern. Ignatius is highly revered among the cultists for his extraordinary powers and knowledge of ancient dragon lore.

2. Dragonbinders: A group of powerful sorcerers and enchanters who specialize in harnessing and controlling the dragon's heart's magical energies. They are skilled in the ancient arts of dragon-binding and are responsible for conducting the cult's most potent rituals.

3. The Cult's Inner Circle: Comprising influential members and trusted advisors to Ignatius, the Inner Circle oversees the day-to-day operations of the cult, including recruitment, gathering resources, and guarding the secrets of the dragon's heart.

Cult Motives: The Fire Heart Cult's primary motive revolves around obtaining and harnessing the immense power they believe resides within the long-lost dragon's heart. Their beliefs are centred on the idea that the heart holds the key to unlocking forbidden and ancient magic, enabling them to gain unparalleled power and dominance.

Cult Objectives:

1. Unleash the Heart's Power: The cult's ultimate objective is to fully tap into the dragon's heart's magic and use it to bolster their own abilities and influence. They envision wielding the heart's power to reshape the world according to their desires.

2. Ascend to Godhood: Some among the cult harbour grandiose ambitions of transcending mortal limitations and attaining godlike status through the dragon's heart's power. They seek to ascend to a higher plane of existence and become immortal beings.

3. Control Sunfire Dominion: The Fire Heart Cult aims to establish a dominating presence in Sunfire Dominion and extend their control over the region, converting the entire nation into a haven of their beliefs and practices.

Cult Enemies: The Fire Heart Cult faces significant opposition and dangers as they pursue their dark and ambitious goals:

1. Sunfire Dominion's Authorities: The cult operates in secret, as their practices often conflict with the traditional religious beliefs of Sunfire Dominion. The ruling authorities seek to suppress their influence and root out their presence.

2. Rival Cults and Magical Orders: Other arcane organizations and secret societies view the Fire Heart Cult as a dangerous and unpredictable threat. These groups may attempt to thwart their plans or eliminate them as competition.

3. Dragon Guardians: Ancient protectors of dragon relics, awakened by the cult's meddling, may see the Fire Heart Cult's actions as sacrilege and actively oppose them, using their own powers to safeguard the world from the cult's reckless pursuits.

4.

Despite the dangers and opposition, they face, the Fire Heart Cult remains steadfast in their devotion to the dragon's heart, seeing it as the key to unlocking their true potential and ascending to unparalleled heights of power and mastery over the arcane arts.

The Cult of the Crystal Spire

The Cult of the Crystal Spire is a mystical and introspective group dedicated to the enigmatic crystal spire that stands tall on a remote mountain peak.

Chief Figures in the Cult

High Priestess Irawanda Moonweaver: Seraphina is the revered leader and spiritual guide of the Cult of the Crystal Spire. She is known for her deep connection with the spirit realm and her ability to communicate with the energies emanating from the crystal spire. Seraphina is seen as a wise and compassionate figure among her followers.

1. Spirit Seekers: These are the skilled mystics and shamans who are tasked with interpreting the messages and visions received from the crystal spire. They are adept at communing with the spirits and seek to understand the spire's guidance to aid the cult's spiritual quests.

2. Guardians of the Spire: A select group of devoted individuals who serve as protectors of the crystal spire. They keep watch over the sacred site, ensuring its safety from any external threats and preserving its sanctity.

Cult Motives: The Cult of the Crystal Spire is driven by a spiritual and philosophical pursuit. Their primary motive is to establish a deeper connection with the realm of spirits through the conduit of the crystal spire. They believe that the spire acts as a bridge between the material world and the ethereal realm, granting them access to profound insights and ancient wisdom.

Cult Objectives:

1. Attainment of Spiritual Enlightenment: The cult seeks to attain a higher level of spiritual enlightenment and understanding through the guidance of the crystal spire. They embark on quests to uncover hidden truths, gain spiritual clarity, and achieve inner harmony.

2. Preserve the Crystal Spire: The cult considers the crystal spire to be a sacred and irreplaceable artifact. They are committed to safeguarding its location and ensuring that it remains undisturbed by those who might misuse its powers.

3. Honouring Ancestral Spirits: The Cult of the Crystal Spire reveres the spirits of their ancestors and seeks to maintain a harmonious connection with them. They believe that the spire allows them to communicate with the spirits of the departed and gain their guidance and blessings.

Cult Enemies: While the Cult of the Crystal Spire prefers a peaceful existence, they face challenges from various sources:

1. Relic Hunters: Adventurers and treasure seekers who seek to exploit the powers of the crystal spire for personal gain may pose a threat to the cult's sacred site.

2. Rival Spiritual Sects: Other mystical orders and spiritual groups may view the cult's beliefs as competition and challenge their interpretations of the crystal spire's messages.

3. Religious Zealots: Some followers of more orthodox religious beliefs might consider the cult's practices as heretical or blasphemous, leading to potential conflicts with zealots seeking to eradicate their presence.

Despite these challenges, the followers of the Cult of the Crystal Spire remain steadfast in their reverence for the enigmatic crystal spire. They continue their spiritual quests, seeking to deepen their connection with the realm of spirits and unlock the profound insights that the spire is said to hold.

The Order of the Revenants

The Order of the Revenants is a secretive and feared cult of necromancers, skilled in the dark arts of manipulating death and reanimating the deceased.

Chief Figures in the Cult

1. Arch master Mortis Blackthorn: Mortis Blackthorn is the enigmatic and formidable leader of the Order of the Revenants. He is a master necromancer who has honed his dark abilities over centuries. Rumoured to have achieved near-immortality through his necromantic practices, he commands unwavering loyalty from his followers.

2. Lady Aria Nightshade: Aria Nightshade is the High Priestess of the Order, second only to Arch master Blackthorn. Her mastery over necromancy and her scholarly knowledge of ancient rituals makes her a respected figure among the cult's members.

3. Lord Dorian Gravesbane: As the Chief Ritualist, Dorian Gravesbane is responsible for overseeing the most complex and potent rituals of the Order. His dark charisma and unwavering devotion to the cult have garnered him considerable influence.

Cult's Motives: The Order of the Revenants is motivated by a profound belief in the cycle of life and death. They view death not as an end but as a passage to another realm of existence. Their necromantic practices are rooted in the desire to preserve ancestral wisdom, memories, and experiences, which they believe hold crucial knowledge and guidance for the living.

Cult's Objectives:

1. Mastery of Necromantic Arts: The cult seeks to continually advance their knowledge of necromancy, delving deeper into the dark arts to unlock greater powers over life and death.

2. Unveiling Ancient Secrets: The Order aims to uncover hidden knowledge and wisdom from the spirits of the deceased. They believe that by communing with the dead, they can gain access to lost histories, forgotten magic, and profound insights.

3. Defying Death's Finality: A primary objective of the cult is to challenge the notion of death as an irreversible event. They seek ways to prolong their existence and that of their loved ones through necromantic practices, striving to achieve a form of immortality.

Cult's Enemies: The Order of the Revenants faces considerable opposition and danger, both from external and internal sources:

1. Holy Orders and Religious Groups: Most religious institutions abhor the necromantic practices of the cult, considering them an affront to the natural order and an offense to the gods.

2. Adventuring Parties and Heroes: Bands of adventurers and champions of light often view the cult as a dark menace that must be eradicated to protect the realm from the potential consequences of their actions.

3. Factions Opposed to Immortality: Other groups, particularly those that believe in the sanctity of death and the transient nature of life, perceive the cult's pursuit of immortality as a blasphemous transgression.

The Order of the Revenants remains hidden in the shadows, moving discreetly to achieve their objectives. As they continue to manipulate the powers of dark magic, they remain shrouded in mystery and danger, ever mindful of the potential consequences of their necromantic practices.

The Wailing Sisters

The Wailing Sisters is a shadowy and vengeful cult composed of mourning women who possess a mysterious connection to the spirits of the deceased.

Chief Figures in the Cult

1. Lady Annia Duskwillow: Seraphina Duskwillow is the enigmatic leader of The Wailing Sisters. She is rumoured to have lost her entire family in a tragic incident and has since dedicated her life to mastering the art of communing with the dead. Her deep grief and desire for revenge have led her to gather like-minded women to form the cult.

2. Mistress Arodiesi Shadowbrook: Isadora Shadowbrook is the High Priestess of The Wailing Sisters. Her haunting beauty and commanding presence make her a formidable figure within the cult. She serves as an intermediary between the mourners and the spirits, guiding the women in their communication with the deceased.

3. Elara Nightshade: Elara Nightshade is a skilled seer and one of the most potent mediums among The Wailing Sisters. Her ability to glimpse into the realm of spirits has earned her reverence and respect within the cult.

Cult's Motives: The Wailing Sisters are driven by profound grief and the desire for revenge. They seek to harness their unique ability to communicate with the spirits of the deceased, allowing them to find closure for their losses and to seek justice for the slain.

Cult's Objectives:

1. Seeking Vengeance: The cult's primary objective is to avenge the deaths of their loved ones by uncovering the truth behind their killings and bringing those responsible to justice. They believe that by seeking revenge, the spirits of the deceased can find peace.

2. Unravelling Secrets: The Wailing Sisters aim to uncover hidden secrets and untold stories surrounding the deaths of their kin. They believe that understanding the true circumstances of these tragedies will empower them to fulfil their vengeance.

3. Honouring the Departed: The cult conducts elaborate ceremonies and rituals to honour the memory of their fallen loved ones. They see their ability to communicate with the spirits as a way to maintain a connection with the departed and provide them with solace.

Cult's Enemies: The Wailing Sisters face numerous adversaries who stand in the way of their quest for revenge and justice:

1. Rival Cults and Orders: Other cults or religious groups often view The Wailing Sisters as a dangerous and dark faction, in direct opposition to their own teachings and beliefs.

2. Law Enforcement and Authorities: The cult's pursuit of vengeance may bring them into conflict with the law, as they seek justice through means outside the legal systems of the realm.

3. Families of Those Accused: The families or allies of those accused of harming the cult's members may take up arms against The Wailing Sisters, seeing them as threats to their own safety and well-being.

The Wailing Sisters remain shrouded in mystery and sorrow, their rituals veiled in darkness as they seek to forge connections with the spirits of the departed. As they continue their quest for revenge and justice, their path is fraught with danger and uncertainty.

The Cult of the Eternal Shadow

The Cult of the Eternal Shadow is a malevolent and secretive organization that operates in the darkest corners of Emberfrost. The cult's inner workings are shrouded in darkness, and few dare to speak its name.

Chief Figures in the Cult

1. Lord Malachai Darkborne: Malachai Darkborne is the enigmatic and sinister leader of the Cult of the Eternal Shadow. His true origins and identity are obscured in shadow, making him a mysterious and feared figure among his followers. He is a master manipulator, cunningly orchestrating the cult's plans from the shadows.

2. Lady Ravenna Nightshade: Ravenna Nightshade is the High Priestess of the cult, a sorceress well-versed in dark and forbidden magics. Her beauty is said to be mesmerizing, luring unsuspecting souls into the cult's grasp. She channels the power of the Eternal Shadow, using it to bend others to the cult's will.

3. Theron Blackthorn: Theron Blackthorn is the cult's enforcer, a skilled assassin and ruthless enforcer of their malevolent schemes. His loyalty to the cult and its leader is unwavering, and he carries out their bidding without hesitation.

Cult's Motives: The Cult of the Eternal Shadow seeks to plunge the lands of Emberfrost into eternal darkness and chaos. Their motives are deeply malevolent, driven by a thirst for power, domination, and destruction. They believe that the current order is flawed and must be torn down to make way for their dark vision of a new world.

Cult's Objectives:

1. Ascendancy to Power: The cult seeks to overthrow the existing rulers and powers, usurping their authority and establishing themselves as the ruling force in Emberfrost. They aim to instill fear and subjugation among the people, bending them to their will.

2. Awakening the Eternal Shadow: The cult believes in the existence of an ancient and powerful entity known as the Eternal Shadow. They seek to awaken this malevolent force and harness its dark energies to further their nefarious goals.

3. Spread of Chaos: The cult aims to sow discord and chaos throughout the land, undermining the stability and order that have long held Emberfrost together. They exploit any opportunity for unrest and strife, seeking to weaken their enemies from within.

Cult's Enemies: The Cult of the Eternal Shadow has made many enemies due to their malevolent actions and malicious intent:

1. The Order of the Radiant Sun: A powerful and ancient order of knights and protectors who stand against the forces of darkness. They see the cult as a grave threat to the safety and well-being of Emberfrost's inhabitants.

2. The Council of High Mages: A council of arcane scholars and wielders of powerful magic who oppose the cult's dark sorcery and seek to protect the realm from its influence.

3. The Underground Resistance: A group of rebels and dissidents who resist the cult's tyranny and strive to thwart their plans for domination.

The Cult of the Eternal Shadow remains a sinister and elusive force, working from the shadows to bring about their dark vision for Emberfrost. Their presence is a constant source of fear and unease, and those who dare to oppose them risk facing the wrath of the Eternal Shadow.

Guilds

Being a guild member in Emberfrost holds significant importance, as guilds are not merely professional organizations but also influential social entities. Here's what being a guild member entails, along with the laws of the guilds and the advantages and disadvantages:

1. **Guild Membership:**

   - Guilds are selective, and joining requires demonstrating proficiency in the respective craft or skill.

   - Aspiring members must undergo rigorous training or apprenticeships under experienced guild members.

   - Once accepted, guild members are expected to uphold the guild's values and traditions.

2. **Guild Laws:**

   - Guilds have their own codes of conduct and internal regulations to maintain professionalism and discipline.

   - Violating guild laws may result in penalties, fines, suspension, or even expulsion from the guild.

3. **Advantages of Being a Guild Member:**

   - **Skill Development:** Guilds provide access to advanced training and knowledge, helping members hone their craft to perfection.

   - **Networking:** Guilds offer valuable connections with other skilled individuals, merchants, and potential employers.

   - **Market Access:** Guild members often enjoy exclusive access to high-paying clients and lucrative contracts.

   - **Protection:** Guilds protect their members from unfair competition and ensure they are not exploited.

   - **Guild Facilities:** Members can use guild facilities and resources to further their work, such as workshops, libraries, or enchanted equipment.

   - **Prestige:** Being a member of a renowned guild brings prestige and respect in the community.

4. **Disadvantages of Being a Guild Member:**

   - **Obligations:** Members must contribute to the guild's funds, participate in guild activities, and adhere to its rules.

   - **Restrictions:** Guild members may face limitations on freelancing or working outside the guild's influence.

   - **Rivalries:** Intense competition may exist between different guilds, leading to tensions or conflicts.

   - **Politics:** Guilds can be influenced by internal politics and power struggles, which might affect members' interests.

   - **Sanctions:** Breaking guild laws can result in harsh penalties or expulsion, affecting one's reputation.

5. **Guild Loyalty and Rivalries:**

   - Guild members are expected to prioritize the interests of their guild, which might conflict with personal goals.

   - Rivalry between guilds can lead to hostilities and sabotage, affecting members' livelihoods.

6. **Guild Specialization:**

   - Different guilds cater to various professions, such as blacksmithing, alchemy, enchanting, healing, etc.

   - Some members might feel confined within their specialization and unable to explore other skills.

7. **Guild Initiation and Fees:**

   - Joining a guild often requires paying an initiation fee or offering proof of skill.

   - For some members, these costs may be prohibitive or might lead to financial strain.

Being a guild member is a matter of pride and skill for individuals in Emberfrost. It opens doors to opportunities and resources, but it also brings responsibilities and expectations. Members must navigate the intricate dynamics of guilds to thrive in their chosen craft and make a name for themselves in the enchanted world of Emberfrost.

1. **The Flameforgers:** Master blacksmiths and metalworkers who craft exceptional weapons, armour, tools and ironmongery. Their work is highly sought after throughout Emberfrost, and they are renowned for their ability to imbue some of their creations with magical properties.

2. **The Whispersong Society:** A secretive guild of bards, minstrels, and storytellers who hold ancient lore and knowledge. They are responsible for preserving the history and legends of Emberfrost and often act as diplomats and mediators between rival factions.

3. **The Artisan's Guild:** A society of craftsmen and artisans who specialize in creating exquisite ice sculptures, intricate jewelry, and other works of art using the region's unique ice and crystal formations.

4. **The Scribes of the Frozen Tome:** A scholarly Guild of historians and archivists who meticulously document the rich history and lore of Emberfrost, preserving the knowledge of past generations.

5. **The Healing Hands:** A guild of skilled healers and herbalists who tend to the sick and injured throughout Emberfrost. They possess vast knowledge of medicinal herbs and magical healing arts.

6. **The Explorer's League:** A society of daring adventurers and explorers who venture into the uncharted regions of Emberfrost, seeking to uncover hidden treasures and ancient relics

7. **The Harvesters' Guild:** A group of skilled farmers and agricultural experts who ensure the bountiful harvests of Emberfrost's hardy crops. They have perfected the art of growing crops even in the harshest winter conditions and play a crucial role in ensuring the region's food security.

8. **The Order of the Enchanters**: A mystical guild of magicians and sorcerers who specialize in the art of enchantment. They are capable of imbuing objects with powerful magical properties, from enhancing the sharpness of a blade to granting protective charms to armour.

9. **The Mercantile Consortium:** A powerful guild of traders, merchants, and bankers who oversee the economic affairs of Emberfrost. They manage the flow of goods and wealth, both within the region and in trade with other lands. This guild works closely, but is aloof from, most of the other guilds, with the exceptions of The whispersong society and The scribes of the Frozen Tome, with whom they seldom have dealings. The guild of course will not admit to working with The Shadowblades,but many merchants have resorted to dealings with individual Shadowblade members, for either protection, intelligence, or revenge..

10. **The Nightwatchers**: A vigilant guild of skilled guards and sentinels who protect the cities and towns of Emberfrost from threats both mundane and supernatural. They are especially trained to deal with creatures that emerge under the cover of darkness.

11. **The Skyweavers:** A guild of talented weavers and textile artisans who create intricate and warm garments to withstand the harsh cold of Emberfrost's winters, and superb silks to keep out the heat of the desert. They are known for their skill in crafting enchanted fabrics that provide protection against extreme weather conditions.

12. **The Alchemical Society:** A group of alchemists and potion-makers who study the mysteries of magical elixirs and concoctions. They are sought after for their ability to create potions that heal, enhance abilities, or bestow temporary magical powers.

13. **The Shadowblades**: A secretive guild of highly skilled assassins and spies who operate in the shadows, carrying out clandestine missions and gathering intelligence for those who can afford their services.

14. **The Sea Serpents:** A maritime guild of sailors, fishermen, and navigators who dominate the waters around Emberfrost. They are experts at sea navigation, fishing techniques, and shipbuilding.

15. **The Hearthkeepers:** A guild of skilled cooks, bakers, and brewers who are renowned for their ability to create delicious meals and drinks using the region's local ingredients, such as frostberries and glacier water. They are linked to both The Harvester's Guild and The Sea Serpents. The rivalry is often a love, hate relationship.

Societies

Emberfrost, a realm shrouded in mystery and enchantment, is a land of diverse cultures, magical wonders, and ancient traditions. Within this fascinating world, numerous societies have emerged, each driven by their unique motives and purpose. These societies are not merely organizations; they are the lifeblood of Emberfrost's social fabric, shaping its destiny and safeguarding its values.

Societies in Emberfrost emerged to fulfil distinct roles:

1. Unity and Cooperation: In a land of unpredictable magic and diverse cultures, societies provided a platform for individuals to come together, transcending boundaries of race, class, and beliefs. They fostered unity, promoting a sense of shared purpose and responsibility.

2. Preservation of Knowledge: The ancient lands of Emberfrost are riddled with untold secrets and forgotten lore. Societies like the Enigma Keepers and the Whispersong Society emerged as custodians of knowledge, preserving the realm's history, magic, and traditions.

3. Protection and Guardianship: As threats loomed from the darkness beyond, societies like the Emberwatch Sentinels and the Order of the Silver Falcons took up arms to protect the realm and its inhabitants, becoming guardians of peace and justice.

4. Exploration and Discovery: In their quest for knowledge and resources, the Explorer's League and the Frostwardens ventured into uncharted territories, uncovering hidden treasures and ancient relics that shaped the realm's destiny.

5. Magical Mastery: Magic courses through the very veins of Emberfrost, and societies like the Moonshadows and the Veilweavers harnessed its arcane power. They sought to master the enigmatic forces and use them for various purposes, both noble and sinister.

6. Celebration and Cultural Identity: Societies such as the Emberfire Carnival and the Harvestmoon Feast provided a space for celebration, fostering a sense of cultural identity and offering respite from the realm's challenges.

7. Navigating Harsh Landscapes: The unforgiving frozen landscapes of Emberfrost demanded unique skills for survival. The Frostwardens emerged to navigate these treacherous terrains and protect the realm from the dangers that lurk within.

Each society is a reflection of Emberfrost's tapestry, weaving together a vibrant narrative of diversity, magic, and ambition. Though their motives may differ, they all contribute to the realm's intricate balance and shape the destinies of its inhabitants.

1. **The Emberwatch Sentinels:** A society of skilled warriors and rangers who guard the borders of Emberfrost, keeping a vigilant eye out for any threats that may come from beyond the realm.

2. **The Order of the Silver Falcons:** A chivalric order of knights and warriors who are dedicated to protecting the weak and upholding the principles of honour and justice.

3. **The Frostwardens:** A guild of skilled and hardy individuals who specialize in surviving and navigating the treacherous frozen landscapes of Emberfrost. They are skilled in Arctic survival, ice fishing, and tracking dangerous beasts that roam the tundra.

4. **The Moonshadows:** A guild of skilled thieves and spies who operate in the shadows, gathering information and undertaking covert missions. They are known for their agility, stealth, and cunning tactics.

5. **The Silverclaw Mercenaries:** A formidable society of mercenaries and warriors for hire. They take contracts to protect caravans, explore dangerous territories, and assist in conflicts when needed.

6. **The Enigma Keepers:** A band of scholars, researchers, and arcane experts who delve into the mysteries of ancient artifacts and magical phenomena. They are the custodians of lost knowledge and secrets of Emberfrost's past.

7. **The Nightfall Cult:** A sinister and malevolent cult that worships the dark and malefic entities that dwell in the shadows. The Nightfall Cult embraces dark rituals and sinister magic to serve their malevolent patrons. They seek to sow chaos and darkness throughout Emberfrost, believing that by bringing about the realm's demise, they will gain favour with their sinister deities.

8. **The Veilweavers:** The Veilweavers are a clandestine and mysterious society of arcane spellcasters and illusionists. They possess the ability to manipulate reality through their mastery of illusions and deception. Cloaked in secrecy, the Veilweavers operate discreetly, concealing their true intentions and weaving intricate webs of illusion to further their enigmatic agenda.

The Emberwatch Sentinels

The Emberwatch Sentinels is a revered society of highly skilled warriors and rangers who have sworn to protect the borders and territories of Emberfrost from any external threats that may loom beyond its realm. Dedicated to preserving the safety and sovereignty of their land, these vigilant guardians stand as a formidable force against those who would dare to trespass or bring harm to the people of Emberfrost.

Key Members of the Society:

1. **Commander Haldor Ironclad:** An esteemed and seasoned veteran, Commander Haldor leads the Emberwatch Sentinels with wisdom and valour. He is respected by his peers and revered by the younger members for his courage and dedication to the protection of Emberfrost.

2. **Sylvia Swiftarrow:** A skilled ranger and scout, Sylvia is known for her uncanny ability to track and anticipate potential threats. Her keen instincts and archery prowess make her an invaluable asset to the society.

3. **Erik the Bold:** A daring and charismatic warrior, Erik is renowned for leading his fellow Sentinels into daring raids and strategic battles. He instils courage in those around him, making him an inspiring figure within the society.

Society's Motives:

1. **Protection of Emberfrost:** The primary motive of the Emberwatch Sentinels is to safeguard the land of Emberfrost and its people from any external harm, whether it be marauding invaders or dangerous creatures.

2. **Preservation of Sovereignty:** They are dedicated to upholding the sovereignty of Emberfrost, ensuring that its borders are respected, and no hostile forces gain a foothold within its territory.

Society's Goals and Achievements:

1. **Secure Borders:** The Sentinels strive to maintain well-protected borders, making it difficult for any intruders or threats to breach Emberfrost's defences.

2. **Eliminate Threats:** They actively seek out and neutralize dangerous creatures and entities that may pose a menace to the citizens of Emberfrost.

3. **Peacekeeping:** In addition to guarding against external threats, they act as peacekeepers within the realm, mediating conflicts and maintaining law and order.

Society's Rivals / Enemies:

1. **The Darkfrost Raiders:** A group of notorious bandits and mercenaries that periodically attempt to breach Emberfrost's borders to pillage and plunder its resources.

2. **The Cursed Coven:** A malevolent cult residing beyond the borders, seeking to unleash dark forces upon Emberfrost. The Emberwatch Sentinels actively counter their attempts to breach the realm.

3. **The Blizzertooth Clan:** A tribe of aggressive and territorial Yeti-like creatures residing in the northern wilderness. The Sentinels clash with them to protect the northern borders.

The Emberwatch Sentinels are a stalwart and revered society, deeply rooted in the traditions of honour, bravery, and loyalty. Their unwavering dedication to the protection of Emberfrost has made them an indispensable force, instilling a sense of security and pride in the citizens they defend.

The Order of the Silver Falcons

The Order of the Silver Falcons is a revered chivalric order of knights and warriors in Emberfrost. With an unwavering commitment to protecting the weak and upholding the principles of honour and justice, they are seen as the embodiment of virtue and bravery.

Key Members of the Society:

1. **Sir Tristan Stormrider:** The esteemed Grand Master of the Order, Sir Tristan embodies the chivalric virtues of valour, wisdom, and humility. His inspiring leadership has garnered respect and admiration from all members of the society.

2. **Lady Isabella Dawnsworn:** A skilled and compassionate knight, Lady Isabella leads the Falcons with unwavering dedication to justice and mercy. Her wisdom and fair judgments have earned her the title of Chief Justiciar.

3. **Sir Gideon Silverhelm:** A formidable warrior and expert tactician, Sir Gideon commands the Silver Falcons' military forces. He is renowned for his strategic prowess on the battlefield.

Society's Motives:

1. **Protection of the Weak:** The primary motive of the Silver Falcons is to ensure the safety and protection of the vulnerable and oppressed, championing those in need.

2. **Upholding Honor and Justice:** They are bound by a strict code of chivalry, striving to uphold honour and justice in all their actions, both on and off the battlefield.

Society's Goals and Achievements:

1. **Defending the Realm:** The Silver Falcons are devoted to defending Emberfrost from all manner of threats, including marauders, monsters, and external enemies.

2. **Promoting Peace and Order:** They work tirelessly to maintain peace within Emberfrost's borders, intervening in disputes and mediating conflicts.

3. **Training New Recruits:** Part of their duty involves mentoring and training young knights and warriors, passing down the traditions and values of the order.

Society's Rivals / Enemies:

1. **The Shadowblade Brotherhood:** A covert and ruthless band of mercenaries, the Shadowblade Brotherhood often opposes the Silver Falcons' efforts to maintain order, leading to clashes between the two factions.

2. **The Darkcrown Cult:** A malevolent cult seeking to spread chaos and fear, the Darkcrown Cult targets the principles of justice upheld by the Silver Falcons, making them natural adversaries.

3. **The Iron Fist Company:** A mercenary guild known for their brutal methods, they occasionally clash with the Silver Falcons over differing views on law and order.

The Order of the Silver Falcons stands as a beacon of hope and courage in Emberfrost. Their valor and unwavering dedication to justice make them the guardians of honour, and they are respected and admired throughout the realm for their noble deeds.

The Frostwardens

The Frostwardens are a revered guild of skilled and hardy individuals who have honed their expertise in surviving and navigating the unforgiving frozen landscapes of Emberfrost. They possess a profound understanding of Arctic survival techniques, ice fishing, and tracking dangerous beasts that prowl the icy tundra. Their knowledge and skills make them indispensable in the challenging environment of Emberfrost's frozen domains.

Key Members of the Society:

1. **Eira Frostfang:** A seasoned and wise leader, Eira serves as the head of the Frostwardens. Her vast knowledge of the icy wilderness and her ability to lead her fellow members with confidence and wisdom have earned her the respect of the entire guild.

2. **Magnus Iceheart:** An expert ice fisherman and trapper, Magnus's keen understanding of tracking and hunting has saved the Frostwardens on numerous occasions. He is a reliable and skilled member of the society.

3. **Sylva Stormsong:** A gifted navigator and explorer, Sylva possesses an innate sense of direction and an unwavering determination to brave the harshest of winter storms. She has made significant contributions to the guild's mapping and exploration efforts.

Society's Motives:

1. **Survival Expertise:** The primary motive of the Frostwardens is to develop and share their expertise in Arctic survival with their members, ensuring they are well-equipped to endure the harsh conditions of Emberfrost.

2. **Preserving the Balance:** The Frostwardens also strive to maintain the delicate ecological balance of the frozen wilderness, safeguarding both the natural resources and the creatures that inhabit the tundra.

Society's Goals and Achievements:

1. **Training and Development:** The Frostwardens aim to continually train their members in Arctic survival skills, ensuring they can withstand the rigors of Emberfrost's frozen terrains.

2. **Mapping and Exploration:** They endeavour to expand their knowledge of Emberfrost's frozen lands through exploration, creating detailed maps that aid in navigating the tundra.

3. **Protecting the Tundra:** The Frostwardens actively engage in tracking and monitoring dangerous beasts to protect the inhabitants of Emberfrost and maintain the delicate balance of nature.

Society's Rivals / Enemies:

1. **The Frostbite Raiders:** A group of opportunistic thieves and mercenaries who often clash with the Frostwardens over control of vital resources found in the icy wilderness.

2. **The Frostclaw Clan:** A tribe of formidable yeti-like creatures that roam the frozen north. The Frostwardens must remain vigilant to prevent conflicts with these territorial beings.

3. **The Frozen Serpent Cult:** A secretive cult that seeks to awaken and control ancient frost serpents. The Frostwardens are dedicated to thwarting their dark machinations and preserving the harmony of Emberfrost's frozen lands.

The Frostwardens are highly esteemed in Emberfrost for their exceptional survival skills and their dedication to protecting the frozen wilderness. Their role is indispensable in ensuring the safety and prosperity of the people who call Emberfrost's icy domains their home.

The Moonshadows

The Moonshadows is a secretive and elusive guild of skilled thieves and spies in Emberfrost. Operating from the shadows, they excel in espionage, information gathering, and undertaking covert missions with precision and finesse.

Key Members of the Society:

1. **Silas Shadowstep:** The enigmatic leader and mastermind behind the Moonshadows. Silas is a master of disguise and manipulation, with an uncanny ability to orchestrate complex operations.

2. **Evelyn Nightshade:** An expert thief and infiltrator, Evelyn is the guild's second-in-command. She is known for her agility and stealth, making her an indispensable asset in executing covert missions.

3. **Lucian Whisperwind:** A brilliant strategist and tactician, Lucian oversees the guild's intelligence operations. His extensive knowledge of espionage techniques and information networks keeps the Moonshadows one step ahead of their enemies.

Society's Motives:

1. **Information Gathering:** The primary motive of the Moonshadows is to collect valuable information, which they leverage for various purposes, including selling it to the highest bidder, using it as leverage against rivals, or protecting Emberfrost from internal and external threats.

2. **Covert Operations:** They specialize in clandestine missions, such as heists, sabotage, and assassinations. These tasks are often commissioned by wealthy clients, shadowy figures, or factions seeking to influence the political landscape of Emberfrost.

Society's Goals and Achievements:

1. **Amassing Wealth and Power:** The Moonshadows aim to accumulate considerable wealth and influence through their covert activities, allowing them to expand their network and solidify their position as a significant player in the underworld.

2. **Outmanoeuvring Rivals:** They seek to maintain an upper hand over rival guilds, criminal organizations, and spies from other lands, always staying ahead in the intricate game of information warfare.

3. **Protecting Their Secrets:** One of their primary goals is to safeguard their clandestine operations and the identities of their members, ensuring their anonymity and security.

Society's Rivals / Enemies:

1. **The Silver Falcons:** The order of chivalric knights considers the Moonshadows to be a threat to Emberfrost's security and the rule of law, leading to constant clashes and attempts to expose their operations.

2. **The Eyes of the Hawk:** A group of elite investigators and spies, the Eyes of the Hawk are determined to dismantle the Moonshadows and bring their illegal activities to an end.

3. **The Arcane Watchers:** A powerful organization of mages and wizards, the Arcane Watchers view the Moonshadows as a potential danger to the stability of Emberfrost, leading to occasional confrontations.

The Moonshadows' operations are a dance of shadows and intrigue, impacting the politics and balance of power in Emberfrost. Their agile manoeuvres, skilled infiltration, and intelligence gathering make them both a formidable adversary and a valuable ally for those who can secure their services.

The Silverclaw Mercenaries

The Silverclaw Mercenaries are a renowned society of battle-hardened warriors and skilled fighters, offering their services as mercenaries for hire. From safeguarding caravans through perilous lands to undertaking daring explorations and intervening in conflicts, they are known for their formidable combat prowess and their unwavering dedication to fulfilling their contracts.

Key Members of the Society:

1. **Alistair Stormclaw:** The charismatic and honourable leader of the Silverclaw Mercenaries. Alistair is a veteran warrior with exceptional tactical skills, inspiring loyalty and camaraderie among his fellow mercenaries.

2. **Sylvia Swiftblade:** Second-in-command, Sylvia is a skilled swordswoman and an expert in hand-to-hand combat. She is known for her quick thinking and decisive actions on the battlefield.

3. **Gareth Ironheart:** As the chief strategist, Gareth devises battle plans and ensures the successful execution of missions. His wisdom and experience make him a trusted advisor to Alistair.

Society's Motives:

1. **Profit and Sustenance:** While they hold to a code of honour, the primary motive of the Silverclaw Mercenaries is to earn a living and sustain their organization. They take contracts that offer fair pay and promise a degree of excitement or challenge.

2. **Honourable Reputation:** They strive to maintain a reputation for integrity and reliability. Fulfilling their contracts with skill and honour ensures a steady flow of new clients seeking their services.

Society's Goals and Achievements:

1. **Gaining Renown:** The Silverclaw Mercenaries seek to establish themselves as the go-to mercenaries in Emberfrost. They aim to become synonymous with dependable and competent fighters for hire.

2. **Expansion and Influence:** As they take on more lucrative and challenging contracts, the society seeks to expand its network and influence within the realm and beyond its borders.

3. **Championing Causes:** While driven by profit, the Silverclaw Mercenaries occasionally take on missions that align with their sense of justice and honour. They may offer their services to protect innocent civilians or uphold the values they believe in.

Society's Rivals / Enemies:

1. **The Crimson Blades:** Another mercenary group in the region, the Crimson Blades are fierce rivals of the Silverclaw Mercenaries. The competition for contracts can sometimes lead to intense clashes between the two societies.

2. **The Order of the Silver Falcons:** The chivalric knights view mercenaries with disdain and mistrust. The Silver Falcons often look down upon the Silverclaw Mercenaries, considering them as mere sell-swords.

3. **The Frostwardens:** The Frostwardens occasionally clash with the mercenaries when their interests collide. The two societies hold differing perspectives on the handling of dangerous creatures that roam the tundra.

The Silverclaw Mercenaries' reputation as skilled fighters and honourable warriors ensures their services are in high demand across Emberfrost. While they may walk the line between opportunism and noble deeds, their dedication to fulfilling contracts has carved them a respected niche in the ever-changing landscapes of the realm.

The Enigma Keepers

The Enigma Keepers are an esteemed society of scholars, researchers, and arcane experts who dedicate their lives to unravelling the mysteries of ancient artifacts and magical phenomena. With their vast knowledge and relentless pursuit of wisdom, they safeguard the secrets of Emberfrost's past, seeking to preserve and understand the enigmatic forces that shape the realm.

Key Members of the Society:

1. **Arch mage Elara Moonweaver:** The venerable leader of the Enigma Keepers, Arch mage Elara possesses unparalleled expertise in arcane arts and ancient lore. Her guidance and wisdom have steered the society towards profound discoveries.

2. **Thaddeus Stonegaze:** A master historian and curator of the society's extensive library. Thaddeus is meticulous in documenting every piece of knowledge unearthed, and he ensures the preservation of ancient texts and artifacts.

3. **Lysandra Nightshade:** A prodigious arcanist and skilled artifact investigator, Lysandra is the driving force behind many successful explorations and breakthroughs. She is renowned for her daring and inquisitive spirit.

Society's Motives:

1. **Unravelling the Enigmas:** The primary motive of the Enigma Keepers is to delve into the secrets of Emberfrost's past and understand the mystical phenomena that shape the realm's history and present.

2. **Preserving Lost Knowledge:** The society aims to safeguard the wisdom of ages past and ensure that it is not lost to time or malevolent forces.

Society's Goals and Achievements:

1. **Unlocking Ancient Artifacts:** The Enigma Keepers relentlessly seek to unlock the hidden potential and purpose of ancient artifacts scattered throughout Emberfrost.

2. **Mastering Arcane Phenomena:** They strive to comprehend the magical phenomena that exist within the realm and harness these forces responsibly.

3. **Advancing Magical Understanding:** Through their research and studies, the society aims to advance the overall understanding of magic and its intricacies.

Society's Rivals / Enemies:

1. **The Order of the Obsidian Eclipse:** The secretive and malevolent cult harbours an interest in ancient artifacts and arcane knowledge. The Enigma Keepers are wary of their intentions and seek to protect valuable artifacts from falling into their hands.

2. **The Frostwardens:** While not necessarily enemies, the Enigma Keepers and the Frostwardens occasionally find themselves at odds when their respective interests intersect. The Frostwardens' focus on survival in the frozen landscape contrasts with the Enigma Keepers' pursuit of ancient knowledge.

3. **The Cult of the Eternal Shadow:** This malicious cult seeks to install a new order over the lands, and their disruptive actions sometimes jeopardize the historical sites and artifacts the Enigma Keepers aim to preserve.

The Enigma Keepers' insatiable curiosity and profound commitment to the pursuit of knowledge have earned them the respect of many, including rulers, scholars, and even adventurers. Their willingness to share their findings with other guilds and societies contributes to a harmonious pursuit of wisdom across Emberfrost. Yet, they remain vigilant, knowing that powerful secrets can attract both allies and adversaries in equal measure.

The Nightfall Cult

A sinister and malevolent cult that worships the dark and malefic entities that dwell in the shadows. The Nightfall Cult embraces dark rituals and sinister magic to serve their malevolent patrons. They seek to sow chaos and darkness throughout Emberfrost, believing that by bringing about the realm's demise, they will gain favour with their sinister deities.

Key Members of the Cult:

1. **High Priestess Lilith Shadowborne:** The ruthless and charismatic leader of the Nightfall Cult, High Priestess Lilith is a master of dark magic and a devout servant of the malevolent entities the cult worships.

2. **Darkblade Kael Drakemourn:** A high-ranking enforcer within the cult, Darkblade Kael is a skilled assassin and warrior. He is fanatically loyal to the cult's cause and carries out their most nefarious deeds.

Cult's Motives:

1. **Chaos and Destruction:** The Nightfall Cult's primary motive is to spread chaos, destruction, and fear throughout Emberfrost to pave the way for their dark deities' ascension.

2. **Summoning Dark Entities:** They seek to summon and unleash malevolent entities into the realm, believing that their presence will bring about the realm's downfall.

Cult's Goals and Achievements:

1. **Dark Rituals:** The Nightfall Cult conducts dark rituals and sacrifices to appease their malevolent patrons and strengthen their connection to the dark forces they serve.

2. **Infiltration and Manipulation:** They aim to infiltrate key positions of power and manipulate unsuspecting individuals to further their dark agenda.

Cult's Rivals / Enemies:

1. **The Emberwatch Sentinels:** The vigilant and skilled warriors of the Emberwatch Sentinels are a significant threat to the Nightfall Cult's plans, as they strive to protect the realm from malevolent forces.

2. **The Order of the Silver Falcons:** The noble knights of the Order of the Silver Falcons stand in direct opposition to the Nightfall Cult's sinister schemes. They clash over their conflicting beliefs and goals for Emberfrost's future.

As darkness descends upon the realm, the Veilweavers and the Nightfall Cult cast ominous shadows, their true intentions concealed, and their actions threatening the peace and stability of Emberfrost.

The Veilweavers

The Veilweavers are a clandestine and mysterious society of arcane spellcasters and illusionists. They possess the ability to manipulate reality through their mastery of illusions and deception. Cloaked in secrecy, the Veilweavers operate discreetly, concealing their true intentions and weaving intricate webs of illusion to further their enigmatic agenda.

Key Members of the Society:

1. **Grand Illusionist Seraphina Nightshade:** The enigmatic leader of the Veilweavers, Grand Illusionist Seraphina is an unmatched master of illusion magic. Her identity remains shrouded in secrecy, and only a select few know her true name.

2. **Shadowblade Elrik Shadowstep:** A shadowy figure and the society's chief operative. Shadowblade Elrik is skilled in covert operations, espionage, and intelligence gathering. His stealth and cunning make him a formidable asset to the Veilweavers.

Society's Motives:

1. **Control and Manipulation:** The Veilweavers seek to wield their illusionary powers to manipulate events, perceptions, and information to gain influence and control over Emberfrost's affairs.

2. **Hidden Agendas:** Their motives remain veiled, and they are known to pursue hidden agendas that further their arcane interests.

Society's Goals and Achievements:

1. **Veiling Their Activities:** The Veilweavers have excelled at concealing their true activities and intentions, making it challenging for other societies to uncover their true goals.

2. **Infiltrating Powerful Circles:** They aim to infiltrate key positions of power within Emberfrost's society, allowing them to influence decisions and shape the realm's future from the shadows.

Society's Rivals / Enemies:

1. **The Moonlit Coven:** The rivalry between the Veilweavers and the Moonlit Coven stems from their shared interest in manipulating magic to achieve their ends. Both societies vie for dominance in the realm's arcane affairs.

2. **The Enigma Keepers:** The arcane experts of the Enigma Keepers seek to understand the true nature of the Veilweavers' magic, while the Veilweavers strive to keep their illusionary secrets hidden from prying eyes.

Flora

Non edible, but unusual flora

1. Celestial Glowbloom (Grows in the Astral Moors) Climate: High-altitude moors, often near ley lines Season: Blooms during the rare convergence of two full moons. Unusual Properties: The Celestial Glowbloom emits a soft, ethereal glow that is said to be connected to the astral realm. Its petals can be used to create a unique luminescent ink, which allows the user to write messages visible only under specific celestial conditions. Comparison to Earth: Similar to bioluminescent algae, but with a stronger connection to celestial energies.

2. Phantom Orchid (Grows in the Veiled Forest) Climate: Dense and mist-covered forests Season: Blooms erratically, often during dense fog. Unusual Properties: The Phantom Orchid is nearly invisible to the naked eye and can only be seen through the lens of a special crystal. When viewed through the crystal, the orchid appears as a translucent, ghostly figure. Comparison to Earth: Resembles the real-world orchid family, but with the unique ability to be seen only through a special crystal.

3. Enigma Bramble (Grows in the Enigma Marsh) Climate: Swampy and mist-shrouded marshlands Season: Blooms once every few decades under a blood moon. Unusual Properties: The Enigma Bramble constantly shifts its shape and position, making it challenging to navigate the marsh. It is also rumoured to trap the souls of those who venture too close, causing them to lose their way. Comparison to Earth: Similar to the real-world plant "dancing grass," but with added supernatural properties.

4. Shimmerleaf Vine (Grows in the Luminous Caverns) Climate: Subterranean caves with phosphorescent crystals Season: Blooms whenever exposed to light. Unusual Properties: The Shimmerleaf Vine's leaves reflect and refract light, creating a mesmerizing display of shifting colours. It is often used by enchanters to create iridescent pigments for magical artwork and illusions. Comparison to Earth: Resembles bioluminescent mushrooms, but with an ability to reflect and refract light.

5. Whispering Willows (Grows in the Whispersong Glen) Climate: Calm and serene valleys with gentle breezes Season: Constantly rustles its leaves, even on the stillest days. Unusual Properties: The Whispering Willows emit soft, soothing whispers that seem to carry ancient secrets and forgotten knowledge. Those who listen closely can sometimes gain insights or receive cryptic messages. Comparison to Earth: Resembles real-world willow trees, but with the magical ability to produce whispers.

6. Emberglade Lanterns (Grows in the Emberglade Marsh) Climate: Marshlands near dormant volcanoes Season: Blooms during volcanic eruptions or seismic activity. Unusual Properties: The Emberglade Lanterns emit a warm, fiery glow that illuminates the marshland during volcanic eruptions. The light is said to have protective properties against dark magic. Comparison to Earth: Similar to bioluminescent fungi, but with a connection to volcanic activity.

7. Enchanted Mists (Grows in the Veiled Peaks) Climate: Mountainous regions with frequent fog Season: Blooms during the heaviest mists. Unusual Properties: The Enchanted Mists create an illusionary haze that distorts perceptions and confuses those who wander through them. They are sometimes used by skilled illusionists to create diversionary tactics. Comparison to Earth: Resembles real-world fog-producing plants, but with the added illusionary effect.

8. Mirage Thistle (Grows in the Mirage Dunes) Climate: Arid deserts with shifting sands Season: Blooms during intense heatwaves. Unusual Properties: The Mirage Thistle releases mirage-like illusions, making it appear as though water is nearby. Travelers who fall for the illusion can become disoriented and lose their way. Comparison to Earth: Similar to real-world desert plants, but with the ability to create mirage-like illusions.

9. Ethereal Veil (Grows in the Ethereal Glade) Climate: Misty and otherworldly glades Season: Blooms during a rare alignment of the stars. Unusual Properties: The Ethereal Veil emits a subtle, shimmering aura that allows those who pass through it to temporarily phase into the ethereal plane. This allows them to interact with spirits and ethereal beings. Comparison to Earth: Resembles a combination of real-world ferns and plants that are believed to have connections to the spirit world.

10. Celestial Blossom (Grows in the Celestial Arboretum) Climate: Magical gardens with celestial alignment Season: Blooms during celestial events, such as meteor showers or eclipses. Unusual Properties: The Celestial Blossom releases a burst of stardust-like particles when in full bloom. These particles are said to have transformative properties, temporarily granting the consumer enhanced magical abilities. Comparison to Earth: Resembles real-world chrysanthemums but with the added stardust-like effect.

Edible flora

1. Frostberry Bush (Grows in Frostfall) Climate: Cold and temperate regions Picking Season: Late Frostfall to Snowmelt Preparation: Eaten raw, often used in sweet desserts and preserves Comparison: Similar to blueberries on Earth, with a hint of sweetness and tanginess.

2. Emberroot Vegetable (Grows in Emberfall) Climate: Mild and temperate regions Picking Season: Frostmorn to Firstbud Preparation: Cooked, used in stews, soups, and roasted dishes Comparison: Resembles a cross between a potato and a sweet potato, with a rich and nutty flavour.

3. Sunpetal Lettuce (Grows in Sunfire Dominion) Climate: Hot and arid regions Picking Season: Suncrest to Naturefade Preparation: Eaten raw in salads or used as wraps for fillings Comparison: Similar to a mix of romaine and butter lettuce, with a refreshing and slightly peppery taste.

4. Frostmoss Herb (Grows in Frostfall) Climate: Cold and snowy regions Picking Season: Frostmorn to Firstsnow Preparation: Dried and used as seasoning for various dishes Comparison: Resembles thyme on Earth, with a mild, pine-like aroma and flavour.

5. Emberbloom Flower (Grows in Emberheart) Climate: Mild and temperate regions Picking Season: Firstbud to Naturebloom Preparation: Eaten raw in salads or candied as a sweet treat Comparison: Similar to nasturtium flowers, with a slightly peppery and citrusy taste.

6. Sunburst Fruit (Grows in Sunfire Dominion) Climate: Hot and arid regions Picking Season: Suncrest to Naturefade Preparation: Eaten raw, often sliced or juiced Comparison: Resembles a mix of mango and passion fruit, with a tropical and sweet flavour.

7. Frostpine Nut Tree (Grows in Frostfall) Climate: Cold and temperate regions Picking Season: Frostmorn to Snowdeep Preparation: Roasted and eaten as a snack or used in baking Comparison: Similar to chestnuts, with a slightly sweet and nutty taste.

8. Emberleaf Herb (Grows in Emberfall) Climate: Mild and temperate regions Picking Season: Snowmelt to Firstbud Preparation: Used fresh in salads, soups, and sauces Comparison: Resembles basil, with a peppery and slightly minty flavour.

9. Sunblossom Vine (Grows in Sunfire Dominion) Climate: Hot and arid regions Picking Season: Suncrest to Naturefade Preparation: Eaten raw, often used in fruit salads or as garnish Comparison: Similar to grapes, with a juicy and sweet taste.

10. Frostfern Leaf (Grows in Frostfall) Climate: Cold and snowy regions Picking Season: Frostmorn to Firstsnow Preparation: Steamed or boiled, served as a side dish Comparison: Resembles spinach, with a tender texture and mild earthy taste.

These edible florae add depth and variety to Emberfrost's culinary traditions, with each plant flourishing in its specific climate and season, offering unique and flavourful options for the inhabitants of the land.

Poisonous flora

1. Witherthorn Bush (Grows in Frostfall) Climate: Cold and temperate regions Toxicity: Poisonous by touch and ingestion Comparison: Resembles a mix of holly and blackthorn bushes on Earth. Fatality: Ingesting a handful of berries can be fatal, causing severe internal damage.

2. Embernightshade Flower (Grows in Emberfall) Climate: Mild and temperate regions Toxicity: Poisonous by ingestion and breathing its scent Comparison: Similar to lily-of-the-valley flowers on Earth. Fatality: Ingesting a single flower or inhaling its scent can be lethal, leading to respiratory failure.

3. Sunscorch Thistle (Grows in Sunfire Dominion) Climate: Hot and arid regions Toxicity: Poisonous by touch and ingestion Comparison: Resembles a mix of thistle and nettles on Earth. Fatality: Ingesting a small nember of leaves or thorns can be fatal, causing organ failure.

4. Frostbane Mushroom (Grows in Frostfall) Climate: Cold and snowy regions Toxicity: Poisonous by ingestion Comparison: Similar to the death cap mushroom on Earth. Fatality: Consuming just one mushroom can be deadly, causing severe liver and kidney damage.

5. Embergloom Lily (Grows in Emberheart) Climate: Mild and temperate regions Toxicity: Poisonous by touch and ingestion Comparison: Resembles a mix of tiger lilies and belladonna flowers on Earth. Fatality: Ingesting or handling the petals can lead to fatal respiratory paralysis.

6. Sunscorch Nightshade (Grows in Sunfire Dominion) Climate: Hot and arid regions Toxicity: Poisonous by ingestion Comparison: Similar to belladonna plants on Earth Fatality: Consuming a small amount of the berries can be lethal, causing heart failure.

7. Frostbite Ivy (Grows in Frostfall) Climate: Cold and temperate regions Toxicity: Poisonous by touch and ingestion Comparison: Resembles a mix of poison ivy and English ivy on Earth. Fatality: Ingesting or touching the leaves can cause severe allergic reactions leading to death.

8. Emberthorn Bramble (Grows in Emberfall) Climate: Mild and temperate regions Toxicity: Poisonous by touch Comparison: Similar to blackberry brambles with toxic thorns on Earth. Fatality: Puncture wounds from the thorns can lead to severe infection and, in some cases, death.

9. Sunburnt Fern (Grows in Sunfire Dominion) Climate: Hot and arid regions Toxicity: Poisonous by touch and ingestion Comparison: Resembles a mix of bracken fern and stinging nettle on Earth. Fatality: Ingesting a small number of leaves or touching the fronds can cause fatal reactions.

10. Frostfire Nightshade (Grows in Frostfall) Climate: Cold and snowy regions Toxicity: Poisonous by touch and ingestion Comparison: Similar to the deadly nightshade plant on Earth. Fatality: Ingesting even a small amount of the berries or touching the leaves can be lethal, affecting the nervous system.

These poisonous florae pose significant risks to the inhabitants of Emberfrost, and caution is essential when navigating the wilderness to avoid contact with these dangerous plants.

Healing and Medicinal Flora

1. Frostleaf Herb (Grows in Frostfall) Climate: Cold and temperate regions Season: Spring and early summer Medicinal Properties: Frostleaf herb has potent antiseptic properties and is used to treat wounds and prevent infections. It can also alleviate respiratory issues and reduce inflammation. Comparison: Similar to a combination of echinacea and chamomile on Earth Quantity Needed: A handful of leaves or flowers can be brewed into a healing tea.

2. Emberbloom Petal (Grows in Emberfall) Climate: Mild and temperate regions Season: Late spring to mid-summer Medicinal Properties: Emberbloom petals have soothing and analgesic properties. They are commonly used to relieve pain, treat minor burns, and reduce fever. Comparison: Resembles the petals of calendula flowers on Earth Quantity Needed: A few petals are sufficient for topical applications or infusion in hot water.

3. Sunshimmer Moss (Grows in Sunfire Dominion) Climate: Hot and arid regions Season: Year-round in shaded areas Medicinal Properties: Sunshimmer moss has potent healing properties for the skin. It can soothe burns, reduce inflammation, and promote skin regeneration. Comparison: Similar to a mix of aloe vera and Irish moss on Earth Quantity Needed: A small amount of the gel-like substance from the moss can be applied directly to the skin.

4. Icethorn Berry (Grows in Frostfall) Climate: Cold and snowy regions Season: Late summer to early autumn Medicinal Properties: Icethorn berries are rich in antioxidants and have immune-boosting properties. They are used to strengthen the body's defences and alleviate cold and flu symptoms. Comparison: Resembles a combination of elderberries and blueberries on Earth Quantity Needed: A handful of berries can be consumed daily for their health benefits.

5. Emberheart Root (Grows in Emberheart) Climate: Mild and temperate regions Season: Autumn to early winter Medicinal Properties: Emberheart root is a natural analgesic and anti-inflammatory. It is used to relieve joint pain, migraines, and stomach discomfort. Comparison: Similar to the properties of ginger and turmeric roots on Earth Quantity Needed: A small piece of the root can be grated and used in teas or as a spice in cooking.

6. Sunbeam Fern (Grows in Sunfire Dominion) Climate: Hot and arid regions Season: Year-round in shaded areas Medicinal Properties: Sunbeam fern has a calming effect on the nerves and is used to treat anxiety and insomnia. It can also aid digestion and alleviate stomach cramps. Comparison: Resembles a mix of chamomile and fennel on Earth Quantity Needed: A few leaves can be steeped in hot water to create a soothing tea.

7. Snowdrop Flower (Grows in Frostfall) Climate: Cold and temperate regions Season: Early spring Medicinal Properties: Snowdrop flowers have natural antiviral properties and are used to treat respiratory infections and boost the immune system. Comparison: Similar to the properties of elderflowers on Earth Quantity Needed: A small bunch of flowers can be brewed into a medicinal tea.

8. Emberroot Bark (Grows in Emberfall) Climate: Mild and temperate regions Season: Late summer to early autumn Medicinal Properties: Emberroot bark is known for its anti-inflammatory and pain-relieving properties. It is used to treat joint and muscle pain. Comparison: Resembles the properties of willow bark on Earth Quantity Needed: A small piece of the bark can be ground and brewed into a healing decoction.

9. Sunleaf Herb (Grows in Sunfire Dominion) Climate: Hot and arid regions Season: Year-round in sunny areas Medicinal Properties: Sunleaf herb is a natural diuretic and is used to detoxify the body and treat urinary tract infections. Comparison: Similar to the properties of dandelion leaves on Earth Quantity Needed: A handful of leaves can be infused in hot water to create a cleansing tea.

10. Frostbloom Petal (Grows in Frostfall) Climate: Cold and temperate regions Season: Late spring to early summer Medicinal Properties: Frostbloom petals have calming and sedative properties. They are used to relieve anxiety, stress, and aid sleep. Comparison: Resembles the properties of lavender flowers on Earth Quantity Needed: A few petals can be steeped in hot water to make a relaxing herbal tea.

These healing and medicinal flora are essential resources for the people of Emberfrost, providing them with natural remedies and therapies for various ailments and health concerns. However, proper knowledge and caution are necessary when utilizing these plants to ensure their safe and effective usage.

Magical Flora

1. Emberbloom Lotus (Grows in Emberheart) Climate: Mild and temperate regions Season: Late spring to mid-summer Magical Properties: The Emberbloom Lotus has the ability to amplify fire-based spells and enhance the wielder's fire magic. When infused in an enchanted oil, it can create a potent catalyst for spellcasting or be used to imbue weapons with fiery properties. Usage: The petals of the lotus can be dried and ground to create an enchanted powder, which is then mixed with other ingredients to form magical oils or elixirs.

2. Frostwind Fern (Grows in Frostfall) Climate: Cold and snowy regions Season: Early spring to late summer Magical Properties: The Frostwind Fern carries an innate cold aura that can lower temperatures and create a localized chill. When handled by skilled enchanters, it can be used to craft frost-based spells or even form temporary barriers of ice and frost. Usage: Frostwind Fern needs to be collected and stored in specialized containers to preserve its magical properties. It can be used in its raw form or ground into a fine powder for spellcasting.

3. Moonshadow Orchid (Grows in Moonlit Valleys) Climate: Mysterious and shadowy valleys Season: Only blooms under the light of the full moon Magical Properties: The Moonshadow Orchid is said to grant the ability to move unseen in the moon's glow. Those who possess its essence can become temporarily invisible or blend effortlessly into shadows. Usage: Moonshadow Orchid petals are highly concentrated, and only a few petals are needed to infuse an individual with its magical properties. It is often used in potions or applied directly to the skin.

4. Sunfire Lily (Grows in Sunfire Dominion) Climate: Hot and arid regions Season: Mid-summer to early autumn Magical Properties: The Sunfire Lily radiates a warm, healing energy. Its essence can be harnessed to accelerate the growth of plants and heal wounds or ailments. Usage: Sunfire Lily petals are typically infused in oils, which can then be applied to plants or used for healing purposes. A small vial of the oil is enough to heal minor injuries.

5. Shadowmoss (Grows in Dark Enclaves) Climate: Dark and shaded areas Season: All year round Magical Properties: Shadowmoss has an affinity for darkness and shadows. When properly enchanted, it can be used to create illusions and even cloak individuals in shadow, rendering them temporarily invisible. Usage: Shadowmoss needs to be prepared under the cover of darkness to preserve its magical potency. It is often used as a key ingredient in invisibility potions and illusions.

6. Starlight Blossom (Grows in High Altitudes) Climate: Mountainous regions with clear night skies Season: Late spring to early summer Magical Properties: Starlight Blossom glows faintly in the dark, and its petals emit a soft, calming light. When consumed, it can enhance focus and concentration, making it useful for mages and scholars. Usage: Starlight Blossom petals can be steeped in hot water to create a calming tea. For a more potent effect, they can be ground into a fine powder and mixed with other magical herbs.

7. Thunderroot Vine (Grows in Thundering Valleys) Climate: Valleys with frequent thunderstorms Season: All year round, but thrives during rainy seasons Magical Properties: Thunderroot Vine has an electric charge that can be harnessed for lightning-based spells. Its essence can also grant temporary immunity to electrical attacks. Usage: Thunderroot Vine needs to be handled with caution due to its electrical properties. It is often infused into wands, staffs, or gloves to channel lightning spells safely.

8. Everbloom Blossom (Grows in Enchanted Glades) Climate: Enchanted forests and glades Season: Blooms once every hundred years Magical Properties: The Everbloom Blossom is a source of potent life magic. Its essence can rejuvenate plants and heal nature itself. It is said to have the power to revive dying forests and purify corrupted lands. Usage: The Everbloom

Blossom is incredibly rare, and only a small amount of its essence is needed to perform powerful healing or restoration spells.

9. Voidshade Fern (Grows in Forbidden Caves) Climate: Dark and mysterious caves Season: All year-round Magical Properties: Voidshade Fern can create temporary portals to other dimensions. Its essence allows skilled enchanters to step briefly into the Void, gaining insight and knowledge from other realms. Usage: Voidshade Fern needs to be combined with special reagents and magical circles to create portals. Using it requires precise knowledge and considerable magical skill.

10. Dreamweaver Ivy (Grows in Dreamer's Grove) Climate: Lush and dreamlike groves Season: Blooms in the ethereal moonlight Magical Properties: Dreamweaver Ivy can induce vivid and prophetic dreams. Its essence can grant individuals the ability to enter the dreams of others and communicate through the realm of dreams. Usage: Dreamweaver Ivy leaves need to be brewed into a dream-enhancing tea or applied as an ointment on the skin. A small dose is sufficient to induce dreams with magical properties.

Fauna

Non edible but unusual fauna

1. Glitterwing Wyverns (Found in the Crystal Peaks) Habitat: High-altitude Mountain ranges, often near crystal formations Behaviour: Solitary creatures that are rarely seen due to their elusive nature Unusual Characteristics: Glitterwing Wyverns have iridescent wings that refract light, creating a shimmering display when they fly. Legends speak of their ability to vanish from sight, akin to the mythical wyverns of folklore.

2. Starlit Stags (Roam in the Starfall Forest) Habitat: Enchanted forests, particularly those with celestial alignments Behaviour: Solitary creatures that prefer to roam beneath the stars during the night Unusual Characteristics: The antlers of Starlit Stags emit a soft, star-like glow, guiding their way through the darkest forests. They are known for their affinity to ancient magic and are said to be the guardians of hidden stardust springs.

3. Embergale Drakes (Inhabit the Emberglade Marsh) Habitat: Volcanic marshlands with geothermal activity Behaviour: Fiercely territorial creatures that travel in small family units Unusual Characteristics: Embergale Drakes breathe scorching embers instead of fire, making their presence known in the marshlands. Their scales are heat-resistant and shimmer with a mesmerizing display of fiery hues.

4. Moonshadow Felines (Found in the Moonlit Glades) Habitat: Moonlit glades and enchanted groves Behaviour: Solitary and elusive creatures that prefer the cover of darkness Unusual Characteristics: Moonshadow Felines have luminescent fur that glows faintly under moonlight, allowing them to move stealthily through the shadows. They are said to have a deep connection to the moon and the realm of spirits.

5. Mistral Hares (Roam in the Enigma Marsh) Habitat: Mist-shrouded marshlands and swamps Behaviour: Agile and swift creatures that travel in large hare families Unusual Characteristics: Mistral Hares have the ability to phase in and out of the ethereal plane, making them appear and disappear like wraiths in the mist. Their fur is pure white, blending seamlessly with the marshland fog.

6. Lumoraft Whales (Migrate through the Lumoraft Sea) Habitat: Lumoraft Sea and coastal areas with floating luminescent plants Behaviour: Majestic creatures that migrate across the Lumoraft Sea in large pods Unusual Characteristics: Lumoraft Whales have bioluminescent skin that illuminates the sea around them, creating a breathtaking spectacle during their migrations. Their deep calls are said to resonate with the magical energies of the ocean.

7. Shimmerfin Koi (Inhabit the Celestial Ponds) Habitat: Celestial Ponds found in celestial-aligned glades and valleys Behaviour: Solitary and elusive, often appearing only during celestial events Unusual Characteristics: Shimmerfin Koi have scales that reflect the constellations, creating the illusion of stars moving within their bodies. They are believed to bring good fortune to those who catch a glimpse of them during celestial occurrences.

8. Shadowtalon Ravens (Roam in the Whispering Peaks) Habitat: Mountainous regions with misty peaks and dark forests Behaviour: Highly intelligent birds that form complex social hierarchies Unusual Characteristics: Shadowtalon Ravens have feathers that absorb light, making them

appear as dark silhouettes in the sky. They are known for their ability to mimic human speech and are often associated with mystical prophecies.

9. Glimmerhoof Unicorns (Found in the Glimmerwood Glades) Habitat: Enchanted glades filled with bioluminescent plants and magical energies Behaviour: Solitary creatures that are rarely seen by humans Unusual Characteristics: Glimmerhoof Unicorns have hooves that leave behind trails of sparkling stardust, imbuing the glades with an otherworldly aura. They are considered protectors of the glades and are associated with purity and magic.

10. Spectral Serpents (Inhabit the Ethereal Caves) Habitat: Subterranean caves with connections to the ethereal plane Behaviour: Elusive and ghostly creatures that are rarely encountered Unusual Characteristics: Spectral Serpents have semi-transparent bodies that seem to flicker in and out of existence. Their venom is rumoured to have mystical properties and is highly sought after by alchemists and enchanters.

Edible fauna

1. Frostback Caribou (Found in the Frostfall Tundra) Habitat: Vast open tundra and taigas. Behaviour: Herd animals that migrate seasonally to find food and avoid harsh winters Description: Frostback Caribou have thick white fur and impressive antlers, adapted to withstand the cold climate. They are similar to Earth's reindeer.

2. Sunfire Cactostrich (Inhabits the Sunfire Dominion Desert) Habitat: Arid deserts and sandy dunes. Behaviour: Solitary creatures that can go for long periods without water Description: Sunfire Cactostrich have a unique blend of cactus-like spikes and ostrich-like appearance. They are well-adapted to the desert's scorching temperatures and are reminiscent of Earth's ostriches.

3. Crystalwing Quetzals (Found in Emberheart's Enchanted Forests) Habitat: Enchanted woodlands with magical energy. Behaviour: Colourful and elusive birds that flit among the shimmering trees Description: Crystalwing Quetzals have iridescent plumage, reflecting the magical energies of their surroundings. They bear a resemblance to Earth's resplendent quetzals.

4. Icelake Salmon (Inhabit the Frostfire's Icelakes) Habitat: Icy freshwater lakes and rivers. Behaviour: Migratory fish that travel upstream to spawn Description: Icelake Salmon have a silvery-blue hue and are known for their size and flavour. They are comparable to Earth's salmon species.

5. Moonlit Foxgloves (Roam in the Moonlit Glades) Habitat: Moonlit glades and shadowy forests. Behaviour: Solitary creatures that prefer the cover of darkness Description: Moonlit Foxgloves have luminescent fur and large eyes that allow them to see clearly in low light. They are fox-like in appearance, but their glowing fur sets them apart.

6. Frostbite Boars (Found in the Frostfall Woodlands) Habitat: Temperate woodlands and snowy forests. Behaviour: Herd animals that forage for food year-round Description: Frostbite Boars have white fur and distinctive tusks, well-adapted to their environment. They are similar to Earth's wild boars.

7. Emberhide Bison (Roam in the Emberglade Plains) Habitat: Grassy plains and open savannas. Behaviour: Herd animals that migrate in search of grazing lands Description: Emberhide Bison have shaggy, ember-coloured fur, and sturdy horns that make them appear imposing. They are reminiscent of Earth's bison.

8. Celestial Tuna (Found in the Lumoraft Sea) Habitat: Luminescent waters and open seas. Behaviour: Schooling fish that migrate through the Lumoraft Sea Description: Celestial Tuna have scales that seem to shimmer like the stars in the night sky. They are comparable to Earth's tuna species.

9. Shadowveil Gazelles (Roam in the Whispering Peaks) Habitat: High-altitude mountains and rocky plateaus. Behaviour: Agile creatures that can quickly navigate rocky terrain Description: Shadowveil Gazelles have a sleek, dark coat that camouflages them among the shadows. They resemble Earth's mountain gazelles.

10. Enigma Snappers (Inhabit the Enigma Marsh) Habitat: Mist-shrouded marshlands and murky waters. Behaviour: Solitary creatures that prefer the cover of mist and fog Description: Enigma Snappers have a unique shell pattern that resembles intricate puzzles. They are reminiscent of Earth's snapping turtles.

Predator fauna

1. Frostfang Sabertooth (Found in the Frostfall Tundra) Habitat: Frozen tundra and snow-covered plains. Behaviour: Solitary predators that roam large territories. Prey: Hunts large herbivores like Frostback Caribou Size: Large and powerful, with sharp fangs and claws Description: Frostfang Sabretooths resemble Earth's prehistoric sabretooth cats, adapted to the cold climate.

2. Emberclaw Wyvern (Inhabits the Emberglade Forests) Habitat: Dense forests and mountainous regions. Behaviour: Solitary predators with keen eyesight and flying ability. Prey: Hunts smaller mammals, birds, and reptiles Size:

3. Shadowwing Nightstalker (Roams in the Whispering Peaks) Habitat: Dark and misty mountainous regions. Behaviour: Nocturnal hunters that prefer the cover of darkness. Prey: Hunts smaller animals like Moonlit Foxgloves Size: Medium-sized with large wings and stealthy movement Description: Shadowwing Nightstalkers have bat-like features and are well-adapted to hunting at night.

4. Frostfire Wyrm (Found in the Frostfire Icelakes) Habitat: Frozen lakes and icy waters. Behaviour: Solitary hunters that lie in wait beneath the ice. Prey: Ambushes Icelake Salmon and other aquatic creatures Size: A large and serpentine creature with icy scales Description: Frostfire Wyrms have similarities to mythical water serpents and dragons.

5. Sunfire Sandstalker (Roams in the Sunfire Dominion Desert) Habitat: Scorching deserts and sandy dunes. Behaviour: Solitary and ambush predators with excellent speed. Prey: Hunts smaller creatures and desert-dwelling species Size: A medium-sized creature with sandy-coloured scales Description: Sunfire Sandstalkers are reminiscent of Earth's sand vipers and lizards.

6. Starshroud Panther (Inhabits the Enchanted Forests of Emberheart) Habitat: Enchanted woodlands and mystical glades. Behaviour: Solitary hunters with stealth and agility. Prey: Hunts smaller animals and magical creatures Size: A medium-sized creature with sleek fur and keen senses Description: Starshroud Panthers have magical markings on their fur, making them blend into the forest's shadows.

7. Emberblade Lion (Roams in the Emberglade Plains) Habitat: Grassy plains and savannas. Behaviour: Hunts in prides with complex social structures. Prey: Hunts Emberhide Bison and other large herbivores Size: A large and majestic creature with a fiery mane Description: Emberblade Lions resemble Earth's lions but with a fiery appearance.

8. Moonshadow Direwolf (Found in the Moonlit Glades) Habitat: Moonlit glades and shadowy forests. Behaviour: Pack hunters with keen senses and nocturnal habits. Prey: Hunts smaller animals like Celestial Tuna and Moonlit Foxgloves Size: Large and powerful, with a dark, silvery coat Description: Moonshadow Direwolves have a mystical aura and are larger than typical wolves.

9. Frostbite Spider (Inhabit the Frostfall Woodlands) Habitat: Dense forests and cold woodlands. Behaviour: Solitary predators that spin intricate webs to catch prey. Prey: Hunts insects, smaller creatures, and sometimes Frostback Caribou Size: Medium-sized with a frosty white carapace and venomous fangs Description: Frostbite Spiders have unique frost-based adaptations and resemble Earth's spiders.

10. Enigma Panthera (Roams in the Enigma Marsh) Habitat: Mysterious and fog-covered marshlands. Behaviour: Solitary and stealthy hunters that move with eerie silence. Prey: Hunts animals that wander into the misty marsh Size: Large and mysterious, with a coat that seems to shift in the shadows Description: Enigma Panthera are cryptic and enigmatic creatures with magical properties.

Magical fauna

1. Celestial Gryphons (Found in the Whispering Peaks) Habitat: High Mountain ranges and celestial skies. Behaviour: Solitary and migratory creatures, soaring across the skies Magical Aspect: They possess ethereal wings that shimmer with starlight, granting them the ability to travel between realms. Size: Large and majestic, with a wingspan as wide as 15 feet Description: Celestial Gryphons have a radiant appearance, resembling a blend of eagle and lion, with glowing, feathered wings.

2. Luminescent Sea Serpents (Inhabit the Emberfrost Coast) Habitat: Deep Ocean waters and bioluminescent reefs. Behaviour: Solitary, often seen glowing in the dark waters Magical Aspect: They produce a soothing bioluminescent glow, used to attract prey and communicate. Size: Long and slender, reaching lengths of up to 30 feet Description: Luminescent Sea Serpents have iridescent scales that shimmer in various colours, and they can emit mesmerizing light patterns.

3. Arcane Owlbears (Roams in the Enchanted Forests of Emberheart) Habitat: Enchanted woodlands and mystical glades. Behaviour: Solitary creatures, wise and elusive Magical Aspect: They have the ability to cast minor spells, using a combination of hoots and arcane symbols. Size: Medium-sized, with feathered wings and sharp talons Description: Arcane Owlbears are a fusion of owls and bears, with magical feathers and intelligent eyes.

4. Ember Phoenix (Found in the Sunfire Dominion Volcanoes) Habitat: Fiery volcanoes and molten landscapes. Behaviour: Solitary and reborn from their ashes Magical Aspect: They can harness the power of fire and are reborn from their own ashes upon death. Size: Large and fiery, with brilliant plumage Description: Ember Phoenixes are radiant and stunning, appearing like a mythical bird engulfed in flames.

5. Astral Elk (Roams in the Starlit Plains of Frostfire) Habitat: Starlit grasslands and frosty meadows. Behaviour: Solitary and elusive, often seen under starlit skies Magical Aspect: They possess the ability to blend into the night sky, vanishing from sight. Size: Large and graceful, with antlers that seem to twinkle like stars Description: Astral Elks have a mystical appearance, with stardust patterns adorning their fur.

6. Verdant Drakes (Inhabit the Moonlit Glades) Habitat: Moonlit glades and shadowy forests. Behaviour: Solitary and often seen gliding through the moonlight Magical Aspect: They have the power to manipulate plant life, causing flora to grow or wither at their will. Size: Medium-sized with emerald scales and vine-like wings Description: Verdant Drakes are connected to the realm of nature, resembling a fusion of dragons and ancient trees.

7. Ethereal Jellyfish (Found in the Enigma Marsh) Habitat: Mysterious marshlands and shimmering ponds. Behaviour: Solitary and elusive, floating through the marsh waters Magical Aspect: They emit a soft, otherworldly glow and can phase through solid objects. Size: Transparent and ethereal, varying in size from small to medium Description: Ethereal Jellyfish have an otherworldly and ghostly appearance, resembling jellyfish made of shimmering light.

8. Soaring Moonbats (Roams in the Frostfall Woodlands) Habitat: Dense woodlands and moonlit clearings. Behaviour: Solitary nocturnal creatures, taking flight during full moons Magical Aspect: They have the ability to glide effortlessly through the air, creating a mesmerizing sight under moonlight. Size: Small to medium-sized, with wings covered in moonlit patterns Description: Soaring Moonbats have an enchanting appearance, akin to bats with iridescent, moonlit wings.

9. Luminous Harefolk (Inhabit the Emberglade Forests) Habitat: Lush woodlands and radiant glades. Behaviour: Solitary creatures with keen senses, active during both day and night Magical Aspect: They possess the ability to create illusions to confuse and protect themselves from predators. Size: Small and agile, with glowing patterns on their fur Description: Luminous Harefolk have an ethereal and mystical appearance, resembling humanoid hares with auras of light.

10. Enchanted Tigersharks (Found in the Sunfire Dominion Coastal Waters) Habitat: Coastal waters and magical coral reefs. Behaviour: Solitary creatures, often associated with magical phenomena Magical Aspect: They have the power to manipulate water currents and are occasionally found near mysterious underwater portals. Size: Large and fierce, with glowing stripes on their dorsal fins Description: Enchanted Tigersharks have a formidable presence, resembling a cross between tigers and sharks, with a hint of enchantment in their aura.

Magical Places

1. The Crystal Spire: A towering crystalline structure that rises from a remote mountain peak in the Whispering Peaks. It is believed to be a conduit to the realm of spirits and holds great mystical significance for the Moonlit Coven.

2. The Veilwood: An ancient and enchanted forest in Emberheart, where the trees seem to shimmer with a faint glow. It is said that the boundaries between the mortal world and the spirit realm are thinnest in this mystical woodland.

3. The Starfall Lake: A breathtaking lake in Frostfire, known for its shimmering, starlit waters. During certain celestial events, such as meteor showers, the lake's surface reflects the night sky above, creating a mesmerizing sight.

4. The Celestial Observatory: Located on a high cliffside in Sunfire Dominion, this observatory is renowned for its ability to predict celestial events and uncover the secrets of the stars. It is often visited by astronomers and stargazers.

5. The Dreamer's Nexus: A hidden cavern deep within the Enchanted Glacier, where dreams take tangible form. Travelers who sleep here often experience vivid and prophetic dreams that hold deep significance.

6. The Portal Ruins: Scattered across Emberfrost, these ancient ruins are said to have been gateways to other realms long ago. Many seek to unlock their secrets and harness their powers.

7. The Luminous Caves: Found in the Emberglade Forests, these caves are illuminated by luminescent crystals that create an enchanting and surreal glow.

8. The Ephemeral Oasis: A mysterious oasis that appears and disappears in the shifting sands of Sunfire Dominion's desert. Those who find it are said to be granted visions of the future.

9. The Frozen Cathedral: A magnificent ice structure hidden deep within Frostfall's glaciers. It emits a hauntingly beautiful melody when the winds blow through its icy spires.

10. The Eternal Flame: A mysterious and eternal flame that burns atop a remote mountain peak in Frostfire. It is believed to be a source of divine power and is the focal point of pilgrimages by devoted followers.

11. The Whispersand Dunes: Vast, shifting dunes in Sunfire Dominion that emit a haunting hum when the winds blow through them. Legend says that those who listen closely can hear the whispers of ancient spirits.

12. The Enchanted Lagoon: A hidden lagoon in Emberheart, surrounded by mystical flora that glows softly in the moonlight. The waters are said to possess healing properties and bring clarity to those who bathe in them.

13. The Eternal Frostfall: A region in Frostfall where time seems to stand still, and perpetual winter reigns. It is home to rare and mythical creatures that thrive in the everlasting cold.

14. The Celestial Falls: A waterfall in Frostfire that cascades from the heavens, its waters sparkling with starlight. It is a place of wonder and awe, often sought by those seeking divine inspiration.

15. The Forgotten Library: A vast underground library hidden beneath the ruins of an ancient city. It contains ancient tomes and scrolls that hold long-lost knowledge and powerful spells.

16. The Moondance Meadow: A meadow in Emberheart where the moon's glow shines brightly even during the day. It is said that dancing in this meadow under the moonlight can grant temporary magical abilities.

17. The Oracle's Grotto: A mysterious cave in the Whispering Peaks, where a reclusive oracle dwells. Those who seek her wisdom often journey through treacherous terrains to receive her cryptic prophecies.

18. The Aurora Nexus: A realm accessible only during the Northern Lights in Frostfall. It is a realm of shimmering colours and shifting dimensions, where time and space seem to meld.

19. The Harmonic Glade: A grove in Emberheart where music and nature intertwine. Each plant and creature here emit musical notes that form an ethereal symphony when the wind rustles through.

20. The Searing Abyss: An otherworldly chasm in Frostfire, where volcanic activity and raw magical energy converge. It is said that the bravest adventurers can harness the potent magic within for a short time.

Magical Events in Emberfrost

1. The Celestial Convergence: Once every few centuries, the stars align in a rare celestial formation, casting a radiant glow across the entire realm. During this event, ancient constellations come alive, guiding and empowering those who look to the night sky.

2. The Whispering Winds: On certain nights, the winds carry a mystical melody that can only be heard by those with a pure heart. Those who listen closely may gain insights into the future or uncover hidden truths.

3. The Dancing Aurora: During the heart of winter, the Northern Lights dance with vibrant colours across the sky. As the lights weave and sway, they leave behind a trail of magical dust that grants temporary levitation to anyone who walks beneath them.

4. The Feywild Migration: Once a year, a portal to the Feywild opens, allowing mystical creatures to pass through and roam freely in Emberfrost. It is a time of wonder and enchantment, but also a test of harmony between the two realms.

5. The Luminous Blossoms: In a secluded glade, otherworldly flowers bloom under the full moon. These radiant blossoms glow in the dark and release a gentle luminescence, guiding lost travellers to safety.

6. The Mirror Pools: On midsummer nights, certain reflective pools in Emberheart act as portals to mirror worlds. Gazing into the waters can reveal alternate realities or glimpses of distant lands.

7. The Song of the Elements: During the equinox, the elements themselves seem to harmonize, creating a mesmerizing symphony of fire crackling, water babbling, earth rumbling, and air whispering. Those attuned to nature can communicate with the elements during this event.

8. The Timeless Grove: In the heart of Frostfall's dense forest, a grove remains in perpetual autumn. Its leaves change colour and fall without ceasing, but never wither away. Visitors can experience the sensation of time standing still in this magical place.

9. The Ephemeral Mirage: Under the scorching sun of Frostfire, an illusionary mirage appears, depicting an ancient city long-lost to time. Brave explorers who venture into the mirage may uncover lost treasures or even unlock forgotten magic.

10. The Aurora Veil: During the spring equinox, a shimmering veil of light descends from the heavens, covering the entire land. Under this enchanting curtain, illusions become reality, and dreams may come to life for a fleeting moment.

Magic and Emberfrost

In Emberfrost, magic is not just a force wielded by individuals; it permeates the very fabric of the land itself. The realm is rich with mystical ley lines, invisible channels of magical energy that crisscross the landscape. These ley lines act as conduits, connecting various magical places and events mentioned elsewhere in this Volume. The presence of ley lines enhances the potency of magic, making certain locations more attuned to specific magical phenomena.

1. Ley Line Nexus: At certain points where multiple ley lines intersect, ley line nexuses are formed. These are powerful centres of magic, where the energy of the land is most concentrated. These nexuses can be found in some of the magical places mentioned earlier, such as the Celestial Convergence or the Dancing Aurora.

2. Resonant Enclaves: Along ley lines, there are areas known as resonant enclaves. In these places, the magic seeps into the environment, imbuing the flora and fauna with supernatural properties. Here, one might find flora with healing properties or animals with unique abilities, such as the magical fauna mentioned before.

3. Elemental Convergence: Emberfrost's ley lines connect with the elemental planes, which can influence the weather and natural occurrences. During the Whispering Winds event, the convergence of ley lines may intensify the wind's enchanting melody, creating a magical symphony of sound.

4. Temporal Ripples: Ley lines' influence can bend the fabric of time, causing temporary time loops or shifting the perception of time in certain locations. The Timeless Grove, a place in Frostfall, could be a result of such temporal ripples.

5. Enchanted Bonds: Inhabitants living near ley lines may have a natural affinity for certain types of magic. For instance, those residing near the Mirror Pools may develop talents for scrying and divination, as the ley lines enhance their abilities to tap into reflective surfaces.

6. Crossover of Realms: The ley lines can act as portals, connecting Emberfrost to other planes of existence, like the Feywild during the Feywild Migration event. This transient connection allows the fey creatures to traverse between the two realms.

7. Synchronized Magic: During certain magical events, ley lines act like a web, amplifying the energy across Emberfrost. The Aurora Veil, for example, could be a result of synchronized magic flowing through ley lines during the equinox.

8. Mutable Places: Some ley line nexuses are known to shift position over time, causing magical events to manifest in different regions of Emberfrost, adding an element of unpredictability to the magical occurrences.

Overall, the interplay between ley lines and magical events in Emberfrost fosters a deep connection between the land, its inhabitants, and the supernatural. Magic is not just a tool to be wielded, but an intrinsic part of the world that influences and shapes the lives of those who dwell within its boundaries.

Magical Spells in Emberfrost

The following is suggested for those Games Masters who want to add an additional layer to their usual system rules.

In Emberfrost, the unpredictability of magic spells is a direct consequence of the intertwined relationship between the magical ley lines and the casting of spells. When spellcasters tap into the ley lines to channel magic, the ever-shifting nature of these conduits can cause alterations and variations in the spells cast. This inherent unpredictability adds an element of excitement and mystery to the practice of magic in the land.

The alterations to magic spells can range from subtle changes in their effects to more dramatic and unexpected outcomes. Here are some examples of how magic spells might be altered:

1. Amplification: The spell's power is enhanced, resulting in a more potent effect than intended.

2. Elemental Surge: The spell may gain an elemental aspect, imbuing it with properties related to fire, ice, lightning, or other elemental forces.

3. Temporal Distortion: The spell's duration may be altered, either shortened or extended, affecting its efficacy.

4. Illusory Mirage: The spell might create illusions or deceptive images, confusing both the caster and the targets.

5. Wild Convergence: The spell combines with nearby ley lines, causing additional magical phenomena to manifest unexpectedly.

6. Unintended Targets: The spell may affect unintended targets or objects nearby, spreading its effects in unpredictable ways.

7. Chaos Twist: The spell's effects may become chaotic and unpredictable, making it challenging to control or contain.

8. Reversed Intent: The spell's effect might reverse, having the opposite outcome of what was initially intended.

9. Dreamweaver's Whim: The spell's manifestation might be influenced by the caster's subconscious, incorporating elements from their dreams or fears.

10. Nature's Embodiment: The spell may be infused with the essence of the surrounding nature, taking on a more organic and primal form.

It is suggested that these changes do happen often, rather use them for dramatic effect within an adventure. If you want to randomise when they occur, then a factor such as 1 in 6, or better still, 1 chance 10, depending on the dice used in your game system.

Table showcasing some examples of alterations to magic spells in Emberfrost:

Original Spell	Alteration	Effect
Fireball	Elemental Surge - Ice	Creates a blast of ice instead of fire.
Invisibility	Illusory Mirage	The caster appears as multiple illusions.
Healing Touch	Amplification	Heals twice the intended amount.
Levitation	Chaos Twist	The target levitates uncontrollably.
Teleportation	Temporal Distortion	The destination is shifted in time.
Mind Reading	Unintended Targets	The caster hears thoughts of others nearby.
Summon Familiar	Nature's Embodiment - Fauna	The familiar takes the form of an animal native to the area.
Enchantment	Dreamweaver's Whim	The enchanted object reacts to the caster's emotions.
Shielding Ward	Reversed Intent	The ward deflects magic aimed at the caster back at them.
Lightning Bolt	Wild Convergence	Lightning bolts split into multiple smaller bolts mid-air.

The dynamic interplay between spellcasters and the magical ley lines in Emberfrost adds an extra layer of complexity and wonder to the art of magic, creating an ever-changing and mesmerizing experience for those who wield its mystical power.

History of Emberfrost

The Lost Age of Emberfrost: A Prelude to Mystery

Long before the current civilizations of Emberfrost, in the annals of history shrouded in mystery, the land was graced by the presence of ancient kingdoms, now lost to time. This forgotten era predates the cataclysmic event of the meteor strike at Meteor Crater, a defining moment that altered the course of Emberfrost's destiny forever.

The Enigmatic Kingdoms: During this epoch, the lands of Emberfrost were ruled by three enigmatic kingdoms, each with its unique culture, traditions, and magical practices. They were known as the Kingdom of Frostfire, the Realm of Moonshadow, and the Dominion of Sunfire. These powerful and awe-inspiring kingdoms thrived in harmony with nature, harnessing the ancient magic of the land.

The Era of Prosperity: For centuries, these kingdoms flourished, sharing knowledge and trade with one another, creating an era of unparalleled prosperity and enlightenment. Each kingdom had its sacred sites, revered monuments, and mystic keepers of ancient wisdom, the secrets of which were passed down through generations.

The Meteor Strike at Meteor Crater: However, this golden age of Emberfrost met its untimely end with the catastrophic meteor strike at Meteor Crater. The meteor impact brought devastation upon the land, unleashing a torrent of natural disasters. The skies darkened, and the once-vibrant kingdoms were engulfed in chaos, destruction, and inexplicable magical anomalies.

The Vanishing Kingdoms: In the aftermath of the meteor strike, the once-mighty kingdoms of Frostfire, Moonshadow, and Sunfire vanished from the face of Emberfrost, leaving behind only the remnants of their once-great civilizations. The reasons for their disappearance remain veiled in obscurity, lost to the ravages of time and the cataclysmic event that befell the land.

Legacy of a Lost Age: Though the kingdoms may have vanished, echoes of their legacy remain in the ruins scattered across the land. Ruined cities, ancient artifacts, and mystical relics hold the whispers of an age long forgotten, tempting scholars and adventurers with the allure of ancient knowledge.

Mysteries Unravelled: The story of the lost age of Emberfrost continues to captivate the minds of the present inhabitants, sparking curiosity and wonder about the events that unfolded in the distant past. Scholars, historians, and archaeologists relentlessly seek to unravel the mysteries of the vanished kingdoms, hoping to uncover the truth behind the meteor strike and the fate of the once-great civilizations.

In Emberfrost, the memory of the lost age lingers, leaving its mark on the present, where the echoes of ancient magic and the whispers of forgotten kingdoms intertwine, waiting to be discovered by those brave enough to venture into the depths of the past.

The Shroud of Shadows

The Shroud of Shadows was a mysterious and tumultuous era that followed the devastating meteor strike but preceded the rise of the Flameheart dynasty. The first 250 years of this period were marked by a haze of forgotten memories and fragmented history, as the people of Emberfrost struggled to rebuild their shattered world.

Amidst this turmoil, ancient artifacts of great power were discovered, remnants of a forgotten time known as the Nether Time. These relics were said to hold unimaginable magical abilities, but their origins and true purpose remained shrouded in mystery. They were jealously guarded by those who found them, and their presence added an aura of mystique to the already tumultuous era.

As the first few centuries passed, scattered city-states began to emerge, each ruled by powerful warlords or charismatic leaders. Some of these leaders claimed to be descendants of legendary figures from the Nether Time, adding an air of divine lineage to their rule. The people clung to these stories as a source of hope and inspiration in the face of adversity.

Amidst the struggle for power, there were tales of legendary warriors who wielded enchanted weapons, gifted to them by ancient spirits. These brave souls fought against marauding beasts and hostile tribes, defending the fragile settlements that dotted the land.

During this time, there were also whispers of elusive and enigmatic sorcerers who could manipulate the very fabric of reality. Legends spoke of their ability to bend time, control the elements, and summon mystical creatures to aid them in their quests.

Yet, despite the glimmers of greatness and the tales of valour, much of the history of The Shroud of Shadows remained obscured. Wars, alliances, and intrigues unfolded in the shadows, and the true extent of the magical artifacts' powers was known only to a select few.

During the first 250 years of The Shroud of Shadows, the history of Emberfrost was filled with legends of brave heroes, cunning heroines, and epic events that shaped the course of the land's destiny. While many of these tales have become fragmented over time, their echoes still resonate throughout the realm:

1. The Tale of Elinor the Fearless: Elinor was a warrior maiden known for her unmatched courage and combat prowess. She single-handedly defended her village from hordes of marauding beasts, earning her the title of "Elinor the Fearless." Legends say that she wielded a legendary sword forged from a fallen star, which blazed with a brilliant light in the darkest nights.

2. The Ballad of Seraphina the Enchantress: Seraphina was a gifted sorceress with the ability to control the elements. She used her powers to protect her people from harsh winters and summon gentle rains during droughts. It was said that she had formed a pact with the spirits of nature, becoming a guardian of the wild lands.

3. The Saga of Brynjar the Explorer: Brynjar was a renowned explorer who ventured deep into uncharted territories, seeking the lost knowledge of the Nether Time. He discovered ancient ruins and unearthed artifacts of immense power, but the knowledge he acquired remained a closely guarded secret, passed down through generations only to his heirs.

4. The Song of Lysander the Bard: Lysander was a charismatic bard whose enchanting melodies could soothe the angriest storms and heal the deepest wounds. His songs became a beacon of hope for those lost in the darkness of The Shroud of Shadows, reminding them that light and warmth would return to the land.

5. The Chronicle of the Twilight Keepers: The Twilight Keepers were an order of mysterious guardians who protected the remnants of ancient magical artifacts. They sought to prevent the misuse of these powerful relics and preserve their knowledge for future generations. Their fortress, the Twilight Keep, was said to be hidden in the heart of a dense forest, shielded by powerful enchantments.

6. The Legend of the Frozen Phoenix: The Frozen Phoenix was a mythical creature said to rise from the coldest of winters, bringing with it a promise of renewal and rebirth. The sight of the phoenix soaring across the sky was considered an omen of hope, inspiring people to endure the harsh conditions of The Shroud of Shadows.

7. The Fable of the Moonlit Twins: According to legend, the Moonlit Twins were mystical beings who were both blessed and cursed by the moon. They possessed an otherworldly beauty and the power to control illusions, but they were bound by a mysterious fate that kept them forever separated, visible only when the moon was at its fullest.

Years 250 to 500 of The Shroud of Shadows were a time of transformation and upheaval in Emberfrost. The once scattered tribes and settlements started to coalesce into more organized societies, laying the groundwork for the first kingdoms to emerge. During this period, legends became intertwined with historical events, blurring the lines between myth and reality:

1. The Battle of Frostpeak Pass: In the year 275, two rival clans clashed in a fierce battle at Frostpeak Pass. It was said that the skies darkened as the armies collided, and the very mountains shook with the intensity of their conflict. The outcome of this battle would shape the balance of power in the region for generations to come.

2. The Sword of Eternity: During the years 300 to 350, a mysterious sword known as the "Sword of Eternity" appeared in the hands of a humble farmer named Darius. Legends claimed that the sword possessed the power to cut through the Shroud of Shadows itself, revealing glimpses of forgotten truths. Darius became a legendary figure, known as the "Eternal Guardian," as he used the sword to protect the innocent and uphold justice.

3. The Rise of the Snow Serpents: From the frozen wastelands, tales of the Snow Serpents spread. These enigmatic creatures were said to be colossal serpents made entirely of ice, with eyes that glowed with an ethereal light. Some legends whispered that those who dared approach them could learn the secrets of the Nether Time, while others warned of their icy wrath.

4. The Weaver's Prophecy: In the year 400, a mysterious figure known as the Weaver emerged. She was said to be gifted with the ability to see into the threads of fate, and she prophesized a great cataclysm that would shape the destiny of Emberfrost. Her cryptic words sparked fear and hope in equal measure, and her predictions became the subject of heated debate among sages and seers.

5. The Council of Five Tribes: In the year 420, leaders from five powerful tribes gathered in a historic meeting to discuss the formation of a united alliance. The council aimed to create a confederation that would protect their lands from external threats while respecting each tribe's autonomy. However, tensions ran high, and the council's unity was tested as old rivalries resurfaced.

6. The Lost Tome of Melandor: In the year 450, rumours circulated of a lost tome known as the "Chronicles of Melandor," believed to contain knowledge of the Nether Time and forgotten magical arts. Adventurers and scholars embarked on quests to find the elusive tome, hoping to unlock its secrets and gain unparalleled power.

7. The Cursed Moonstone: Legends spoke of a bewitched moonstone that granted incredible magical abilities but exacted a terrible price from its wielder. As whispers of its existence spread, covetous individuals sought to harness its power, unaware of the dark fate that awaited those who dared to possess it.

The leaders from The Council of Five Tribes were:

1. Chief Gorm Blackthorn: Leader of the Blackwolf Clan, a fierce and proud tribe that settled in the vast forests of what they called "Ravenshroud."

2. High Shamaness Selene Frostgale: Spiritual leader of the Frostmoon Tribe, a group of nomads who found sanctuary in the icy tundras they called "Starfrost."

3. Chieftain Kael Stoneheart: Ruler of the Stoneshield Clan, a sturdy and resilient tribe that made their home in the rugged mountains known as "Stonepeak."

4. Lady Eira Stormwatch: The head of the Stormrider Tribe, a seafaring people who inhabited the coastal regions they referred to as "Wavewind."

5. King Torin Emberbrand: The monarch of the Emberforge Clan, a tribe known for their craftsmanship and metalworking skills. They settled in the volcanic plains they named "Firescar."

The five tribes had a long history of rivalries and territorial disputes, but they recognized the need for unity in the face of external threats that loomed over Emberfrost. The historic meeting of The Council of Five Tribes was a pivotal moment in the land's history, where they attempted to put aside their differences and form a united alliance for mutual protection and prosperity.

However, old tensions resurfaced during the negotiations, testing the council's unity. Personal ambitions, conflicting interests, and historical grievances threatened to unravel the delicate balance they sought to achieve. Only through compromise, diplomacy, and a shared vision for a stronger Emberfrost did they manage to solidify the alliance, eventually laying the foundation for the first confederation that would shape the future of the land.

As the centuries passed, The Council of Five Tribes' alliance grew stronger, and they began to expand their influence and territories. Over time, the tribes' names and the lands they settled in evolved into the names that Emberfrost is known by today. Here is how the transformation occurred from years 500 to 750:

Year 500 - 550: The tribes' leaders recognized the need for a centralized authority to better coordinate their efforts and ensure a cohesive defence against external threats. In a landmark decision, they established a rotating council of representatives from each tribe to govern collectively. This council was known as "The Circle of Unity," and it played a crucial role in shaping the future of the land.

Year 550 - 600: Under the guidance of The Circle of Unity, the tribes embarked on ambitious infrastructure projects, connecting their territories through roads and trade routes. As they established peaceful relations and fostered cultural exchange, they adopted a common language known as "Frosthaven Tongue" to facilitate communication among the tribes.

Year 600 - 650: During this era, the tribes' cultures and traditions began to intermingle, creating a unique blend of customs that would define the emerging civilization of Emberfrost. The original names of the tribes' settlements evolved into more symbolic and poetic titles, reflecting the land's breathtaking beauty and awe-inspiring landscapes.

For instance:

- Ravenshroud transformed into "Moonhaven," signifying the mystical allure of their dense, moonlit forests.

- Starfrost evolved into "Auroradale," celebrating the magical auroras that danced across their frigid skies.

- Stonepeak became "Highhelm," a tribute to the towering mountain peaks they called their home.

- Wavewind took on the name "Seabreeze Bay," in honour of the soothing ocean winds that caressed their shores.

- Firescar changed to "Emberforge," a nod to their people's skilled craftsmanship and the heart of their metalworking industry.

Year 650 - 700: As Emberfrost continued to flourish, The Circle of Unity worked to strengthen their confederation further. They codified laws to ensure justice and fairness, and a council of mages was established to study and regulate the use of magic in the land.

Year 700 - 750: Emberfrost became renowned for its unique cultural heritage, where various artistic expressions, myths, and tales thrived. With each passing generation, the names of settlements and tribes took on a more poetic and resonant tone, invoking the land's enchanting nature and storied history.

By the year 750, Emberfrost had emerged from the tumultuous period of The Shroud of Shadows into a thriving and united realm. The tribes' transformation into a confederation marked a turning point in history, paving the way for the rise of powerful kingdoms and noble dynasties, including the Flameheart dynasty that would shape Emberfrost's destiny for centuries to come.

Years 750 to 1,000 marked a period of significant changes and upheavals in the history of Emberfrost. Here are the major events that took place during this time:

Year 750 - 800: The unity among the tribes, which had been the cornerstone of Emberfrost's strength, began to fracture. The Circle of Unity faced internal divisions and struggles for power. Disputes arose over resources, territory, and leadership, leading to conflicts that strained the alliance. However, the tribes managed to maintain a delicate balance, wary of the potential consequences of further disunity.

Year 800 - 850: Tensions within The Circle of Unity escalated, and the tribes struggled to reach consensus on critical decisions. In a pivotal event known as the "Great Schism," the Circle ultimately split into two factions, each vying for control over Emberfrost. The "Northern Circle" sought to maintain the original confederation, while the "Southern Circle" advocated for more decentralized governance, granting greater autonomy to individual tribes.

Year 850 - 900: The struggle for supremacy between the two circles intensified, leading to open hostilities and territorial conflicts. The once-united alliance was now divided, and battles were fought across the land. Many legendary warriors and generals emerged during this time, seeking to protect their respective tribes and prove their strength and leadership.

During the period of 900 to 1,000 AE, Emberfrost witnessed a momentous transformation as the once-united Circle of Unity that had experienced a profound split was heading to the rise of the six distinct city-states. The catalyst for this monumental change was a series of events that culminated in what would be known as the Breaking of the Two Rings.

Year 900: Internal strife and irreconcilable differences among the tribes within the Circle of Unity reached a boiling point. Despite efforts to find common ground, the rift between the Northern Circle and the Southern Circle grew wider. The two factions, each determined to assert its vision of governance, could no longer coexist harmoniously.

Year 920: Tensions escalated further, and the Breaking of the Two Rings became inevitable. The Northern Circle, led by the charismatic and strategic Lord Garrick Frostborne of Frostfall, sought to create a unified realm that upheld a central authority while respecting the autonomy of each city-state. Their motive was to establish a stable and powerful entity capable of withstanding external threats.

On the other hand, the Southern Circle, headed by the enigmatic Lady Elara Shadowblade of Frostfire, believed in decentralization and empowering individual tribes with greater autonomy. Their vision was to foster diversity and regional identities, promoting cultural uniqueness within Emberfrost.

Year 940: As the divisions deepened, a series of diplomatic attempts to mend the rift failed, and the Circle of Unity fractured into two separate rings. The Northern Ring, composed of Frostfall, Riven and Emberheart stood resolute in their pursuit of unity and strength.

The Southern Ring, comprised of Emberfall, Frostfire and Sunfire Dominion, was equally steadfast in their pursuit of individual sovereignty and cultural preservation.

Year 960: The six city-states emerged as distinct entities, each with its own ruler and governing principles. As the years passed, Frostfall's leadership fell to Lady Freya Snowmantle, known for her fierce dedication to her people and her unwavering belief in unity through shared prosperity.

Riven found its ruler in Lord Belgrin Riven, who remained a loyal advocate of decentralization and sought to establish a society that valued individual freedoms.

Emberheart's leadership was vested in the wise and benevolent Lord Eadric Stormborne, whose priority was to create a realm where knowledge and wisdom thrived.

Emberfall's ruler was the charismatic Lady Arya Firewind, who embraced diplomacy and trade, envisioning a city-state that connected the realms through commerce and cultural exchange.

Frostfire was governed by the ambitious and resourceful Lord Ustace Ironhart, who sought to harness the land's natural resources to forge a powerful and prosperous domain.

Sunfire Dominion, led jointly by the sisters Arwala and Imara Ishulay. aimed for Sunfire Dominion to be a centre of knowledge, magic, and spiritual enlightenment.

Year 980: With the six city-states now established, the dynamics of Emberfrost had shifted dramatically. The period of upheaval had passed, and the quest for identity, autonomy, and strength defined the new era. As the first millennium approached its end, each city-state faced its unique challenges and opportunities, carving its own path toward greatness, shaping Emberfrost's destiny for generations to come.

Year 990: After many battles the leaders of the six city-states are:

Frostfall – Magnus Flameheart	Emberfall – Eadric Delemar
Riven – Garret Riven	Frostfire – Ustace Canarveon
Emberheart – Eadric Stormborne	Sunfire Dominion - Arwala and Imara Ishulay

The Unification of Emberfrost: An Unsteady Alliance

In the turbulent history of Emberfrost, the once separate city-states were marked by rivalries, territorial disputes, and even wars that tore the realm apart. Each city-state, governed by its Lord or Lady, fiercely guarded its sovereignty, and unity seemed like an unattainable dream. However, destiny had other plans.

The Raging Wars: For generations, Frostfall, Sunfire Dominion, Riven, Emberfall, and Frostfire were embroiled in bitter conflicts over resources, land, and power. The realm was plagued by bloodshed, and animosity between the noble houses ran deep. The once tranquil lands were marred by the scars of war, and their people suffered under the constant turmoil.

King Magnus Flameheart and Queen Imara's Union: It was amidst this chaotic backdrop that King Magnus Flameheart, the ruler of Frostfall, and Queen Imara, the sovereign of Sunfire Dominion, united in a powerful alliance. What began as a strategic marriage to solidify their claims to the throne soon blossomed into a genuine love, bound by a shared vision of a unified Emberfrost. Their marriage marked the beginning of a new era, one where love and ambition intertwined.

The Iron Rule of King Magnus: Inspired by their union, King Magnus and Queen Imara set out to bring about an unprecedented unification of Emberfrost under their rule. With cunning diplomacy, strategic alliances, and unmatched military prowess, King Magnus waged campaigns against the other city-states. He demonstrated that unity could be achieved through strength, and slowly but surely, Emberfrost's once-warring kingdoms began to fall under his iron rule.

An Unsteady Alliance: Though King Magnus succeeded in uniting Emberfrost, the alliance remains fragile. The scars of past wars are not easily forgotten, and deep-rooted animosities continue to smoulder beneath the surface. The uneasy peace is most palpable between Lord Garret Riven and Lord Eadric Delemar, once close friends and now wary rivals.

Tensions Amongst Nobles: Lord Garret, the ruler of Riven, still carries the weight of lost battles and territories at the hands of King Magnus's forces. Meanwhile, Lord Eadric, once a staunch supporter of King Magnus, now struggles with a sense of betrayal over the decisions made in the pursuit of unity. Their friendship is shadowed by a sense of resentment, and the once harmonious relationship between them is now strained.

The Future of Emberfrost: The realm of Emberfrost stands united, but its unity is not without its challenges. King Magnus and Queen Imara's alliance brought hope for a brighter future, but the realm must now navigate the complexities of its newfound harmony. The people of Emberfrost look to their rulers with hope and apprehension, yearning for a lasting peace and prosperity that transcends the trials of the past.

In this land of magic and uncertainty, the uneasy alliance between the city-states teeters on a delicate precipice. Only time will tell whether Emberfrost will embrace a new era of enduring unity or succumb once more to the echoes of its turbulent past.

The Rebirth of Emberfrost: History of Kings, Generals & Magic

Tally of Years: The modern Calendar of Years: 0 AE (After Emberheart)

0 AE: The Rise of the Flameheart Dynasty

- King Magnus Flameheart, a charismatic and visionary ruler, ascends to the throne of Emberfrost. He unites the fragmented city-states under his rule, establishing the Flameheart Dynasty.

2 AE: Queen Imara of Sunfire Dominion

- Queen Imara, a powerful sorceress and former ruler of the Sunfire Dominion, marries King Magnus, solidifying the alliance between their once-separated lands. Their union marks a turning point in the relations between the city-states.

5 AE: The Enigma Keepers Discovered

- The Enigma Keepers, a group of scholars, and arcane experts, are founded. They dedicate themselves to uncovering the mysteries of ancient artifacts and magic, aiming to preserve lost knowledge.

8 AE: The War of Frost and Fire

- Tensions between Lord Garret Riven of Riven and Lord Eadric Delemar of Emberfall escalate, culminating in the War of Frost and Fire. The conflict ravages the lands, leaving a scar on the unity of Emberfrost.

9 AE: The Treaty of Frozen Unity

- After a decade of bitter conflict, the Treaty of Frozen Unity is signed, bringing an uneasy peace between Riven and Emberfall. Both lords, once close friends, now maintain a wary coexistence.

11 AE: The Silverclaw Mercenaries

- The Silverclaw Mercenaries, a formidable society of warriors for hire, are officially established. They begin taking contracts to protect caravans, explore dangerous territories, and assist in conflicts.

14 AE: The Frostwardens Expedition

- The Frostwardens organize a daring expedition into the uncharted and perilous Frozen Wastes, seeking to discover hidden secrets and dangerous beasts that roam the frozen landscapes.

16 AE: The Moonshadows' Coup

- The Moonshadows orchestrate a daring and covert coup against a corrupt noble, seizing control of an important city-state. Their agility, stealth, and cunning tactics prove formidable.

18 AE: The Battle of Emberwatch

- The Emberwatch Sentinels face their greatest challenge as a horde of monstrous creatures breaches the borders of Emberfrost. The Sentinels stand united, repelling the invasion and protecting the realm.

20 AE: The Lost Artifacts Resurface

- Ancient magical artifacts, rumoured to have disappeared during the Nether Time, start resurfacing across Emberfrost. The Enigma Keepers play a crucial role in their recovery.

24 AE: The Unseen Threat

- Rumours of an elusive cult, the Cult of the Eternal Shadow, begin to spread. Whispers speak of their malevolence and hidden agendas, causing unrest among the populace.

26 AE: The Silver Falcons' Quest

The Order of the Silver Falcons embarks on a noble quest to protect the weak and uphold justice across Emberfrost, earning the respect and admiration of the people.

It is suggested that Games masters might start their campaigns with the current year set at 27 AE. A battle has begun between Emberfall and Riven. The results of the feud between Riven and Emberfall will be that Lord Eadric Delemar betrays Lord Garret Riven by framing him for treason and then seizing his lands and wealth. Valtor Riven, Garret's son and heir, escapes and goes into hiding. The other city states look on. A few suggested future events, depending on player interactions in the lands could be:

Possible Future Events in Emberfrost:

1. **The Riven Uprising:** As Valtor Riven gathers support from the people of Riven, a growing rebellion against Lord Eadric Delemar's rule takes shape. The people, fuelled by their desire for justice and loyalty to the Riven family, unite to reclaim their lands and restore the rightful ruler.

2. **The Battle of Frostfire:** As Lord Eadric sets his sights on invading Frostfire, he underestimates the strength of the Frostfire forces. The invasion sparks a fierce and pivotal battle, leading to a turning point in the conflict between the two lords.

3. **The Shifting Alliances:** As news of Lord Eadric's invasion spreads, other city-states in Emberfrost are forced to choose sides. Some may support Eadric, seeing an opportunity for their own gain, while others may stand with Frostfire, seeking to maintain the balance of power.

4. **The Secret of Betrayal:** Clues emerge about Lord Eadric's betrayal of Lord Garret Riven, revealing a deeper and more sinister plot. Players might uncover evidence of Eadric's hidden alliances and manipulations, leading to a hunt for the truth and possible justice for Garret Riven.

5. **Valtor's Quest for Redemption:** Valtor Riven's journey to reclaim his family's honour and lands is fraught with challenges. The players might aid him in his quest, battling not only against Lord Eadric's forces but also the doubts and fears plaguing Valtor's heart.

6. **The Unravelling of Dark Secrets:** Delving into the Nether Time and ancient prophecies, the players might stumble upon dark secrets that connect the current conflicts with events from Emberfrost's distant past. The truths they unearth could change the course of the realm's history.

7. **The Emergence of a Greater Threat:** While Emberfrost faces internal conflicts, a greater threat looms on the horizon. An ancient evil, awakened by the shifting balance of power, begins to influence events from the shadows, forcing the city-states to put aside their differences to combat a common enemy.

8. **A World in Flux:** The consequences of the players' actions and the unfolding events reshape the geopolitical landscape of Emberfrost. New alliances form, old rivalries intensify, and the future of the realm hangs in the balance.

9. **The Search for the Lost Heir:** As Valtor Riven fights to reclaim his birthright, whispers spread of a long-lost heir to the throne of Emberfrost. The players might embark on a quest to find this hidden descendant and restore the rightful lineage.

10. **A Time of Reckoning:** In the years leading up to 50 AE, Emberfrost faces a moment of reckoning. The events set in motion by Valtor's uprising, Lord Eadric's ambitions, and the looming ancient threat culminate in a climax that will shape the future of the realm for generations to come.

As the players navigate through these potential future events, the web of relationships, hierarchies, and obligations in Emberfrost becomes increasingly complex, and their decisions hold the power to determine the fate of the entire realm.

Some other possible future events in the other city-states of Emberfrost:

1. **Frostfall: The Frozen Council:** In Frostfall, a significant event looms as the council of influential mages and scholars convene to discuss the resurgence of ancient magic in the region. Players might find themselves entangled in a quest to uncover the source of this magic and its potential consequences.

2. **Emberheart: The Festival of the Eternal Flame:** A grand festival is set to take place in Emberheart, celebrating the eternal flame that burns at the heart of the city. However, mysterious occurrences threaten to extinguish the sacred fire, and the players are tasked with ensuring the festival's success and uncovering the cause of the disturbances.

3. **Emberfall: The Elemental Disruptions:** In Emberfall, the elements seem to be in turmoil, with sudden storms, blazing fires, and earth tremors becoming more frequent and intense. The players must investigate the cause of these disruptions and prevent a potential catastrophe.

4. **Frostfire: The Frozen Crypt Expedition:** A renowned archaeologist announces a daring expedition to uncover the long-lost secrets of an ancient frozen crypt in Frostfire. Players may join the expedition, navigating through treacherous icy landscapes and confronting ancient guardians.

5. **Sunfire Dominion: The Celestial Conjunction:** As the sun and stars align in a rare celestial event, the Sunfire Dominion prepares for a time of great significance. The players may get involved in the rituals and ceremonies related to this event, discovering hidden celestial powers that may be awakened.

6. **The Enigma Keepers' Quest:** In the Enigma Keepers' society, an enigmatic artifact is discovered, said to possess the power to rewrite history. The players might embark on a dangerous journey to safeguard or harness this artifact, all while avoiding its malevolent potential.

7. **The Moonlit Coven's Vision Quest:** The Moonlit Coven is visited by prophetic visions that foretell a looming threat to their magical practices. Players must undergo a mystical vision quest to interpret the meaning of these visions and take action to protect their ancient traditions.

8. **The Order of the Silver Falcons: Trials of Chivalry:** In the Order of the Silver Falcons, a series of rigorous trials is held to determine the true heir to the throne of a neighbouring kingdom. The players might be invited to participate or investigate possible foul play amidst the knights' ranks.

9. **The Flameforgers: Forge of Legends:** The Flameforgers craft a legendary weapon of ancient power, and the players may be tasked with aiding in its creation or safeguarding it from those who seek to exploit its potential.

10. **The Wailing Sisters' Lament:** The Wailing Sisters, in their dark cult of mourning, invoke a potent ritual to communicate with the spirits of the deceased. The players must navigate through the veil between life and death, uncovering the secrets that lie beyond.

These future events add depth and unpredictability to the world of Emberfrost, allowing players to immerse themselves in a living and evolving realm with numerous engaging storylines and challenges to face.

Details by City State

Frostfall

City State – Frontier lands of Frostfall

Frostfall is on the edge of the vast and frozen demesne of the northern tundra. It is capital city of the Frostfall region and stands as the central hub of power and governance, embodying the spirit and resilience of its inhabitants. In the city of Frostfall areas of interest are:

1. Frostholm: Frostholm is the central district of the city of Frostfall and also represents the heart of the frontier lands of Frostfall. Frostholm is where the ruling authority and important institutions are located. The city sits at the confluence of multiple rivers, with bridges and canals crisscrossing its landscape. The architecture of Frostholm reflects the rugged nature of the region, with sturdy stone buildings and fortifications.

2. Ice Citadel: At the heart of Frostholm stands the imposing Ice Citadel, a grand structure made of frost-veined stone and adorned with intricate ice sculptures. This formidable fortress serves as the seat of power, housing the ruling monarch and their advisors. The Ice Citadel is both a symbol of authority and a testament to the resilience of Frostfall.

3. Frostheart Plaza: The main square of Frostholm, Frostheart Plaza, serves as a gathering place for public events and celebrations. It features a grand fountain made of ice, constantly flowing with crystal-clear water that never freezes, serving as a symbol of life amidst the cold. The plaza is surrounded by shops, taverns, and bustling markets, offering a vibrant atmosphere for locals and visitors alike.

4. Hall of Frostfall: The Hall of Frostfall is a majestic structure that serves as the seat of governance and administration. Within its halls, council meetings, public hearings, and diplomatic negotiations take place. The architecture showcases the rich history and culture of Frostfall, with intricate ice carvings and tapestries depicting heroic legends and notable events.

5. Frostfall Academy: A renowned institution of learning and magical study, the Frostfall Academy is a prestigious centre of knowledge and training for wizards, scholars, and mages. The academy offers a comprehensive curriculum, specializing in elemental magic, frost manipulation, and understanding the mysteries of the tundra. It attracts students from far and wide seeking to harness the power of ice and master their craft.

6. Iceweaver Gardens: These meticulously landscaped gardens surrounding the Ice Citadel offer a serene oasis amidst the bustling city. Iceweaver Gardens are adorned with vibrant ice sculptures, exotic plants that thrive in the cold climate, and enchanting pathways that wind through frozen waterfalls and serene ponds.

7. Frostfall Archives: A vast repository of knowledge and history, the Frostfall Archives house ancient tomes, scrolls, and records. Scholars and historians from across the realm visit this revered institution to study the history, culture, and magical heritage of Frostfall. The archives hold secrets and insights that contribute to the understanding of the region's past and guide its future.

8. Frostspire Cathedral: A magnificent cathedral dedicated to the Frostfall faith, Frostspire Cathedral stands as a beacon of spiritual guidance and devotion. Its towering spires, adorned with ice crystals, reach toward the heavens. The cathedral hosts grand ceremonies, religious rituals, and acts as a sanctuary for worshipers seeking solace and guidance.

9. Frosthaven Docks: Situated along the frozen shores, Frosthaven Docks serve as a crucial point of trade and commerce. Ships from distant lands dock here, bringing goods and resources to the capital. The docks bustle with activity as merchants, sailors, and traders negotiate deals and unload their cargo, ensuring a steady flow of goods into and out of Frostholm.

10. Frostfall Royal Gardens: These sprawling gardens adjacent to the Ice Citadel are a lush sanctuary of beauty and tranquillity. They feature meticulously manicured hedges, colourful flower beds, and serene ponds frozen into delicate ice sculptures. The royal family and esteemed guests often stroll through the gardens, seeking respite from the weight of governance and enjoying the serene ambiance.

Other key towns and villages in Frostfall

Stormholm: The rugged and weather-beaten northern port city situated on a cliff side. overlooking the stormy seas. It is a bustling trade hub, known for its resilient inhabitants who have mastered the art of sailing through treacherous waters. Stormholm boasts a sturdy harbor and is home to a diverse community of merchants, sailors, and adventurers. It is notorious for its tumultuous seas and unpredictable storms, making it a treacherous but lucrative trade destination.

Frostreach: A fortified town located deeper within the frontier lands. It serves as a central hub for adventurers, providing supplies and shelter for those venturing into the tundra. Frostreach is known for its skilled hunters, trappers, and guides who navigate the harsh terrain.

Snowfall: Nestled at the foot of a mountain range, Snowfall is a tranquil village surrounded by picturesque snowy landscapes. Its inhabitants are skilled craftsmen and artisans who produce exquisite ice sculptures, textiles, and other crafts unique to the region. The village is also known for its hot springs, which offer warmth and respite from the cold.

Frostbrook: A frontier outpost located near the border of the northern tundra. It serves as a strategic defence point against potential threats from the wilds. Frostbrook is primarily inhabited by soldiers, scouts, and rangers who patrol the borders and maintain the security of the region.

Frostglade: A hidden village nestled deep within an ancient forest. Its inhabitants are skilled in the arcane arts and have a close bond with nature. The village is guarded by powerful enchantments and wards to keep intruders at bay. Frostglade is a sanctuary for those seeking knowledge and guidance in magic.

Snowpine: A mountainous village perched high above the tree line. Its brave inhabitants are adept mountaineers and expert climbers. Snowpine is a hub for adventurers and treasure hunters, as it provides access to hidden caves, ancient ruins, and valuable resources found within the peaks.

Frosthaven: A small trading outpost that serves as a stopping point for caravans traveling to and from the northern tundra. Frosthaven offers shelter, supplies, and a place to rest for weary travellers. It is known for its market, where rare goods from the tundra and beyond can be found.

Coldharbour: A remote village situated in a valley, surrounded by towering snow-capped peaks. Coldharbour relies on agriculture and animal husbandry, cultivating resilient crops and raising hardy livestock. The villagers are known for their resourcefulness and self-sufficiency, adapting to the challenges of the cold climate.

Key figures in power and influence in the city of Frostfall

Town Officials:

1. **Lady Freya Snowmantle:** The Lady of Frostfall's frontier lands, Lady Freya is a respected and powerful figure. She is known for her cunning tactics in protecting the borders of Frostfall.

2. **Captain Ulfar Icebane:** Captain Ulfar is a brave and skilled warrior. He leads the Frostwardens, a guild specializing in surviving the frozen landscapes of Emberfrost.

3. **Arch mage Elara Frostweaver:** The head of the Frostfall Mages Guild, Arch mage Elara is a powerful mage and a scholar of ancient magic. She advises the rulers and keeps the city safe from magical threats.

4. **Commander Bjorn Stormblade:** The leader of the Frostfall Guards, Commander Bjorn is a fierce and loyal soldier. He maintains law and order in the city and ensures the safety of its inhabitants.

5. **High Priestess Isolde Iceheart:** The spiritual leader of Frostfall's temples, High Priestess Isolde is deeply devoted to the worship of the Frost Mother. She guides the people in matters of faith and rituals.

Influential Merchants:

1. **Gareth Ironforge:** A prominent blacksmith and merchant in Frostfall, Gareth is renowned for crafting exceptional weapons and armour.

2. **Lysandra Frostglade:** A skilled jeweller and gem trader, Lysandra's exquisite jewelry is highly sought after in Frostfall.

3. **Orik Frostbeard:** The owner of a successful trading company, Orik oversees the import and export of goods in Frostfall.

4. **Evelyn Riversong:** A respected herbalist and apothecary, Evelyn provides the city with medicinal herbs and potions.

5. **Thane Goldenleaf:** An influential merchant dealing in rare and exotic artifacts, Thane's collection includes valuable magical items.

6. **Elissa Swiftwind:** A skilled tailor and designer, Elissa's elegant and enchanting clothing is favored by nobles and elites.

7. **Cedric Stormborne:** A prominent ship captain and trader, Cedric manages Frostfall's thriving sea trade.

8. **Olivia Frostborne:** An accomplished artist and sculptor, Olivia's ice sculptures and artworks grace the city's galleries.

9. **Silas Stormwood:** An enterprising lumber merchant, Silas supplies the city with timber from the vast Emberfrost forests.

10. **Veronica Moonshadow:** A shrewd businesswoman, Veronica runs a successful inn and tavern in Frostfall, frequented by travellers and adventurers.

These individuals, both town officials and influential merchants, play crucial roles in shaping the prosperity and cultural vibrancy of Frostfall. Their decisions and actions impact the daily lives of the city's inhabitants and contribute to the city's position as a prominent hub of commerce and culture in Emberfrost.

Key figures in the lands of Frostfall

1. **Merchants**:

   - Galen Silverforge: Found in Frostfall City, where his exquisite magical artifacts and enchanted gems shop stands.

   - Isadora Nightshade: Operates her apothecary in the village of Moonbrook, known for her mystical elixirs and potions.

   - Thane Ironhelm: Can be found in the bustling town of Iceholm, where he runs a prominent armour and shield emporium.

   - Elara Frostwood: Her apothecary is located in the village of Frostgrove, providing medicinal herbs and potions.

2. **Cult Leaders**:

   - Alistair Shadowblade: Leads the Nightshade Coven, a secretive cult, in their hidden sanctuary deep within the Darkwood Forest.

   - Thaddeus Bloodmoon: Guides the Cult of the Eternal Night in their moonlit rituals within the mysterious Waning Caves.

3. **Adventurers and Heroes**:

   - Lyra Stormwind: A wandering rogue, known to traverse the wilderness around Frostfall City and aid those in need.

   - Darian Iceheart: Frequents the Frostwarden Lodge in the town of Frostpeak, sharing tales of his daring quests.

   - Astrid Stonefist: Often found at the grand Coliseum in Frosthold, showcasing her combat prowess to the crowds.

   - Finn Evergreen: Roams the forests near the village of Whisperbrook, revered for his ability to communicate with animals.

4. **City Officials**:

   - Councilor Lucius Dawnhammer: Holds office within Frostfall City, handling trade and diplomatic matters.

   - Magistrate Isolde Thistledown: Oversees the village of Everdale, ensuring justice and law enforcement.

   - Chancellor Corwin Emberveil: Resides in Frostfall City, serving as an advisor to the lord and managing diplomacy.

5. **Prominent Citizens**:

   - Delia Starling: Often found at the Frostfall Explorer's Guild, plotting expeditions into the uncharted tundra.

   - Garrick Wildwood: Performs at the lively Frostfall City's "Moonlit Serenade" tavern, captivating the audience.

6. **Guild Leaders**:

- Helga Ironbeard: Rules over the Flameforgers Guild from the well-known forge in Frostfall City.

- Thalia Moonwhisper: Leads the Whispersong Society, based in the library of the ancient village of Lorehaven.

7. **Tavern Owners**:

- Gideon Frostbeard: Owns "The Frosted Tankard" tavern in Frostfall City, a popular spot for adventurers.

- Elowen Nightshade: Manages the mysterious "Moonlit Grove Inn" in the secluded village of Twilight's End.

8. **Scholars and Sages**:

- Archivist Roland Blackwood: Devotes himself to the archives in Frostfall City, preserving ancient knowledge.

- Professor Alaric Frosthelm: Resides in the village of Crystalbrook, studying Emberfrost's prehistoric civilizations.

These key residents inhabit various towns and villages across Frostfall, contributing to the diverse tapestry of life in the realm.

Commerce of Frostfall

The main commerce of the city of Frostfall revolves around the trade of exquisite weaponry, armour, and magical artifacts. With Bloodstone Delve and Emberstone Mine, being just through the mountain passes, Frostfall is renowned for its skilled blacksmiths, artisans, and mages, who craft exceptional weapons and armour infused with magical properties. These fine creations are highly sought after throughout Emberfrost and beyond, attracting adventurers, warriors, and nobles from all corners of the realm.

Furthermore, Frostfall's reputation as a nexus of mystical craftsmanship extends to the creation and trade of enchanted weaponry and artifacts. Skilled enchanters and mages, who have honed their craft over generations, work in tandem with blacksmiths and artisans to infuse weapons, armour, and magical trinkets with potent spells and arcane abilities. These unique and powerful creations find their way into the hands of not only local defenders but also renowned adventurers and renowned scholars seeking to harness the extraordinary potential contained within these items. The alluring presence of such enchanted relics ensures that Frostfall remains a beacon for those in search of the extraordinary and the otherworldly, driving its reputation as a city of unparalleled mystic commerce.

The city's strategic location near the Frostwardens' territory also makes it a central hub for the trade of Arctic survival gear and specialized equipment for traversing the treacherous frozen landscapes. Merchants from Frostfall supply essential gear such as insulated clothing, ice cleats, and enchanted items to travellers, explorers, and the Frostwardens themselves.

Moreover, Frostfall boasts a thriving market for rare and magical artifacts discovered during expeditions into the ancient ruins of Emberfrost that exist in the northern tundra. The Enigma Keepers, a society of scholars and arcane experts, have their headquarters in Frostfall, making it an ideal place for trading and studying these enigmatic relics.

In addition to trade, Frostfall also benefits from its sea access to the west and east coasts. As a result, it enjoys a thriving maritime commerce, with ships transporting goods, passengers, and cultural influences between different regions and city-states. The port of Frostfall is bustling with merchants, traders, and seafarers, further enriching the city's economy and cultural diversity.

Local festivals of Frostfall

In the lands of Frostfall, the inhabitants celebrate unique festivals and events that are deeply rooted in their culture and the challenges they face in their wintry domain. Here are some festivals and events local to Frostfall:

1. **Crystal Frost Festival**: Held at the beginning of winter, this festival celebrates the beauty of frost and ice. The towns and villages are adorned with intricate ice sculptures, and competitions are held for the most exquisite creations. The festival also features ice skating, snowboarding, and other winter sports.

2. **Aurora's Embrace**: During the peak of winter, the skies of Frostfall are often adorned with mesmerizing auroras. The Aurora's Embrace event involves nighttime gatherings to watch the spectacular display of lights and celebrate the mystical connection between the people and the northern lights.

3. **Snowstorm Feast**: In the heart of winter, as blizzards rage outside, the Snowstorm Feast is a tradition where families and friends gather in warm and cozy homes to share a grand feast. This event celebrates the spirit of togetherness and survival during the harshest weather.

4. **Starlight Revelry**: During the clear and crisp nights of mid-winter, the Starlight Revelry takes place. Residents venture into the wilderness away from the city lights to stargaze and enjoy enchanting performances by bards and fire dancers under the stars.

5. **Frostfall Equinox**: At the end of winter, the Frostfall Equinox marks the transition to spring. The event celebrates the return of longer days and milder temperatures. It is a time for hope and renewal, with communal bonfires and festivities that symbolize the victory over the harsh winter.

6. **Ice Fishing Frenzy**: As the ice begins to thaw, the people of Frostfall participate in the Ice Fishing Frenzy. This competitive event challenges individuals to showcase their ice fishing skills and catch the largest and rarest fish from the icy lakes.

7. **Runes and Relics Expo**: Held in Frostfall's ancient catacombs, this event gathers mages, scholars, and collectors to showcase magical runes, relics, and artifacts from ages past. The expo offers a rare opportunity to learn about the region's history and its arcane mysteries.

8. **Frostheart Carnival**: This carnival takes place in the heart of Frostfall's capital and involves thrilling rides, games of skill, and magical performances. It is a time of joy and celebration, with merchants from all over Frostfall offering their wares.

9. **Snowbound Solstice**: The Snowbound Solstice is a time of reflection and spiritual connection. Citizens gather in ancient glacial caves to meditate and pay homage to the spirits of their ancestors, seeking guidance for the coming year.

10. **Whiteout Race**: As the snow begins to melt and the land emerges from winter's grasp, the Whiteout Race is a renowned event. Participants compete in a challenging cross-country race through snowy landscapes, testing their endurance and survival skills.

These festivals and events add colour, camaraderie, and a sense of wonder to the lives of the people of Frostfall, bringing them together to celebrate their unique culture and the magic of their icy realm.

Fauna and Flora specific to Frostfall

Flora:

1. **Frostbloom Fern**:

   - Description: A rare fern with delicate silver-white fronds that shimmer like frost. It emits a faint, enchanting glow in moonlight.

   - Unusual Trait: The Frostbloom Fern only blooms during the coldest nights of winter when the full moon illuminates the land.

   - Location: Found in the remote regions of Frostfall, particularly near glacial caves and frozen lakes.

2. **Glacier Orchid**:

   - Description: This ethereal orchid has petals that resemble translucent ice, reflecting the colours of the surrounding environment.

   - Unusual Trait: The Glacier Orchid thrives near ancient ice formations and emits a soothing, low hum when touched.

   - Location: Mostly found near the Frostfall Glacier and high-altitude mountain meadows.

Fauna:

1. **Frostwing Owls**:

   - Description: These majestic owls have iridescent blue and silver feathers and striking amber eyes.

   - Unusual Trait: The Frostwing Owls are capable of harnessing the cold winds to fly faster during winter nights.

   - Location: They inhabit the snowy woodlands of Frostfall, nesting in ancient trees and cliffside caves.

2. **Glacial Hare**:

   - Description: This swift hare has a pure white coat and large, expressive black eyes adapted to see in dim light.

   - Unusual Trait: The Glacial Hare's footprints leave behind a subtle glowing trail due to a luminescent substance on their paws.

   - Location: Commonly found in open tundra and icy plains across Frostfall.

3. **Spectral Icefish**:

   - Description: A translucent fish with an otherworldly glow, moving gracefully through the icy waters.

   - Unusual Trait: The Spectral Icefish is not only capable of surviving in near-freezing waters but can also emit light signals to communicate with other members of its shoal.

   - Location: Inhabits the frozen lakes and rivers, as well as subterranean ice caves.

4. **Frostbound Wolf**:

   - Description: These resilient wolves have thick white fur and eyes that gleam like the stars.

   - Unusual Trait: The Frostbound Wolves can camouflage themselves in the snow, making them formidable hunters.

   - Location: Roaming the vast snowy plains and forests of Frostfall in family packs.

These unique flora and fauna add to the mystique of Frostfall, thriving in the frozen landscapes and captivating the imaginations of travellers and inhabitants alike.

Local laws of Frostfall

In Frostfall, with its unique environment and challenges, the local laws are tailored to ensure the safety and well-being of its inhabitants. Here are some specific local laws that might exist in Frostfall:

1. **Winter Curfew**: During the coldest and darkest nights of winter, a curfew is enforced in Frostfall. Citizens are required to stay indoors after sundown to avoid getting lost or facing dangerous creatures lurking in the shadows.

2. **Fire Safety Measures**: Due to the prevalence of wooden structures and the risk of blizzards, there are strict regulations regarding the use of open flames. Citizens must take precautions with heating sources and avoid fire hazards, with regular inspections by city officials.

3. **Protection of Glacial Caves**: The glacial caves of Frostfall are considered sacred and fragile natural formations. It is strictly prohibited to harm or disturb these caves, and special permits are required for explorations.

4. **Harvest Preservation**: As the growing season is short, Frostfall has laws to protect agricultural resources. Farmers are encouraged to use magical preservation methods for crops, allowing food to be stored and distributed throughout the harsh winters.

5. **Snowpack Removal**: All residents are required to remove snow from their rooftops and walkways regularly to prevent the buildup of dangerous ice formations, ensuring safe passage for everyone.

6. **Healing Herb Cultivation**: To maintain a steady supply of medicinal herbs, Frostfall promotes the cultivation of certain plants with magical healing properties. These herbs are essential for the well-being of the community, and their trade is closely monitored.

7. **Protection of Magical Wildlife**: Certain unique magical creatures inhabit Frostfall, and harming or capturing them is strictly forbidden. The punishment for violating this law is severe, as these creatures are considered vital to the balance of the ecosystem.

8. **Ancient Artifact Handling**: Frostfall is known for its many ancient artifacts of unknown origin. Citizens are required to report any discoveries to the Enigma Keepers for examination and safekeeping to prevent any unwanted magical effects.

9. **Magical Dueling Regulations**: Due to the presence of powerful mages, magical dueling is permitted only in designated areas and under the supervision of the Mage Council to prevent collateral damage or harm to civilians.

10. **Trade with Outsiders**: Frostfall has established strict protocols for trading with merchants from other realms to prevent the introduction of dangerous or invasive species, diseases, or harmful magical artifacts.

These local laws help create a structured and safe environment for the people of Frostfall, ensuring their survival and prosperity in the challenging and magical realm they call home.

Cults and religions of Frostfall

In the lands of Frostfall, where the icy tundra holds an aura of mystery and wonder, various cults and religions have emerged, each with its unique beliefs and practices. Some cults and religions specific to Frostfall:

1. **The Frostweavers**: A secretive cult that worships the ancient spirits of ice and snow. The Frostweavers believe that these spirits hold the key to harnessing the power of the winter elements. They perform intricate rituals in remote icy caves and use ice crystals as conduits to commune with the spirits.

2. **The Order of the Frozen Heart**: This religious order venerates a mythical entity known as the Frozen Heart, believed to be the embodiment of Frostfall's resilience and strength. The Order conducts ceremonies during the coldest nights of winter to pay homage to the Frozen Heart and seek its blessings for protection and prosperity.

3. **The Frostwalkers**: A nomadic cult that roams the frozen landscapes, guided by their belief in the spirits of ancient Frostwalkers. They are known for their exceptional survival skills in extreme cold conditions and are said to be able to communicate with spirits of animals that inhabit the tundra.

4. **The Crystal Seers**: This cult reveres the mystical properties of Frostfall's unique ice crystals. The Crystal Seers believe that gazing into these crystals can reveal glimpses of the future or hidden knowledge. They gather in crystalline grottoes for meditative practices and divination ceremonies.

5. **The Icebound Guardians**: A cult dedicated to safeguarding ancient ice formations and sacred glaciers. The Icebound Guardians view themselves as protectors of the delicate balance between the forces of ice and the living world. They seek to prevent any harm to Frostfall's natural ice structures.

6. **The Frostwhisperers**: A religious group that believes in the power of icy winds and howling blizzards. The Frostwhisperers perform rituals atop high cliffs during intense winter storms, seeking visions and guidance from the spirits of the winds.

7. **The Aurora Seekers**: A cult fascinated by the elusive auroras that dance in Frostfall's skies. The Aurora Seekers embark on quests to witness and study these magical lights, associating them with the presence of celestial beings or divine blessings.

8. **The Frostborn Ascendants**: A reclusive cult that follows a path of spiritual enlightenment through physical endurance in the icy wilderness. The Frostborn Ascendants undertake extreme tests of endurance and survival to achieve spiritual growth and transcendence.

9. **The Frozen Oracle**: This religious sect believes that a mystic figure called the Frozen Oracle holds the wisdom of past ages and the secrets of Frostfall's creation. Devotees make pilgrimages to an ancient frozen lake, seeking visions from the Oracle through reflection.

10. **The Ice Phoenix Cult**: A cult that venerates the legendary Ice Phoenix, said to rise from the ashes of a massive ice volcano. The Ice Phoenix Cult sees the mythical bird as a symbol of rebirth and renewal, and they gather in volcanic caves for ceremonial rites during rare eruptions.

These cults and religions add depth and complexity to the cultural fabric of Frostfall, shaping the beliefs and practices of its inhabitants amidst the chilling beauty and mystique of the icy realm.

Rumours and adventure hooks for Frostfall

These rumours and adventure hooks add depth and intrigue to the world of Frostfall, enticing adventurers to brave the icy landscapes in search of glory, treasure, and the unknown.

1. **The Frozen Relic**: Rumours circulate about an ancient relic hidden deep within the heart of Frostfall, said to possess the power to control the winter elements. Adventurers seek to locate this artifact, but caution that it's guarded by the spirits of ice and may trigger an eternal blizzard if mishandled.

2. **The Glacier Maze**: Tales of a mysterious glacier maze that shifts its icy corridors draw daring explorers. The maze is rumoured to lead to a hidden chamber containing an otherworldly crystal said to grant the power of cryomancy to its possessor.

3. **The Frostfallen Wraith**: A vengeful wraith is said to roam the frozen wastelands, seeking retribution against those who defile the sacred glaciers. Adventurers may be hired to either appease the spirit or confront it and put its tormented soul to rest.

4. **The Aurora Wyrm**: Whispers of an ethereal creature, the Aurora Wyrm, have caught the attention of treasure hunters. This creature is said to emerge only during the most vibrant auroras, and legends claim it guards a treasure hoard hidden beneath the ice.

5. **The Hidden Temple of Ice**: Stories of a long-lost temple hidden within a glacial cavern have piqued the interest of archaeologists and treasure hunters alike. The temple is said to hold ancient knowledge or even house the remains of a powerful ice deity.

6. **The Frostfall Ritual**: A secretive cult, known as the Frostfall Ritualists, seeks a rare and sacred herb that tales say grants eternal youth. Adventurers might be approached to procure the herb for the cult or to thwart their sinister intentions.

7. **The Frostborn Trials**: Brave warriors are drawn to the Frostborn Trials, a series of physical and mental challenges held by the Icebound Guardians to test those seeking to join their ranks. Success in the trials is said to bestow unique powers and recognition from Frostfall's spirits.

8. **The Icicle Labyrinth**: Legend speaks of a perilous Icicle Labyrinth hidden beneath Frostfall's surface, filled with crystalline traps and formidable guardians. The challenge for adventurers is to navigate the maze and claim the ancient treasures rumoured to lie at its heart.

9. **The Winter Mage's Enclave**: Whispers tell of a secluded enclave of powerful winter mages, capable of shaping the very fabric of Frostfall's climate. Those seeking to master the arcane arts may attempt to gain entry to this secretive society.

10. **The Heart of Ice**: As the legend goes, a heart of pure ice lies at the centre of Frostfall's coldest glacier. Possessing the heart is said to grant immeasurable power, but it comes at a cost, for whoever wields it will forever be bound to the tundra, becoming one with the ice.

Riven

City State – Riven

In the city of Riven, areas of interest are:

1. **Riven Castle**: A grand fortress atop a rocky hill, serving as the seat of power for Lord Garret Riven and his family. The castle overlooks the city, and its impressive architecture showcases the history of Riven's ruling nobility.

2. **Market Square**: A bustling hub of commerce and trade, where merchants from all over Riven and neighbouring regions gather to sell their goods. Here, one can find exotic spices, fine fabrics, and rare treasures from distant lands.

3. **The Sable Tower**: A mysterious structure shrouded in legends and folklore. The Sable Tower is rumoured to be an ancient magical observatory that holds powerful artifacts from a bygone era. Many adventurers seek its secrets.

4. **Temple of the Silver Moon**: A sacred place of worship dedicated to the moon deity. The temple's elegant architecture and serene atmosphere draw devout followers and curious visitors seeking blessings or spiritual guidance.

5. **The Enchanted Garden**: A beautiful and secluded garden located within Riven's walls. It is said that the flowers and plants here possess magical properties, and the garden is frequented by alchemists and herbalists seeking rare ingredients.

6. **The Scarlet Rose Inn**: A popular establishment that offers fine food, drinks, and lodging for travellers. The inn is renowned for its warm hospitality and the best entertainment in Riven, courtesy of talented bards and performers.

7. **The Labyrinthine Catacombs**: A vast network of underground tunnels beneath Riven, containing ancient burial chambers and hidden treasures. Many adventurers and tomb raiders venture into these catacombs seeking riches and glory.

8. **The Misty Moors**: A hauntingly beautiful landscape on the outskirts of Riven, characterized by rolling hills and a constant ethereal mist. Local legends speak of ghostly apparitions and the spirits of ancient warriors.

9. **The Guildhall of Shadows**: A discrete building where the secretive Moonshadows guild conducts its covert operations. This guild of spies and thieves has a clandestine influence over Riven's affairs. Despite the rulers' best efforts to eradicate the Moonshadows, this constantly moving headquarters, has still not been shut down.

10. **The Arkanum Academy**: An esteemed magical institution where aspiring mages and scholars learn the arcane arts. The academy's towers and spires dominate the city's skyline, and its graduates often become influential figures in Riven.

These are just a few of the areas that make Riven an intriguing and diverse city, offering endless opportunities for adventure and exploration.

Other key towns and villages in Riven

In the region of Riven, nestled amidst rugged landscapes and picturesque scenery, several towns and villages form the backbone of this land. Each settlement offers a unique charm and character, reflecting the diverse people who call Riven their home. Some of the main towns and villages in Riven:

1. **Ironspire**: The largest town in Riven, Ironspire is a bustling trade hub located near the base of the towering mountain range. Its strategic location makes it a crucial centre for commerce and defence. Ironspire is known for its skilled blacksmiths and metalworkers, who craft exceptional weapons and armour sought after throughout Emberfrost.

2. **Mistwood**: Nestled within a dense and mysterious forest, Mistwood exudes an aura of enchantment and mystique. The village is home to skilled woodworkers and herbalists who harness the natural resources of the forest. Legends speak of ancient spirits that dwell within the woods, adding to the village's air of magic.

3. **Silverbrook**: A quaint and picturesque village known for its silver mines and skilled miners. The village thrives on its mining operations and the production of fine jewellery and ornaments. The people of Silverbrook are hardworking and deeply connected to the land.

4. **Amberfield**: A peaceful farming village located amidst fertile plains and rolling hills. Amberfield's inhabitants are known for their agricultural prowess, growing bountiful crops and raising livestock. The village hosts a lively market day where locals gather to trade goods.

5. **Riversong**: Nestled along the banks of a serene river, Riversong is a tranquil village known for its skilled fishermen and boat makers. The villagers have a strong connection to the water and the wildlife that thrives in and around the river.

6. **Stonehaven**: Perched on the cliffs overlooking the vast sea, Stonehaven is a maritime village that thrives on fishing and maritime trade. Its people are known for their seafaring skills and craftsmanship in shipbuilding.

7. **Highforge**: A secluded mountain village situated high up in the peaks of the mountain range. Highforge is known for its skilled miners who extract precious gemstones and rare minerals from the heart of the mountains.

8. **Emberbrook**: A village located near the border of Riven, known for its hot springs and healing waters. The village is a popular destination for travellers seeking relaxation and rejuvenation.

9. **Stormwatch**: An outpost built on the edges of Riven, overlooking the vast wilderness beyond. Stormwatch serves as a watchtower and defence point against potential threats.

10. **Whisperwind**: A hidden village tucked away in a valley, known for its reclusive inhabitants who are said to possess unique talents in nature magic and communication with animals.

Each town and village in Riven plays a significant role in shaping the character of this region. They form a tightly knit network of communities, working together to survive and thrive amidst the challenges and wonders of Riven's diverse landscapes.

Key figures in power and influence in the city of Riven

In the city of Riven, the key figures in power and influence are:

1. **Lord Garret Riven**: The ruling lord of Riven, known for his fierce determination and tactical prowess. He is well-respected by the people and has earned their loyalty through just governance and protection from external threats. Although Garret may be dead, depending on when the Games Master sets the adventures, in which case either Lord Eadric Delemar, or Valtor Riven rule.

2. **Lady Isabella Darrow**: A powerful and influential noblewoman, Lady Isabella is the head of one of the most prominent noble families in Riven. She is renowned for her keen political acumen and ability to navigate the intricate web of alliances and rivalries.

3. **Commander Valerius Blackthorn**: The head of Riven's elite guard, Commander Valerius is a skilled warrior and tactician. He is fiercely loyal to Lord Garret Riven and is known for his unwavering dedication to the city's defence.

4. **Archmage Selene Nightshade**: The esteemed leader of the Arcane Society in Riven, Arch mage Selene is a powerful mage and scholar. She delves into the secrets of ancient artifacts and magical phenomena, guiding the city's efforts in harnessing mystical energies.

5. **Merchant Guildmaster Ulric Stonehaven**: As the head of the Merchant Guild, Ulric wields significant economic influence in Riven. He is known for his shrewd business acumen and ability to strike profitable trade deals, contributing to the city's prosperity.

6. **High Priestess Elara Moonshadow**: The spiritual leader of Riven, High Priestess Elara guides the city's religious practices and provides counsel to both Lord Garret Riven and the people. Her wisdom and devotion to the divine aspects of life are highly regarded.

7. **Captain Aric Stormrider**: In charge of Riven's navy, Captain Aric is responsible for safeguarding the city's coastal borders and trade routes. He is a skilled sailor and has earned a reputation for fearlessness and strategic brilliance on the high seas.

8. **Lord Commander Cedric Ironhelm**: As the head of the city's army, Lord Commander Cedric is a formidable warrior and military strategist. He ensures Riven's military strength remains unparalleled and trains soldiers to defend the realm.

9. **Mistress Marianne Whitewood**: The influential head of the Council of Advisors, Mistress Marianne holds considerable sway in shaping the city's policies and laws. Her counsel is often sought on matters of governance and diplomacy.

10. **Guildmaster Thalia Swiftblade**: The leader of the Thieves' Guild, Guildmaster Thalia oversees the underground network of thieves and spies in Riven. Though her activities are shrouded in secrecy, her influence in the city is undeniable.

These key figures in Riven hold positions of authority and influence, and their actions and decisions shape the destiny of the city and its people. While some may be allies, tensions and rivalries among them often lurk beneath the surface, adding intrigue and complexity to the political landscape of Riven.

Key figures in the lands of Riven

In the lands of Riven, the key figures in power and influence are:

City Officials:

1. **Lady Elara Blackthorn**: The High Councillor of Riven, Lady Elara is a skilled diplomat and advisor to Lord Garret, providing wise counsel on matters of governance.

Prominent Citizens:

1. **Sir Cedric Stonehelm**: A renowned knight and hero of Riven, Sir Cedric is admired for his valor and chivalry in protecting the people.

2. **Lady Isabella Windwood**: A prominent noblewoman, Lady Isabella is a patron of the arts and a philanthropist, known for her charitable works.

3. **Merchant Guildmaster, Harlan Goldcoin**: A wealthy and influential merchant, Harlan is the leader of the Merchant Guild and controls much of Riven's trade.

Cult Leaders:

1. **High Priestess Lilith Nightshade**: The leader of the secretive Cult of the Shadow Veil, High Priestess Lilith is shrouded in mystery, with rumours of dark rituals and forbidden knowledge.

Guild Leaders:

1. **Thane Ironforge**: The head of the Guild of Artisans, Thane is a skilled craftsman and is responsible for overseeing the city's craftsmanship and trade.

2. **Lady Seraphina Stoneforge**: Head of the Stoneforge Smithing Guild. Lady Seraphina is a master blacksmith and a skilled enchanter, and she has earned a reputation for her meticulous craftsmanship and the ability to imbue items with powerful enchantments.

Adventurers and Heroes:

1. **Erik Stormblade**: A seasoned adventurer and dragon slayer, Erik is a local hero celebrated for his bravery and daring feats.

2. **Lyra Silverleaf**: A skilled elven ranger, Lyra is known for her keen tracking abilities and her tireless efforts to protect the forests of Riven.

Tavern Owners:

1. **Grim Ironfist**: The owner of the Hammer and Hearth Tavern, Grim is a boisterous and welcoming host, known for serving the finest ales in the city.

Scholars and Sages:

1. **Arch mage Alaric Mystborne**: A wise and powerful arch mage, Alaric is the head of the Arcane Order, responsible for magical research and education.

These key figures in Riven hold significant power and influence over the city's governance, economy, and culture. They play pivotal roles in shaping the destiny of Riven and the adventures that unfold within its borders.

Commerce of Riven

Commerce in the Lands of Riven revolves around a diverse array of precious goods and skilled craftsmanship. The region is renowned for its rich deposits of iron ore and coal, which, combined with the expertise of its blacksmiths, results in high-quality iron and steel products, including formidable weapons, sturdy armour, and essential tools. The mines also produced Copper, Lead, Tin, and Zinc. The city of Riven and its surrounding towns flourish as major centres for the iron and steel trade, supplying the realm and beyond.

Riven boasts a thriving textile industry, where talented weavers and artisans create an enchanting variety of fabrics and textiles. From opulent silks that shimmer like moonlight to sturdy woollens that ward off winter's chill, Riven's textiles are sought after for their beauty and craftsmanship. Additionally, the region's mountains hold a treasure trove of precious gemstones, such as dazzling sapphires, mesmerizing amethysts, and radiant topazes. Expert jewellers in the city of Riven meticulously craft exquisite jewellery, drawing wealthy buyers and traders to their glittering wares.

The vast forests surrounding Riven provide an abundant supply of timber, supporting a thriving woodwork industry. Master carpenters and skilled woodworkers create finely crafted furniture, intricate carvings, and sturdy wooden goods that find appreciation both within the realm and beyond. Furthermore, Riven's colder regions offer a bounty of furs and pelts from various creatures, including wolves and bears. These luxurious furs are highly coveted by traders for their warmth and prestige.

Riven's thriving mining industry cements its position as a hub for the production and sale of mining equipment. Stalwart pickaxes, reliable lanterns, and efficient mining carts are crafted and traded within the city, essential tools for ambitious miners and explorers. While agriculture is not the primary focus of Riven's economy, the fertile lands outside the mountainous regions yield crops like grains, vegetables, and fruits, traded within the region.

The city of Riven is also known for its skilled enchanters and mages, who craft an assortment of magic items, including enchanted weapons, protective amulets, and mystical artifacts. These rare and powerful items attract the attention of adventurers, nobles, and even distant lands, adding to Riven's allure as a centre of commerce.

Moreover, Riven's strategic location between mountain passes makes it a hub for transportation services. Caravan guides, horse breeders, and pack animal handlers cater to the needs of traders and travellers alike, facilitating the movement of goods and people across Emberfrost. Furthermore, Riven's history of conflicts and struggles has given rise to a thriving mercenary market. Skilled warriors and fighters for hire can be found in the city, ready to undertake missions and contracts for those in need.

As a bustling trade hub, Riven plays a pivotal role in connecting the various towns and villages scattered throughout its lands. The commerce of Riven fosters prosperity, cultural exchange, and cooperation, making it a thriving and dynamic cornerstone of the realm's economy. Traders, merchants, and adventurers from all over Emberfrost converge upon Riven, forging bonds and fuelling the pulse of commerce that enriches the entire realm.

In addition to its thriving commerce, Riven is also home to the "Loreseekers' Consortium," a prestigious guild of scholars and sages dedicated to the pursuit of knowledge and wisdom. Led by the venerable Sage Alaric, this consortium serves as an intellectual beacon within the city. Its members delve into the mysteries of Emberfrost's ancient ruins, decipher cryptic texts, and uncover forgotten lore. The artifacts and knowledge they unearth often find their way into Riven's bustling markets, attracting collectors, historians, and curious minds from distant lands who seek to unravel the secrets of the realm. The Loreseekers' Consortium not only contributes to Riven's reputation as a centre of learning but also fuels the demand for rare and esoteric artifacts, further enriching the city's vibrant commerce.

Local festivals of Riven

In the lands of Riven, the locals celebrate a variety of vibrant festivals that reflect their rich cultural heritage and the spirit of unity within their community. Among the most anticipated festivals are:

1. Forgefire Festival: Held in honour of Riven's skilled blacksmiths and artisans, the Forgefire Festival showcases the art of metalworking and craftsmanship. The festival takes place in the heart of the city, where elaborate demonstrations of weapon forging and armour crafting are displayed. Visitors can purchase finely-crafted weapons, armour, and tools, and participate in friendly competitions to test their own blacksmithing skills.

2. Tapestry of Colours: This annual event celebrates Riven's thriving textile industry. The city's weavers and artisans display their most intricate tapestries, fabrics, and garments. The streets are adorned with colourful banners and flags, creating a visually stunning atmosphere. The festival culminates in a grand parade where people dress in costumes made from the finest textiles, and performances of traditional dances and music fill the air.

3. Gemstone Gala: Riven's Gemstone Gala is a glittering affair that highlights the city's abundant precious gemstones. Expert jewellers showcase their exquisite creations, attracting collectors and nobles from all over Emberfrost. The gala features gemstone exhibitions, auctions, and opportunities to purchase unique and dazzling jewellery.

4. Harvest Festival: Celebrated in the surrounding towns and villages of Riven, the Harvest Festival marks the bountiful harvest season. Farmers present their best crops, fruits, and vegetables in a lively market fair. The festival is filled with feasts, traditional dances, and gratitude for the abundance provided by the land.

5. Riven's Tournament of Blades: This thrilling tournament showcases the combat prowess of Riven's warriors. Knights, mercenaries, and adventurers from far and wide come to participate in epic duels and battles. The grand champion receives a prestigious title and rewards, while the crowd cheers on the awe-inspiring displays of swordsmanship and combat skills.

6. Night of Enchantment: As the year comes to a close, Riven embraces the Night of Enchantment, a magical celebration of music, dance, and spectacle. The city is adorned with lanterns and luminous decorations, and the streets are filled with performers, jugglers, and magicians. Revellers don colourful masks and costumes as they dance the night away in a mystical atmosphere.

7. Festival of Unity: The Festival of Unity commemorates the historic meeting of the Council of Five Tribes that united Riven's inhabitants under a common purpose. The festival serves as a reminder of the strength that comes from unity and features cultural displays, speeches, and feasts to celebrate the diversity and harmony among Riven's people.

These festivals bring joy, camaraderie, and a sense of community to the people of Riven.

Fauna and Flora specific to Riven

In the rugged and diverse lands of Riven, a wide array of unique flora and fauna thrive, each adapted to the challenges of the mountainous terrain. Some of the notable fauna and flora specific to Riven include:

Fauna:

1. Mountain Giants: Towering creatures with enormous strength and size, mountain giants are a rare sight in Riven's high peaks. Legends speak of them as ancient protectors of the mountains, and encountering one is considered a blessing by some.

2. Frost Wolves: These large, white-furred wolves are well-adapted to the cold climate of Riven. They travel in packs through the snowy regions, hunting mountain goats and other prey.

3. Stoneback Bears: Known for their grey-brown fur and powerful build, stoneback bears are skilled climbers that inhabit the rocky cliffs of Riven. They are elusive and rarely seen, but their presence is marked by their massive paw prints.

4. Ember Eagles: Majestic birds with fiery plumage, ember eagles are symbols of strength and courage in Riven. They nest in the higher reaches of the mountains and are revered by some tribes as spiritual protectors.

5. Frostbloom Foxes: Smaller than regular foxes, frostbloom foxes have snowy-white fur and large, intelligent eyes. They are known for their playful nature and are sometimes kept as companions by the mountain communities.

Flora:

1. Frostwood Trees: These tall and sturdy trees thrive in Riven's cold climate, with their wood being highly sought after for its resilience and strength. Riven's skilled woodworkers use frostwood to craft exceptional furniture and durable items.

2. Iceblossom Flowers: Delicate and radiant, iceblossoms bloom in the early spring, despite the lingering cold. They are known for their luminescent petals, which emit a soft glow at night, adding an ethereal touch to Riven's landscape.

3. Silvervein Herbs: Found in the mountain valleys, silvervein herbs possess healing properties and are commonly used by herbalists to create medicinal remedies. They are essential for treating injuries sustained in Riven's challenging terrain.

4. Stormcrystal Vines: These shimmering, blue-hued vines grow along the cliffs and rocky outcrops of Riven. Stormcrystal vines are believed to harness the elemental energies of the mountains and are often used in magical rituals.

5. Frostfire Lilies: Blooming near the volcanic regions of Riven, frostfire lilies are striking flowers with fiery red petals and cool blue centres. They symbolize the balance between the heat of the volcanoes and the chill of the snowy peaks.

Riven's unique flora and fauna contribute to the region's allure and mystique, with each species playing a crucial role in the ecosystem and cultural beliefs of the mountain communities. Exploring the diverse wildlife and breathtaking landscapes of Riven is an adventure cherished by those who dare to traverse its rugged terrain.

Local laws of Riven

These laws are crucial for maintaining order, preserving the safety of the realm, and upholding the rights of its inhabitants. Some of the specific local laws in Riven are:

1. Curfew and Night Watch: Riven city enforces a strict curfew after nightfall to ensure the safety of its residents. Citizens must be indoors by a designated hour, and the Night Watch patrols the streets to maintain order and protect against potential threats.

2. Mountain Conservation: Riven is situated near vast and treacherous mountains, which are a valuable resource for the lands. There are strict regulations against illegal mining, logging, or any activity that could harm the natural environment. Those caught exploiting the mountains without proper authorization face severe penalties.

3. Sword and Weapon Control: Given Riven's reputation for crafting exceptional weapons, there are laws that control the possession and carrying of dangerous arms within the city. Only licensed blacksmiths, warriors, and city officials are allowed to bear weapons openly.

4. Respect for Local Traditions: Riven has a rich history and deeply rooted traditions. Visitors are expected to respect local customs and practices, and any acts of disrespect or desecration of cultural symbols are strictly forbidden.

5. Dispute Resolution: Riven has a unique approach to dispute resolution called "Trial by Challenge." In this process, two parties involved in a dispute may opt for a trial of physical skill or prowess rather than a court hearing. A mutually agreed-upon challenge settles the matter, overseen by appointed arbitrators.

6. Sanctuary for Outlaws: Riven has a policy of granting sanctuary to individuals seeking refuge from other realms. However, those who seek refuge in Riven must adhere to its laws and customs and refrain from causing trouble within the city or wider lands.

7. Trade Regulations: Riven is known for its commerce, and specific regulations govern trade and bartering within the city's markets. Unscrupulous merchants engaging in fraudulent practices are subject to penalties and expulsion from the city and lands of Riven.

8. Preservation of Ancient Artifacts: Riven holds a wealth of ancient artifacts from the Nether Time. Tampering with or stealing these relics is strictly prohibited, and the Enigma Keepers have the authority to oversee the preservation and study of these items.

9. Responsible Use of Magic: Riven respects the power of magic and has laws in place to regulate the use of magic within city limits, or town limits in the wider lands of Riven. Unauthorized spellcasting that endangers public safety or property is strictly forbidden.

These laws, while subject to change with time and evolving circumstances, play a crucial role in maintaining the stability, harmony, and unique identity of Riven.

Cults and religions of Riven

In the lands of Riven, a realm of rugged mountains and vast forests, various cults and religions have emerged, each with its unique beliefs and practices. Some of the specific cults and religions in Riven are:

1. The Cult of the Ironheart: This ancient cult venerates the elemental spirit of iron and the forging process. Followers believe that through the mastery of metalwork and craftsmanship, they can harness the power of the Ironheart to strengthen their weapons and armour, granting them exceptional prowess in battle.

2. The Order of the Sylvan Guardians: This religious order worships the spirits of the forests and mountains. They believe in the balance between nature and civilization and seek to protect the wilderness from exploitation while fostering a harmonious coexistence with nature.

3. The Brotherhood of the Blazing Sun: A fire-worshipping cult that reveres the sun as a symbol of power and illumination. Followers believe that by offering prayers and sacrifices to the sun, they can gain its favour, granting them warmth, light, and protection against darkness.

4. The Seekers of the Crystal Veil: This secretive cult is dedicated to unravelling the mysteries of ancient artifacts and arcane knowledge. They believe that by understanding the hidden truths within crystals and ancient relics, they can gain insights into the past and harness powerful magic.

5. The Cult of the Feral Hunt: A nomadic cult that reveres the spirits of the wild and the primal instincts of nature. They practice ancient hunting rituals and believe that by embracing their animalistic nature, they can become one with the wilderness and gain the favour of the spirits.

6. The Order of the Stone Wardens: A martial religious order that worships the spirits of the mountains and stones. They believe in the strength and resilience of the earth and strive to protect their homeland from external threats and maintain the stability of the mountains.

7. The Moonlit Chorus: A mysterious cult that venerates the moon and the stars as celestial beings of guidance and power. They conduct nocturnal rituals and believe that by aligning themselves with the cosmos, they can tap into cosmic energies.

8. The Sisters of the Whispering Grove: An all-female religious sisterhood that resides in secluded groves. They are devoted to healing and herbalism, using the knowledge of plants and natural remedies to cure ailments and aid their communities.

9. Society of the Eternal Forge: This clandestine organization is dedicated to the pursuit of eternal life through the melding of body and metal. Its followers believe that by replacing their frail mortal bodies with finely crafted, enchanted constructs, they can achieve immortality. The society operates from hidden sanctuaries deep within the mountainous terrain of Riven, where they conduct intricate rituals, merging their essence with iron and steel. Outsiders view them with a mixture of awe and fear, as the Society of the Eternal Forge remains shrouded in secrecy, guarding their mystical knowledge of melding flesh and metal closely.

10.

These cults and religions add depth and complexity to the cultural fabric of Riven. Each has its rituals, traditions, and ceremonies that are closely tied to the natural landscape and the challenges faced by the people living amidst the mountains and forests. Some cults may be secretive and mysterious, while others are more open and integrated into the daily lives of the inhabitants of Riven. The beliefs and practices of these cults shape the identities of their followers and influence their interactions with the world around them.

Rumours and adventure hooks for Riven

1. The Lost Mine of Riven: Rumours abound of a long-forgotten mine hidden deep within the mountains of Riven. It is said that this mine once yielded precious gemstones and rare minerals, but it was abandoned centuries ago due to mysterious accidents and supernatural occurrences. Adventurers are enticed by the promise of untold riches, but they must contend with the dangers lurking within the dark depths of the mine.

2. The Cursed Amulet: There's a tale of a cursed amulet that is said to bring misfortune and tragedy to its owners. It is believed to be hidden within the catacombs beneath Riven, protected by ancient guardians and deadly traps. Bravery and wits are needed to navigate the perilous underground labyrinth and break the curse before it claims another victim.

3. The Goliath's Challenge: A fearsome Goliath warrior has issued a challenge to any who dare to face him in combat. He awaits opponents at a secluded gladiator arena within the mountain ranges of Riven. Warriors from near and far are drawn to the challenge, seeking fame and glory, but they must be prepared to face a mighty adversary.

4. The Mysterious Artificer: Whispers spread of a reclusive artificer who has unlocked the secrets of forging powerful magical artifacts. However, the artificer's whereabouts are unknown, and seekers must follow a trail of cryptic clues to find this enigmatic creator. Those who seek to acquire or learn from these powerful items embark on a quest that takes them on a journey across Riven's varied landscapes.

5. The Ghosts of Riven Manor: Riven Manor, an ancient estate in the outskirts of the city, is said to be haunted by vengeful spirits. Eerie lights and ghostly apparitions have been witnessed by locals. Adventurers are called upon to investigate the haunting and put the restless spirits to rest. Unravelling the dark secrets of the manor and its former inhabitants will be crucial to lifting the curse.

Adventure Hooks:

1. The Missing Heir: The rightful heir to a powerful noble family in Riven has vanished, and the city is in turmoil as rival factions vie for control. The players are tasked with finding the missing heir and ensuring their safety amidst a web of political intrigue and dangerous power plays.

2. The Frozen Gate: An ancient portal has been discovered within the mountains of Riven, rumoured to lead to a mysterious and forbidden realm. The players are hired to investigate the portal's origins and purpose, but they soon find themselves entangled in a struggle between powerful factions seeking to exploit the gate's secrets.

3. The Feywild Incursion: Fey creatures from the nearby enchanted forests are spilling into Riven, causing havoc and confusion. The players must venture into the Feywild to negotiate with the elusive fae rulers and uncover the source of the disturbance before the situation worsens.

4. The Mountain Titans: The towering mountain peaks of Riven are home to slumbering titanic beings of immense power. When these giants awaken due to unnatural disturbances, the players must navigate the treacherous terrain and prevent the cataclysmic consequences of their wrath.

5. The Sunshard Relic: Legends speak of a divine artifact known as the Sunshard Relic, said to grant its possessor immense control over sunlight and fire. Various factions, including cults and rival kingdoms, seek to claim the relic for their own ends. The players must race against time to find the relic and decide its ultimate fate in the face of rising tensions and looming conflicts.

These rumours and adventure hooks paint a vivid picture of the mysteries and dangers that await adventurers in the lands of Riven, offering a tapestry of thrilling quests and challenges for those willing to explore its diverse and enchanted landscapes.

Emberheart

City State – Emberheart

Starhaven: The grand capital city and heart of Emberheart, Starhaven stands as a symbol of the kingdom's power and culture. With its impressive architecture, bustling markets, and elegant gardens, Starhaven is a hub of commerce, politics, and the arts. It houses the royal palace, where the king and queen reside, and the seat of the kingdom's governance. In the city of Starhaven, areas of interest are:

1. **Starhaven Palace**: The majestic residence of the ruling monarchs of Emberheart, currently King Magnus Flameheart and Queen Imara. The palace is a stunning architectural masterpiece adorned with intricate carvings and shimmering crystal decorations.

2. **The Astral Plaza**: A central square where people gather to witness astrological events and celestial displays. It serves as a venue for grand celebrations, ceremonies, and the occasional magical performances.

3. **The Luminary Library**: A vast repository of knowledge and ancient tomes. Scholars and sages from across Emberheart come here to research history, magic, and the mysteries of the cosmos.

4. **The Starforge**: A renowned workshop where skilled artisans and blacksmiths create weapons and armour infused with celestial enchantments. Their craftsmanship is highly sought after by adventurers and nobles alike.

5. **The Temple of the Celestial Dawn**: A sacred sanctuary devoted to celestial deities and cosmic forces. Followers come to pay their respects, seek blessings, and participate in celestial-themed ceremonies.

6. **The Luminous Gardens**: A botanical wonderland filled with otherworldly flora that glow with a soft radiance at night. It is a serene and enchanting place, popular for stargazing and moments of reflection.

7. **The Starseeker Observatory**: A remarkable observatory atop a high tower, equipped with telescopes and celestial instruments. Astronomers use this facility to chart the movements of the stars and predict celestial events.

8. **The Arcane Emporium**: A magical emporium filled with all sorts of enchanted trinkets, star-stones, and rare artifacts. It is a favourite spot for those seeking unique and celestial-themed magical items.

9. **The Celestial Bazaar**: A vibrant marketplace where merchants from distant lands trade in celestial artifacts, star charts, and mystical components. Visitors can find everything related to celestial lore and astrological wonders.

10. **The Eclipsed Alley**: A curious and mysterious side street said to have its own peculiar relationship with the stars and the moon. Rumours speak of clandestine gatherings and secret rituals taking place here.

Starhaven is a city that embraces the wonders of the celestial realm, and its fascination with stars, moons, and cosmic energies shapes every aspect of life within its walls. The city's enchanting ambiance and magical aura make it a captivating destination for adventurers and mystics alike.

Other key towns and villages in Emberheart

In the sprawling and majestic lands of Emberheart, ruled over by the king, several towns and villages dot the landscape, each contributing to the vibrancy and prosperity of the region. Here are some of the main towns and villages in Emberheart:

1. **Emberhill**: Nestled in the rolling hills of Emberheart, Emberhill is a quaint and picturesque town known for its warm and inviting atmosphere. The town's fertile lands make it an agricultural centre, producing a variety of crops that are vital to the kingdom's sustenance. The townspeople are skilled farmers, tending to their fields with dedication and care. Emberhill is also renowned for its renowned vineyards and wineries. The town's unique microclimate, with a perfect balance of sunlight and cool breezes, creates the ideal conditions for growing exquisite grapes. The winemakers of Emberhill produce some of the finest wines in the kingdom, and their products are highly sought after by nobles and commoners alike.

2. **Amberwood**: Nestled within a sprawling forest, Amberwood is renowned for its timber and woodworking expertise. The village is surrounded by ancient trees, and its people are skilled craftsmen, crafting exquisite wooden creations sought after throughout Emberfrost.

3. **Silverspring**: Located near a crystal-clear spring, Silverspring is a tranquil village known for its crystal artisans. The villagers specialize in carving and crafting intricate crystal jewellery and ornaments.

4. **Goldengrove**: Surrounded by lush meadows and golden fields, Goldengrove is a farming village known for its abundant harvests. Its people cultivate a variety of crops, and the village is famous for its delicious honey.

5. **Stonemount**: Perched at the foot of a mighty mountain, Stonemount is a mining town known for its rich deposits of precious stones and metals. Skilled miners and jewellers thrive in this village, creating beautiful gemstone works.

6. **Ironhaven**: Situated near the kingdom's iron mines, Ironhaven is a vital centre for metalworking and smithing. The village's blacksmiths produce exceptional weapons and armour used by the kingdom's soldiers.

7. **Brightwater**: A picturesque village located along the banks of a winding river, Brightwater is known for its watermills and skilled millers who produce flour and other goods.

8. **Moonreach**: Built on the coast overlooking the sea, Moonreach is a coastal village with a strong maritime tradition. Its skilled sailors and fishermen contribute to the kingdom's thriving trade.

9. **Emberwatch**: A fortified outpost situated at the edge of the kingdom's borders, Emberwatch serves as a guardian against external threats. Its watchmen are vigilant protectors of Emberheart's safety.

10. **Frostwood**: Tucked within a mystical forest, Frostwood is a village with a unique blend of ice magic and nature enchantments. The villagers have a deep connection to the enchanted flora and fauna of the forest.

These towns and villages, each with their distinct strengths and specialties, form the backbone of Emberheart's prosperity and cultural richness. As they contribute to the kingdom's well-being, they also contribute to the grandeur of the realm ruled over by the king and queen.

Key figures in power and influence in the city of Starhaven

In the city of Starhaven, the key figures in power and influence are:

1. **Lord Alistair Nightwing**: The ruling lord of the Starhaven Council and deputy to the King and Queen in their absence. Lord Alistair is a charismatic and diplomatic leader. He is known for his wise rule and dedication to maintaining harmony among the various factions within the city.

2. **Lady Seraphina Moonstone**: A prominent noblewoman in Starhaven, Lady Seraphina is a patron of the arts and culture. She plays a vital role in promoting education and supporting artists and scholars.

3. **Captain Orion Thunderheart**: As the captain of Starhaven's city guard, Captain Orion is a respected and skilled warrior. He ensures the safety and security of the city's residents, and his bravery on the battlefield is admired by many.

4. **Arch mage Lyanna Frostwillow**: The head of the Arcane Tower in Starhaven, Arch mage Lyanna is a powerful mage and researcher of magical artifacts. She is highly sought after for her knowledge and guidance in matters of the arcane.

5. **Guildmaster Roland Stonebrook**: As the leader of the Merchant Guild, Guildmaster Roland is a savvy and ambitious businessman. He oversees the city's trade and commerce, contributing to the economic prosperity of Starhaven.

6. **High Priest Victoria Dawnswind**: The spiritual leader of Starhaven, High Priest Victoria is deeply devoted to the city's religious practices. She fosters a sense of unity and faith among the people and provides counsel on spiritual matters.

7. **Commander Tristan Ironwood**: In charge of Starhaven's navy, Commander Tristan is a skilled sailor and naval strategist. He safeguards the city's coastal borders and trade routes and is ready to defend Starhaven against any maritime threats.

8. **Councillor Isabella Stormcaller**: A key member of the Council of Advisors, Councillor Isabella holds significant influence in shaping the city's policies and governance. Her sharp intellect and diplomatic skills make her a valuable asset to Lord Alistair.

9. **Guildmaster Lucien Shadowbrook**: The enigmatic leader of the Thieves' Guild, Guildmaster Lucien operates in the shadows and is skilled in espionage and covert operations. His network of spies and informants is a force to be reckoned with.

10. **Master Bard Eliana Silverwood**: A renowned musician and storyteller, Master Bard Eliana is highly respected for her artistry. She uses her talent to inspire and entertain the people of Starhaven, weaving tales of valour and love.

These key figures in Starhaven play crucial roles in shaping the city's culture, governance, and prosperity. While they may collaborate to ensure the well-being of Starhaven, the complexity of their interests and ambitions can also lead to conflicts and intrigues. The delicate balance of power among these influential individuals adds depth and excitement to the city's political and social landscape.

Key figures in the lands of Emberheart

In the lands of Emberheart, the key figures in power and influence are:

City Officials:

1. **King Magnus Flameheart**: The ruler of Emberheart and the entire realm of Emberfrost, King Magnus is a wise and charismatic leader, known for his strong leadership and strategic prowess.

2. **Queen Imara Flameheart**: The Queen of Emberheart, Queen Imara is a skilled diplomat and advocate for the well-being of the people.

3. **Lord Cedric Thornwood**: A respected noble and skilled diplomat, Lord Cedric serves as the ambassador to neighbouring realms, forging alliances and maintaining peace.

4. **Lady Isadora Whitewood**: The High Chancellor and head of the Royal Court, Lady Isadora is a shrewd and wise advisor to King Magnus, overseeing matters of governance and administration.

Prominent Citizens:

1. **Lord William Stormborne**: A noble lord and close advisor to King Magnus, Lord William is renowned for his loyalty and military expertise.

2. **Lady Amelia Fairwind**: A prominent noblewoman and philanthropist, Lady Amelia is dedicated to social causes and charitable endeavours.

Cult Leaders:

1. **High Priest Malachi Darkwood**: The enigmatic leader of the Cult of the Eternal Shadow, High Priest Malachi wields dark powers and has a mysterious agenda.

Guild Leaders:

1. **Master Artificer Thalia Steelweaver**: The head of the Guild of Artificers, Thalia is a master inventor and craftsman, known for her ingenious creations.

2. **Guildmaster Thorian Stonehammer**: The leader of the Miner's Guild, Thorian oversees the mining operations in the rich mines of Emberheart.

Adventurers and Heroes:

1. **Sir Aldric Stormblade**: A legendary knight and hero of Emberheart, Sir Aldric is celebrated for his courage and valour in defending the realm.

2. **Luna Moonshadow**: A skilled elven rogue and adventurer, Luna is known for her stealth and resourcefulness in overcoming challenges.

Tavern Owners:

1. **Galen Fireforge**: The owner of the Dragon's Hearth Inn, Galen is a warm and hospitable host, famous for his hearty meals and cozy ambiance.

Scholars and Sages:

1. **Archmage Isabella Moonfire**: The head of the Arcane Academy, Archmage Isabella is a powerful mage and the foremost authority on magical studies

Commerce of Emberheart

The lands of Emberheart are a realm of grandeur and majesty, and its commerce echoes this sentiment. The heart of the kingdom beats to the rhythm of trade that revolves around the exchange of precious gemstones, exquisite jewellery, and luxurious textiles.

Emberheart boasts rich mines that yield a good quantity of gold and silver, as well as rare and valuable gemstones. The skilled gem cutters and jewellers of the region turn these raw stones into dazzling masterpieces, adorning them with intricate designs and magical enchantments. The jewels of Emberheart are renowned for their unparalleled beauty and are highly sought after by nobles, royalty, and wealthy merchants from all over Emberfrost.

In addition to gemstones, Emberheart is celebrated for its weaving tradition. The kingdom's artisans expertly craft luxurious textiles from the finest materials, creating rich fabrics that are coveted by fashion connoisseurs and royalty alike. The renowned Emberweave is a testament to the mastery of the kingdom's weavers, known for its softness, durability, and vibrant colours.

Furthermore, Emberheart is a centre of alchemical studies and potion-making. The region is blessed with an abundance of rare herbs and magical flora, which the skilled alchemists use to brew potent potions, elixirs, and enchantments. These elixirs hold great value to adventurers, warriors, and scholars, making Emberheart a hub for seekers of mystical knowledge and magical remedies.

Trade caravans and merchant ships from far and wide journey to Emberheart to partake in these treasures, and the city becomes a bustling centre of commerce and cultural exchange. The markets of Emberheart overflow with the vibrant colours of gemstones and textiles, while the air carries the exotic scents of alchemical potions and magical enchantments. In this land of opulence and allure, commerce thrives, weaving a tapestry of prosperity and enchantment.

Local festivals of Emberheart

In the lands of Emberheart, the people celebrate a diverse array of festivals that embody their cultural traditions, spiritual beliefs, and appreciation for nature. Some of the prominent local festivals include:

1. Starlight Celebration: Held under the shimmering night sky, the Starlight Celebration is a joyous event that celebrates the bond between the people of Emberheart and the celestial world. During this festival, lanterns and candles are lit across the city and its villages, illuminating the night with a soft glow. The festival features stargazing sessions, storytelling about constellations, and performances inspired by celestial themes.

2. Emberfest: As the first snowflakes fall and winter approaches, Emberfest marks the beginning of the colder months. This lively celebration features bonfires, feasts, and dancing. People dress in colorful garments and wear masks adorned with embers, symbolizing the warmth and light that will keep them company during the cold season.

3. Day of Remembrance: A solemn festival dedicated to honouring the ancestors and fallen heroes of Emberheart. People gather at sacred sites and cemeteries to offer prayers and light candles for their departed loved ones. This day also serves as a remembrance of important historical events that shaped the land and its people.

4. Blossom Carnival: As spring blankets the lands with blossoms, the Blossom Carnival welcomes the season of renewal and growth. The streets are adorned with floral decorations, and people wear flower crowns and vibrant costumes. The festival features flower markets, music performances, and competitions celebrating nature's beauty.

5. Festival of Spirits: A spiritual celebration where the boundaries between the mortal world and the spirit realm are believed to be thin. People construct altars adorned with offerings for their ancestors and spirits. This festival involves rituals, meditations, and storytelling to connect with the spiritual aspects of Emberheart.

6. Great Hunt: A thrilling event that celebrates the bountiful wildlife and the bond between Emberheart's people and nature. Hunters and adventurers come together for a friendly competition to test their skills in tracking and survival. The Great Hunt showcases feats of bravery and camaraderie among the participants.

7. Emberheart Tournament: A grand martial arts tournament where warriors from different regions compete in various combat styles. Swordplay, archery, and unarmed combat are among the disciplines showcased. The victors receive accolades and recognition for their exceptional skills.

8. Festival of Light: As the days grow longer and summer approaches, the Festival of Light is a joyous occasion of music, dance, and artistic performances. The city is illuminated with elaborate light displays, and people celebrate the warmth and brightness that the summer season brings.

These festivals are an integral part of Emberheart's cultural identity, fostering a strong sense of community, tradition, and harmony among its people.

Fauna and Flora specific to Emberheart

Within the lands of Emberheart, a realm teeming with life and magic, a variety of extraordinary flora and fauna thrive, each intimately connected to the vibrant landscape. Some of the notable fauna and flora specific to Emberheart include:

Fauna:

1. Emberfoxes: These mystical creatures are adorned with fiery-red fur, blending seamlessly with the vibrant landscape of Emberheart. Emberfoxes are known for their cunning intelligence and are often associated with the elemental forces of fire.

2. Crystalwing Hummingbirds: Delicate and resplendent, these small hummingbirds have iridescent wings that shimmer with a kaleidoscope of colours. They are attracted to the nectar of the enchanting Crystal Blossoms that grow in Emberheart's forests.

3. Solarian Stags: Majestic and proud, Solarian stags possess luminous antlers that emit a soft, golden glow. They roam the sunlit glades of Emberheart and are revered as symbols of grace and strength.

4. Celestial Butterflies: These ethereal butterflies are adorned with celestial patterns on their wings. They are believed to be messengers from the spirits of the land, guiding travellers and bringing blessings to the realm.

5. Luminous Serpents: Gliding through the night skies, luminous serpents possess scales that reflect the light of the moon and stars. They are often considered symbols of ancient wisdom and are cherished by Emberheart's mystics.

Flora:

1. Crystal Blossoms: Blossoming in the moonlight, these enchanting flowers radiate a soft, silvery glow. They are imbued with magical properties and are sought after by alchemists and spellcasters for their potent essences.

2. Emberthorn Vines: These vines are adorned with radiant, amber-coloured thorns. Emberthorn vines are used by Emberheart's skilled artisans to craft intricate jewellery and mystical artifacts.

3. Starfire Orchids: Rare and captivating, these orchids bloom under the night sky and emit a soft, celestial light. The essence of starfire orchids is believed to enhance one's connection to the astral planes.

4. Solstice Trees: Towering and majestic, Solstice Trees reach towards the heavens. Their leaves change colour with the seasons, and during the solstices, they release shimmering, luminescent pollen that fills the air with magic.

5. Moonshadow Ferns: Flourishing in the shadowy glades, moonshadow ferns have fronds that sparkle like silver in the moonlight. They are often associated with moonlit rituals and lunar energies.

Emberheart's fauna and flora are deeply intertwined with the mystical essence of the realm. The diverse array of creatures and plants contribute to the magical ambience of Emberheart, inviting adventurers and nature enthusiasts to uncover its wonders and unravel its secrets.

Local laws of Emberheart

In the lands of Emberheart, where the rule of the Flameheart dynasty prevails, several local laws and regulations govern the conduct of its citizens, promoting order, justice, and the well-being of the realm. Some of the specific local laws in Emberheart are:

1. Loyalty to the Crown: Emberheart upholds the paramount importance of loyalty to the ruling monarch and the Flameheart dynasty. Any act of treason, rebellion, or attempts to overthrow the king's authority is punishable by severe consequences.

2. The Right of Hospitality: Emberheart, known for its hospitality, enforces a law that requires citizens to offer food and shelter to travellers in need. Refusal to provide hospitality without valid reason is seen as a breach of the realm's values.

3. Preservation of Ancient Artifacts: Emberheart treasures its ancient relics and magical artifacts. Tampering with or stealing these historical items is strictly prohibited, and the Order of the Silver Falcons is responsible for safeguarding and preserving such valuable heritage.

4. The Rule of Law: Emberheart's justice system adheres to a fair and impartial trial process. Accused individuals have the right to legal representation and a fair hearing before a council of judges.

5. Protection of Sacred Sites: Emberheart is home to sacred locations, temples, and shrines. Any act of desecration or disrespect towards these sites is considered a grave offense, with penalties ranging from fines to exile.

6. Prohibition of Dark Magic: Emberheart has a strong aversion to dark and forbidden magic. Practicing necromancy or other malevolent arts is illegal, with offenders subject to the judgment of the Order of the Silver Falcons.

7. Respect for Tradition: Emberheart places great value on tradition and cultural customs. Disrespect or mockery of cultural practices is discouraged, and outsiders are expected to observe local traditions with reverence.

8. Trade and Taxation: Emberheart regulates trade and levies taxes on merchants and traders entering the city. The revenue generated is used for public welfare, infrastructure, and maintaining the realm's defences.

9. Environmental Protection: Emberheart aims to protect its natural resources and wildlife. Hunting or fishing without permits, as well as unauthorized deforestation, is punishable by law.

10. Duels and Challenges: Emberheart allows duels and challenges to resolve disputes between willing participants. However, such contests must be conducted within designated areas and adhere to strict rules to avoid escalation. This tradition is however on the wane, and seen by the younger residents to be outdated.

These laws, guided by the principles of justice, loyalty, and honour, are instrumental in maintaining the peace and prosperity of Emberheart and upholding the legacy of the Flameheart dynasty.

Cults and religions of Emberheart

In the lands of Emberheart, a realm of diverse landscapes and ancient mysteries, various cults and religions have flourished, each with its own distinct beliefs and practices. Here are some of the specific cults and religions found in Emberheart:

1. The Order of the Ember Flame: This ancient religious order venerates the sacred flame as a symbol of transformation and renewal. Followers believe that the Ember Flame holds the power to purify the soul and grant enlightenment. They conduct sacred rituals around eternal flames, seeking to harness its energy for spiritual growth.

2. The Brotherhood of the Evergreen Grove: A nature-centric cult that reveres the spirit of the ancient forests and the cycle of life. They believe in the interconnectedness of all living beings and seek to protect the forests from harm while promoting sustainable practices.

3. The Cult of the Lunar Tides: This secretive cult worships the moon as a celestial entity of magic and intuition. They believe that the phases of the moon hold the key to unlocking hidden knowledge and accessing mystical energies.

4. The Guild of Artificers: A group of skilled artisans and engineers who revere the art of crafting and invention. They consider their creations to be expressions of divine inspiration and believe in the union of art and technology.

5. The Order of the Star Seekers: This religious order devotes itself to the study of celestial bodies and the mysteries of the cosmos. They believe that the stars hold profound wisdom and seek to understand the cosmic forces that shape their world.

6. The Cult of the Ember Wyrm: A controversial cult that venerates a mythical creature known as the Ember Wyrm. They believe that the Wyrm embodies the primal forces of fire and holds the key to unlocking hidden power.

7. The Keepers of the Ancient Scrolls: A scholarly order dedicated to preserving and deciphering ancient texts and scriptures. They believe that the knowledge contained in these scrolls can reveal forgotten truths and ancient prophecies.

8. The Order of the Crystal Chalice: This cult places great importance on the healing properties of crystals and gemstones. They use crystal elixirs and healing rituals to promote physical and spiritual well-being.

These cults and religions contribute to the diverse tapestry of beliefs in Emberheart. Each cult has its unique practices and rituals that are deeply intertwined with the history, mythology, and natural wonders of the land. Some may be widely accepted and integrated into society, while others might be shrouded in mystery and secrecy. The various cults and religions in Emberheart shape the worldview and actions of their followers, offering different paths to spiritual fulfilment and enlightenment.

Rumours and adventure hooks for Emberheart

1. The Forgotten Library: Whispers of a hidden library filled with ancient tomes and lost knowledge echo through the city of Emberheart. Adventurers are drawn to this enigmatic place, said to be guarded by magical traps and puzzles. Within its depths lie secrets that could alter the course of history, but dangers lurk for those who seek to uncover them.

2. The Rebellion's Secret: Rumours of a growing rebellion against the crown in Emberheart spread like wildfire. The players find themselves entangled in a web of intrigue, torn between their loyalty to the king and their empathy for the rebels' cause. Unravelling the truth behind the rebellion's goals and the identities of its leaders becomes a delicate balance of trust and deception.

3. The Phoenix's Cry: Tales of a majestic phoenix, rumoured to dwell atop the highest peak in the Emberheart mountain range, captivate the hearts of adventurers. Many seek to witness the elusive creature's rebirth from its ashes, believing that it bestows blessings upon those who witness the event. Ascending the treacherous mountains becomes a journey of both spiritual discovery and survival.

4. The Gilded Mask Heist: The city's most prized artifact, the Gilded Mask, has been stolen from Emberheart's grand museum. Suspicion falls upon various individuals, including prominent nobles and skilled thieves. The players are hired to recover the artifact, but the truth behind the heist is more convoluted than anyone could have anticipated.

5. The Timeless Gardens: Whispers speak of a hidden realm where time flows differently, granting immortality to those who find it. As tales spread, adventurers embark on a quest to locate the Timeless Gardens, where eternal life and ancient wisdom are said to await. However, the journey to this mythical place is filled with perilous trials and unforeseen consequences.

Adventure Hooks:

1. The Royal Scion: The rightful heir to the Emberheart throne is missing, and the kingdom's stability hangs in the balance. The players are tasked with finding the scion, whose existence could sway the power dynamics in the realm. Uncovering the truth requires them to navigate a maze of political rivalries and ancient prophecies.

2. The Shadow Sorcerers: A group of mysterious sorcerers with dark intentions are rumoured to be plotting in the shadows of Emberheart. The players must investigate this malevolent cabal and thwart their sinister plans before they plunge the city into chaos.

3. The Heart of Embers: Legends tell of a heart-shaped gemstone hidden deep within Emberheart's sacred forest. Said to hold the essence of fire itself, the gem has become the target of covetous treasure hunters and cultists. The players are called upon to safeguard the gem from falling into the wrong hands and prevent potential catastrophic consequences.

4. The Masked Ball: The annual Masked Ball, a grand celebration in Emberheart, is a feast of lavish costumes and intrigue. Amidst the festivities, an assassination plot is rumoured to be unfolding. The players must navigate the glamorous ballroom to uncover the assassin's identity and prevent a tragedy that could shatter the city's harmony.

5. The Celestial Alignment: As an unusual celestial event approaches, so does a prophecy of great significance. The players become embroiled in a race against time to find the scattered shards of an ancient artifact. With the fate of Emberheart tied to the celestial alignment, the adventurers must decipher clues and face powerful foes to restore the artifact before the appointed day arrives.

These rumours and adventure hooks paint a compelling and dynamic landscape of challenges and mysteries in the lands of Emberheart, enticing adventurers to explore its vibrant cities, sacred forests, and enchanting mountains.

Emberfall

City State – Emberfall

In the city of Emberfall, areas of interest are:

1. **Emberkeep Fortress**: A massive and imposing fortress that serves as the heart of the city's defence. It is manned by skilled soldiers and guards, protecting the city from potential threats and ensuring its safety.

2. **The Ember Market**: A bustling marketplace where merchants from all corners of Emberfall and beyond gather to trade goods and wares. It is a vibrant hub of commerce, with a wide array of products, from exotic spices to magical artifacts.

3. **The Flameheart Plaza**: A grand square at the city centre, named in honour of King Magnus Flameheart. Lord Eadric Delemar had it built to show his subjugation and acknowledgement of the King. It hosts various public gatherings, celebrations, and royal proclamations, creating a sense of unity among the people.

4. **The Enchanted Quarters**: A district known for its proliferation of magic shops, alchemical laboratories, and mystical academies. It is a place where aspiring mages and sorcerers come to hone their craft and study the arcane arts.

5. **The Whispering Glades**: A serene and enchanting park filled with ancient trees and mystical creatures. It is a favourite spot for locals and visitors to relax, meditate, and connect with nature's magical energies.

6. **The Phoenix Theatre**: A renowned venue for performing arts, including plays, concerts, and magical performances. The theatre attracts the most talented artists and is a source of cultural pride for the city.

7. **The Tower of Radiance**: A towering structure where skilled artisans create exquisite stained-glass windows infused with magical luminescence. The windows depict legendary tales and significant events of Emberfall's history.

8. **The Golden Gauntlet**: An arena where skilled warriors, gladiators, and adventurers compete in combat for glory and prizes. The competitions are a spectacle, drawing large crowds and showcasing exceptional combat prowess.

9. **The Sunlit Gardens**: A splendid botanical garden filled with rare and exotic plants, some of which are imbued with magical properties. It is a popular destination for those seeking tranquillity and natural beauty.

10. **The Ember Archives**: A vast repository of historical texts, scrolls, and tomes that chronicle Emberfall's rich history. Scholars and researchers come here to study and unearth forgotten knowledge.

Emberfall is a city teeming with life, culture, and magic. Its citizens take great pride in their heritage, and the city's historical sites, along with its enchanting districts, create a unique and captivating atmosphere. From the Tower of Radiance to the Golden Gauntlet, each location reflects the city's deep connection to its past and its present embrace of magic and the arcane.

Other key towns and villages in Emberfall

In the kingdom of Emberfall, the towns and villages are as diverse as the lands they inhabit. Here are some of the main towns and villages in Emberfall:

1. **Emberstead**: Nestled along the banks of the winding Ember River, Emberstead is a bustling trade hub and a gateway to the heart of Emberfall. Merchants from all over the kingdom converge here to trade their goods, making it a vibrant and lively town. The iconic Ember Bridge, a stunning stone structure, connects Emberstead to other towns across the river, facilitating commerce and travel.

2. **Glimmerbrook**: Tucked away in a dense forest, Glimmerbrook is a village known for its mystical charm and enchanting beauty. The village is home to skilled artisans who craft intricate wooden carvings and exquisite jewellery inspired by the surrounding natural beauty. The villagers revere the ancient trees, believing them to be sacred guardians of their home.

3. **Ironhold**: Standing tall amidst the rocky hills, Ironhold is a fortified town known for its impressive iron mines and skilled blacksmiths. The town's strategic location makes it a vital stronghold for Emberfall's defences. The clang of hammers and the glow of the forge resonate through the town as the smiths' craft powerful weapons and sturdy armour.

4. **Misthaven**: Located near the borders of Emberfall, Misthaven is a village shrouded in a perpetual mist that veils it in an air of mystery. The villagers are known for their expertise in herbal remedies and medicinal concoctions, using the unique plants and herbs found in the misty environment.

5. **Silverpeak**: Perched on the slopes of the Silverpeak Mountains, this village is renowned for its skilled mountaineers and climbers. Silverpeak serves as a base for adventurers exploring the majestic peaks and treacherous terrain of the mountains. The village also houses the Silverpeak Guild, a society of daring explorers and pioneers.

6. **Duskwinds**: Situated on the vast Ember Plains, Duskwinds is a farming village blessed with fertile lands and abundant harvests. The villagers are skilled horse breeders, and the fields are dotted with windmills, harnessing the strong gusts that sweep across the plains.

7. **Rivershade**: Situated along the tranquil banks of the Emberflow River, Rivershade is a picturesque village known for its peaceful atmosphere and lush gardens. The villagers have mastered the art of irrigation, creating an oasis of greenery even in the arid regions of Emberfall. The villagers are skilled botanists and horticulturists, cultivating rare and exotic plants.

8. **Stonehaven**: Carved into the foothills of the Stonewall Mountains, Stonehaven is a town known for its impressive stone architecture and skilled masons. The stone quarries surrounding the town provide an abundance of raw materials, and the town's buildings display intricate stonework. Stonehaven is also home to the renowned Stone Guild, who have mastered the art of stone craft.

9. **Twilight Hollow**: Hidden within a dense forest, Twilight Hollow is a village surrounded by ancient trees that seem to come alive under the shimmering light of the moon. The villagers are skilled woodworkers, creating stunning wooden crafts and instruments that are sought after throughout the kingdom. Twilight Hollow is also known for its unique music festivals held under the moonlit canopy.

10. **Emberwatch**: A strategic outpost perched on the edge of Emberfall's borders, Emberwatch is a key watchtower that guards against potential threats from beyond the kingdom. The village is home to vigilant scouts and skilled archers, who keep a watchful eye on the surrounding lands. Emberwatch acts as the first line of defence for Emberfall and plays a crucial role in maintaining the kingdom's safety.

Key figures in power and influence in the city of Emberfall

In the city of Emberfall, the key figures in power and influence are:

1. **Lord Cedric Ironwood**: The ruling lord deputy of Emberfall council in Lord Eadric Delema's absence. Lord Cedric is a strong and authoritative leader. He is known for his strategic thinking and unwavering dedication to the prosperity and security of Emberfall.

2. **Lady Elara Nightshade**: A prominent noblewoman in Emberfall, Lady Elara is a skilled diplomat and negotiator. She often represents the city in diplomatic matters and fosters alliances with neighbouring regions.

3. **Commander Marcus Stormbourne**: As the head of Emberfall's military forces, Commander Marcus is a seasoned warrior and tactician. He ensures the city's defences are strong and oversees military campaigns when needed.

4. **High Mage Isadora Firestone**: The leader of the Mage Council, High Mage Isadora is a formidable spellcaster and expert in magical arts. She safeguards the city from arcane threats and advises Lord Cedric on magical matters.

5. **Guildmaster Hugo Goldmine**: As the head of the Merchants' Guild, Guildmaster Hugo is a shrewd and ambitious businessman. He plays a vital role in managing the city's trade and commerce, boosting Emberfall's economy.

6. **High Priestess Lysandra Moonweaver**: The spiritual leader of Emberfall, High Priestess Lysandra guides religious practices and rituals in the city. She brings comfort and guidance to the people, promoting unity and faith.

7. **Councillor Roland Stormrider**: A respected member of the Council of Advisors, Councillor Roland is a seasoned statesman and wise counsellor. His knowledge and experience make him an invaluable asset to Lord Cedric.

8. **Master Engineer Percival Ironforge**: The chief engineer of Emberfall, Master Engineer Percival oversees the city's infrastructure and technological advancements. He is known for his ingenuity and innovative solutions.

9. **Guildmaster Seraphina Brightwing**: The leader of the Artisans' Guild, Guildmaster Seraphina is a talented artist and craftsman. She supports the city's cultural development and encourages artistic expression.

10. **Master Tracker Kael Wildborne**: A skilled ranger and tracker, Master Tracker Kael is an expert at navigating Emberfall's wilderness. He aids in exploring and securing the city's outskirts and is instrumental in dealing with threats from the wild.

These key figures in Emberfall hold significant sway over the city's governance, security, and progress. Their interactions and conflicting interests shape the dynamics of Emberfall's society and politics, leading to intricate plots and challenges for adventurers and residents alike.

Key figures in the lands of Emberfall

City Officials:

1. **Lord Eadric Delemar**: The ruling Lord of Emberfall, known for his strategic acumen and ambitions to expand his influence.

2. **Lady Gwendolyn Ashbourne**: The High Chancellor and advisor to Lord Eadric, overseeing matters of law and justice in Emberfall.

Prominent Citizens:

1. **Lady Elara Nightshade**: A talented sorceress and advisor to Lord Eadric, wielding great magical powers.

2. **Sir Aldric Stormwind**: A renowned knight and hero of many battles, respected and admired by the people of Emberfall.

Guild Leaders:

1. **Mistress Isabella Lockwood**: The head of the Merchants Guild, controlling much of the trade and commerce in the region.

2. **Master Thane Stonehammer**: The leader of the Stonemason Guild, responsible for the construction and maintenance of Emberfall's buildings and fortifications.

Merchants:

1. **Eleanor Silverthorn**: An ambitious trader who specializes in precious gemstones and rare artifacts.

2. **Felix Ravenscroft**: A successful merchant known for his exotic goods and mysterious connections to far-off lands.

Tavern Owners:

1. **Astrid Hammersmith**: The proprietor of the Hammersmith Forge and Tavern, offering fine ales and expertly crafted weaponry.

2. **Gareth Blackthorn**: The owner of the Blackthorn Inn, a popular establishment known for its lively atmosphere and talented bards.

Cult Leaders:

1. **High Priestess Lyra Moonshadow**: The leader of the Moonlit Coven, a secretive cult of witches and warlocks who draw power from the phases of the moon.

Adventurers and Heroes:

1. **Talon Shadowbane**: A skilled rogue and renowned treasure hunter, known for daring heists and daring rescues.

2. **Seraphina Sunfire**: A powerful sorceress and protector of the innocent, feared by evildoers and praised by the oppressed.

Scholars and Sages:

1. **Archmage Thaddeus Blackwood**: The foremost arcane scholar and head of the Mage's Guild, responsible for magical research and education in Emberfall.

2. **Lady Adeline Starbrook**: A renowned historian and keeper of ancient knowledge, with access to rare tomes and hidden lore.

Commerce of Emberfall

Commerce in the lands of Emberfall flourishes amidst a diverse range of resources and skilled craftsmanship. The region's fertile lands and temperate climate enable a flourishing agricultural industry, yielding bountiful crops of grains, vegetables, and fruits. Emberfall's produce is highly valued both within the region and in neighbouring city-states, making it a significant contributor to the realm's food supply. The mine of Shadowstrike Depths, produces vast quantities of salt, which helps in the food preservation and tanning.

As a realm rich in history and ancient artifacts, Emberfall fosters a thriving trade in archaeology and antiquities. Adventurers and scholars embark on expeditions to discover rare and magical artifacts within the realm's ancient ruins. These valuable relics are traded, studied, and sometimes exhibited in museums, drawing in knowledge seekers and history enthusiasts from all over Emberfrost.

Furthermore, Emberfall's strategic location at the crossroads of various trade routes makes it a bustling centre for commerce. Caravans laden with goods traverse the realm, trading and exchanging goods from different lands. Merchants from neighbouring city-states pass through Emberfall, making it a melting pot of cultural influences and trade opportunities.

Emberfall's coastline also plays a significant role in its commerce. Fishing is a vital industry, providing a fresh supply of seafood for the local populace and contributing to trade with other coastal cities. The port city of Emberheart serves as the gateway for maritime commerce, with ships transporting goods, passengers, and cultural influences between different regions and city-states.

Furthermore, Emberfall's magical heritage adds to its unique commerce. The city is home to skilled enchanters and mages who create magic items, including enchanted weapons, protective amulets, and other mystical artifacts. The demand for these potent items attracts adventurers, nobles, and traders seeking to harness their magical power. The lands skilled alchemists have just discovered the process of making gunpowder, but this dangerous process is very much in its infancy and several talented alchemists have been killed. Currently this is a little know substance and very little of the powder exists.

Emberfall's vibrant markets and bustling trade hubs create a dynamic and prosperous economy, making it an essential player in the realm's commerce and cultural exchange. Its strategic location, rich resources, and skilled artisans make it a hub for various trades and crafts, attracting traders and merchants from all corners of Emberfrost. The lands of Emberfall stand as a testament to the power of commerce in forging connections, fostering cooperation, and enriching the realm's way of life.

Local festivals of Emberfall

In the lands of Emberfall, the people embrace a variety of festivals that reflect their rich history, deep-rooted traditions, and reverence for nature. Some of the local festivals celebrated in Emberfall include:

1. Harvest Moon Festival: As the bountiful crops are gathered from the fertile lands, the Harvest Moon Festival celebrates the abundance of nature. The festival takes place under the full moon, and people offer thanks to the land for its gifts. There are feasts, dancing, and music to mark the occasion.

2. Dragonfire Carnival: This vibrant and exciting festival commemorates the ancient tale of a dragon that once protected the region. People dress up in dragon-themed costumes and masks, and there are elaborate parades featuring dragon floats. The carnival also includes games, performances, and dragon-themed contests.

3. River's Day Celebration: A festival dedicated to honouring the rivers that nourish the lands of Emberfall. People gather by the riverbanks to clean the water and offer prayers for its purity. There are boat races, river fishing competitions, and water-themed games.

4. Festival of Lights: As the days grow shorter and the winter season approaches, the Festival of Lights brings warmth and cheer to Emberfall. The city and towns are adorned with colorful lanterns and candles, illuminating the streets. People exchange gifts and share stories around cozy fires.

5. Sunflower Festival: In the sun-kissed plains of Emberfall, the Sunflower Festival celebrates the blooming of sunflowers that blanket the fields. People create intricate floral displays and participate in sunflower picking competitions. The festival also showcases local arts, crafts, and traditional music.

6. Masked Masquerade: A mysterious and enchanting festival where people don masks and costumes to conceal their identities. The Masked Masquerade features dancing, enchanting performances, and storytelling. It is believed that wearing masks allows people to let go of their inhibitions and reveal their true selves.

7. Day of Remembrance: A solemn and reflective festival dedicated to honouring the memory of fallen heroes and loved ones. People visit memorials and offer prayers for peace and unity. The Day of Remembrance also serves as a time to reflect on the history and sacrifices that shaped Emberfall.

8. Festival of the Four Elements: Celebrated during the equinoxes, the Festival of the Four Elements pays homage to the balance of nature's elements – earth, water, air, and fire. The festival includes elemental-themed ceremonies, rituals, and artistic expressions representing the interconnectedness of all things.

These festivals in Emberfall bring communities together, fostering a sense of unity, gratitude, and joy among its people. Each celebration is a unique reflection of the region's culture and its harmonious relationship with the natural world.

Fauna and Flora specific to Emberfall

In the lands of Emberfall, a realm of diverse landscapes and enchanting beauty, an array of unique flora and fauna flourish, each intricately connected to the vibrant environment. Here are some notable examples of fauna and flora specific to Emberfall:

Fauna:

1. Emberwing Griffins: Majestic creatures with fiery wings, Emberwing Griffins soar through the skies of Emberfall. These powerful beings are known for their loyalty and are often seen as symbols of strength and protection.

2. Moonshadow Wolves: Moonshadow Wolves are elusive creatures that prowl the shadowy forests of Emberfall. Their fur glimmers under the moonlight, and they are believed to be connected to the mystical energies of the moon.

3. Earthstride Elk: These elegant and agile creatures traverse the grasslands and forests of Emberfall. Their hooves seem to glide effortlessly over any terrain, earning them their name.

4. Luminous Fireflies: As night falls in Emberfall, the air comes alive with the soft glow of Luminous Fireflies. They dance through the dark, enchanting travellers with their ethereal beauty.

5. Emberstone Turtles: Slow-moving and resilient, Emberstone Turtles inhabit the rivers and lakes of Emberfall. Their shells are infused with a radiant, ember-like glow, making them appear as if they carry a piece of the realm's essence.

Flora:

1. Emberblooms: Brilliant flowers that bloom in shades of orange and red, Emberblooms thrive in the warm and fertile lands of Emberfall. They are known for their fragrant and calming aroma.

2. Shadowvine: Twining through the dense forests, Shadowvine is a mysterious and unique plant that seems to shift in the moon's light. It is said to possess magical properties and is often sought after by alchemists and mystics.

3. Starlight Lilies: These luminous lilies only bloom under the night sky, releasing a soft, radiant light. They are associated with celestial energies and are considered sacred by some Emberfall inhabitants.

4. Sunfire Cacti: Thriving in the arid regions of Emberfall, Sunfire Cacti store solar energy during the day and emit a warm, soothing glow at night. They are a vital source of sustenance for both wildlife and travellers.

5. Tranquil Willows: Graceful and serene, Tranquil Willows line the riverbanks of Emberfall. Their drooping branches and leaves create a tranquil atmosphere, making them popular spots for meditation and contemplation.

Emberfall's fauna and flora contribute to the realm's unique charm and allure. As adventurers traverse the lands, they will encounter these magical creatures and plants, each adding to the richness of Emberfall's natural beauty and mystical essence.

Emberfall Migration:

As the warm winds of spring sweep through Emberfall, a spectacle like no other graces the skies. Thousands of graceful, winged creatures take flight in a mesmerizing migration that captivates the hearts of all who witness it. These majestic creatures are known as "Celestial Drifters," and they are a unique species of magical beings native to the lands of Emberfall.

Appearance: The Celestial Drifters are ethereal beings, with iridescent wings that shimmer with a kaleidoscope of colours, reflecting the sun's rays like a dazzling display of gemstones. Their bodies are slender and adorned with intricate patterns that seem to glow with a faint inner light. They vary in size, with some as small as a hummingbird and others as large as eagles, making the migration a mesmerizing dance of shapes and colours across the skies.

Migration Routes: The migration follows a well-established route, starting from the southern coastal regions of Emberfall. As the days grow longer and the temperature rises, the Celestial Drifters emerge from their hidden nesting grounds and take flight in vast flocks. They follow ancient ley lines that crisscross the realm, guiding them through valleys, across plains, and over mountains to settle somewhere in the mountains on the border with Riven and Emberheart.

Their journey: The Celestial Drifters embark on this migration for a purpose known only to them and perhaps the enigmatic forces of Emberfrost. The journey is believed to be tied to the magical energies of the realm, as the winged creatures draw upon the ley lines' energies during their flight. Some scholars speculate that the migration is connected to their breeding cycles, while others believe it is a way for the creatures to cleanse and renew their magical essence.

Festivities and Honor: During the migration, the people of Emberfall celebrate the return of the Celestial Drifters with grand festivities known as the "Wingsong Festival." The skies are filled with vibrant banners and colourful decorations, welcoming the winged creatures back to the land. The festival features music, dances, and performances inspired by the graceful flight of the Celestial Drifters.

Time of Return: The Celestial Drifters' migration usually takes place over a few weeks, and they typically return to Emberfall at the beginning of summer. Their arrival heralds the start of the warm season, symbolizing a time of renewal, growth, and magical abundance in the realm.

The Emberfall Migration is a harmonious convergence of nature's magic and the people's deep-rooted respect for the creatures that grace their skies. It reminds the inhabitants of Emberfall of their connection to the mystical forces that shape their world, and it stands as a testament to the awe-inspiring beauty and wonder that can be found within their enchanted lands.

Local laws of Emberfall

In the lands of Emberfall, where different city-states exist under the united rule of the Flameheart dynasty, various local laws and regulations govern the conduct of citizens and ensure a harmonious society. Here are some specific local laws in Emberfall:

1. Loyalty to the Monarch: Emberfall emphasizes unwavering loyalty to the Flameheart dynasty and its ruling monarch. Acts of treason or rebellion against the crown are considered grave offenses, punishable by severe consequences.

2. Trade and Commerce Regulations: Each city-state within Emberfall has its specific trade and commerce regulations. Merchants and traders are required to adhere to these rules when conducting business within the city's jurisdiction.

3. Sanctity of Sacred Sites: Emberfall houses numerous sacred locations, temples, and shrines. Defiling or desecrating these sites is strictly forbidden and can result in significant repercussions.

4. The Guild System: Guilds play a crucial role in Emberfall, and each guild has its specific laws and codes of conduct. Guild members must abide by these rules, and any disputes within the guild are settled through established protocols.

5. Environmental Conservation: Emberfall values its natural resources and wildlife. Laws are in place to protect the environment, including regulations on hunting, fishing, and logging to maintain ecological balance.

6. Public Conduct and Decorum: Emberfall places importance on maintaining public decorum and respect for others. Disruptive behaviour, public disturbances, or engaging in unruly activities may lead to penalties.

7. Magic Regulation: Emberfall acknowledges and values magic but strictly regulates its usage. Unauthorized or malevolent use of magic can lead to prosecution by the authorities or intervention by the Order of the Silver Falcons.

These laws, guided by the principles of loyalty, justice, and order, contribute to the stability and prosperity of Emberfall, fostering an environment where the Flameheart dynasty's rule is upheld and the interests of its people are protected.

Cults and religions of Emberfall

In the lands of Emberfall, a realm marked by its turbulent history and rugged landscapes, various cults and religions have emerged, each with its own beliefs and practices. Here are some of the specific cults and religions found in Emberfall:

1. The Cult of the Blood Moon: This mysterious and enigmatic cult worships the Blood Moon as a divine entity. They believe that during a lunar eclipse, the Blood Moon grants them heightened magical abilities and spiritual enlightenment. They conduct elaborate rituals during eclipses, seeking to commune with the Blood Moon and receive its blessings.

2. The Circle of the Ancient Stones: A druidic order that reveres the ancient standing stones scattered throughout Emberfall. They believe that these stones hold the memories and wisdom of the land. The Circle conducts rituals to attune themselves with nature and draw power from the stones.

3. The Order of the Silver Serpent: This religious order venerates a mythical serpent said to inhabit the deepest waters of Emberfall's lakes and rivers. They believe that the Silver Serpent embodies the cycle of life, death, and rebirth. They perform water rituals and ceremonies to honour the serpent's influence.

4. The Brotherhood of the Scarlet Blade: A secretive cult of assassins who follow a strict code of honour and loyalty. They consider their art of assassination to be a sacred duty, protecting the balance of power in the realm. They believe that through their actions, they are agents of justice and balance.

5. The Order of the Celestial Scribes: A group of scholars and sages who study the celestial bodies and believe in the interconnectedness of the universe. They seek to unravel the cosmic mysteries and understand the influence of the stars on human destinies.

These cults and religions contribute to the diverse cultural landscape of Emberfall, each with its own rituals, beliefs, and adherents. Some of these groups may be openly practiced and integrated into society, while others might remain hidden and secretive, adding an air of mystery to the realm. The cults and religions of Emberfall shape the spiritual and philosophical perspectives of its people, offering different paths to enlightenment and understanding of the world around them.

Rumours and adventure hooks for Emberfall

1. The Ghost of Ember Keep: Whispers of a restless spirit haunting the ancient Ember Keep spread like wildfire. Adventurers are called upon to investigate this supernatural occurrence, uncovering the tragic past of the keep and the reason behind the ghost's unresolved business. As they delve deeper, they find themselves entangled in a tale of lost love and betrayal.

2. The Lost Relic of Emberfall: Legends speak of a long-lost relic hidden in the heart of Emberfall's enchanted forest. Said to possess immense power, the relic has become the target of treasure hunters and dark cults. The players are tasked with locating the relic before it falls into the wrong hands, leading them on a perilous journey through the mystical woods.

3. The Dragon's Awakening: Rumours of a dormant dragon awakening from its slumber in the Emberfall mountains send waves of fear throughout the region. The players are hired to investigate and determine the truth behind these rumours. Their quest leads them to ancient dragon lore, the forgotten history of Emberfall, and an opportunity to prevent a catastrophic clash between the dragon and the kingdom.

4. The Elemental Rifts: Mysterious elemental rifts begin appearing throughout Emberfall, unleashing destructive elemental energies upon the land. The players must close these rifts before they consume the kingdom in chaos. As they search for the source of the rifts, they uncover a powerful mage manipulating the elements, with intentions that could reshape the kingdom's future.

5. The Cursed Crown: Whispers of a cursed crown, once worn by a long-dead king of Emberfall, have resurfaced. Legends claim that whoever dons the crown will be imbued with immense power but at the cost of their sanity. The players find themselves drawn into a dangerous game of intrigue, as multiple factions vie to possess the crown's power and navigate the treacherous path of corruption and redemption.

Adventure Hooks:

1. The Forbidden Tower: High in the mountains of Emberfall, a tower long forbidden and sealed off from the world holds secrets of ancient magics. The players must navigate the tower's arcane challenges to uncover lost knowledge or seal away its dangerous power once more.

2. The Bandit Queen: A notorious bandit queen has emerged in the outskirts of Emberfall, terrorizing travellers and challenging the kingdom's authority. The players are tasked with apprehending her and unravelling the motivations behind her rise to power.

3. The Enchanted Grove: A mystical grove deep within Emberfall's forests is said to grant a boon to those who prove themselves worthy. The players are drawn to this sanctuary of ancient druids, where they must undergo a series of trials and tests to prove their worthiness and receive a unique blessing.

4. The Vanishing Children: Children from a nearby village in Emberfall have been mysteriously disappearing without a trace. The players are enlisted to solve the puzzle of the vanishing children, revealing a dark secret that threatens the entire realm.

5. The Astral Observatory: A long-lost observatory that can predict celestial events has been discovered in Emberfall's mountain range. The players are invited to assist scholars and mages in studying the observatory's ancient machinery, leading to unexpected revelations about the past and future of Emberfall.

These rumours and adventure hooks invite daring adventurers to explore the lands of Emberfall, braving its forests, mountains, and ancient ruins in pursuit of legendary treasures, uncovering hidden truths, and shaping the kingdom's destiny.

Frostfire

City State – Frostfire

In the city of Frostgate, nestled on a sunlit plain below the ice-capped peaks, areas of interest are:

1. **The Irongate Citadel**: An imposing fortress that crowns the highest hill in Frostgate, serving as the stronghold of the city's ruler. Its tall stone walls and watchtowers overlook the passes, providing a strategic vantage point for defence.

2. **The Boreal Bazaar**: A vibrant marketplace bustling with traders from Frostgate and the surrounding regions. Here, a diverse array of goods is exchanged, from precious gemstones mined in the mountains to spices and exotic fruits from distant lands.

3. **The Arcane Quarter**: A district where skilled wizards, sorcerers, and magicians congregate. It is a hub of magical knowledge, where practitioners of elemental and frost magic come to share their expertise.

4. **The Sapphire Observatory**: A grand tower that houses both an observatory and a library. Sages and astronomers study the night sky, while scholars delve into ancient tomes, seeking secrets of the cosmos and the world.

5. **The Drifting Tavern**: A lively establishment where tales of adventure and daring escapades abound. Adventurers, sailors, and locals gather to share stories and raise tankards of the city's famed Frostfire Ale.

6. **The Arena of Aurora**: A sprawling amphitheatre that hosts various contests and tournaments. From elemental duels to ice sculpting competitions, the arena is always alive with the spirit of friendly competition and excitement.

7. **The Crystal Sanctum**: A breathtaking temple devoted to the worship of the Eternal Sun, the mythical celestial body that brings warmth and prosperity to the land. The temple's grand architecture reflects the city's devotion to their patron deity.

8. **The Enchanted Gardens**: A magical oasis, despite the surrounding icy terrain, the gardens are a sanctuary of tranquillity. Unusual plants from distant lands flourish here, making it a fascinating sight for visitors and botanists alike.

9. **The Guild of Frostsmiths**: A renowned blacksmith guild known for crafting exceptional weapons and armour. Master smiths here imbue their creations with magical properties, making them sought-after by warriors from all across Emberfrost.

10. **The Palace of Gleaming Ice**: The opulent residence of the city's ruling lord or lady, built with rare and shimmering ice crystals. Its architecture reflects the merging of sunlit Spain with the frozen beauty of Emberfrost.

Frostgate, a city of contrast, thrives as a centre of trade, culture, and magical knowledge. The strategic position of the Irongate Citadel, guarding the vital mountain passes, has shaped its identity as a beacon of prosperity and unity within the realm of Emberfrost.

Other key towns and villages in Frostfire

In the lands of Frostfire, where the high mountains remain snow and ice-capped throughout the year, but the plains experience a warm climate, the main towns and villages are:

1. **Frostpeak**: Nestled at the foothills of the towering Frostpeak Mountains, this town serves as a gateway to the icy wonders beyond. It's a bustling trade hub, where merchants exchange precious gemstones and minerals mined from the mountains. The town has a lively market, attracting visitors from all over the kingdom.

2. **Crystalbrook**: Located beside a clear glacial river, Crystalbrook is renowned for its skilled glassblowers and artisans. They create delicate glassware and intricate sculptures inspired by the surrounding natural beauty. The village is known for its picturesque glass gardens and dazzling glass lantern displays during festivals.

3. **Auroravale**: This village is situated in a serene forest where the enchanting Northern Lights often illuminate the night sky. Its people have a deep connection to the celestial display, and they hold nightly celebrations to witness the dancing lights. Auroravale is a place of wonder and spiritual contemplation.

4. **Everfrost**: As a remote village on the edge of the Ice Plains, Everfrost is a place of ancient traditions and mystical rituals. Its wise mystics and shamans harness the power of frost magic to protect their community and seek visions of the future. The village is adorned with ice sculptures and glowing crystals.

5. **Sunshroud**: Located amidst the vibrant plains of Frostfire, Sunshroud enjoys warm and pleasant weather throughout the year. The village is known for its sunflower fields, where colourful blooms sway with the gentle breeze. It's a cheerful place with a rich agricultural heritage.

6. **Glacier's Edge**: Set at the boundary of the icy mountains and the warm plains, Glacier's Edge is a town of contrasts. Its people are skilled hunters and traders who bridge the gap between the two regions. The town's market offers an array of unique goods, from exotic furs to rare spices.

7. **Frostwood**: Embraced by a mystical forest, Frostwood is a village steeped in legend and folklore. Ancient trees surround the village, their branches shimmering with ice crystals. The villagers have a deep respect for nature, and they celebrate their bond with the forest through vibrant feasts and ceremonies.

8. **Whisperwind**: Nestled atop a hill overlooking the plains, Whisperwind is a picturesque village with white stone buildings and intricate wind chimes. The village is known for its skilled wind musicians who create mesmerizing melodies with the natural breezes that sweep through the area.

9. **Warmharbor**: Found along the coast of Frostfire, Warmharbor is a bustling maritime town that thrives on trade and fishing. The harbour is filled with colourful ships from across the realm, bringing goods and travellers to this lively coastal community.

10. **Flamecrest**: High in the mountains, where the air is thin and crisp, Flamecrest is a small village known for its hot springs and geothermal activity. The villagers use the natural heat to grow unique flora and nurture lush gardens amidst the snow-capped peaks.

These towns and villages reflect the diverse and enchanting aspects of Frostfire's lands, where the high mountains and the warm plains coexist, creating a kingdom of wondrous contrasts and unique cultural experiences.

Key figures in power and influence in the city of Frostgate

In the city of Frostgate, the key figures in power and influence are:

1. **Lord Thorian Frostbane**: Thorian is a stern and principled leader. He comes from a long line of respected rulers and is dedicated to upholding the traditions and values of Frostgate. A key advisor to Lord Ustace Canarveon, the ruler of Frostfire.

2. **Lady Isabella Snowdancer**: The wife of Lord Thorian and a prominent figure in Frostgate's high society. Lady Isabella is known for her grace and charm, and she often hosts social events and fundraisers for charitable causes.

3. **Captain Aldric Winterborn**: As the captain of the Frostgate Guard, Captain Aldric is responsible for maintaining law and order within the city. He is a skilled warrior and a fair enforcer of the city's laws.

4. **Archmage Elowen Frostglade**: The head of the Frostgate Academy of Arcane Arts, Archmage Elowen is a powerful spellcaster and scholar. She oversees magical education and research within the city.

5. **Guildmaster Grimald Stoneheart**: The leader of the Frostgate Merchant Guild, Guildmaster Grimald is a shrewd businessman and negotiator. He plays a crucial role in Frostgate's trade and economic growth.

6. **High Priest Orlaith Frostwhisper**: The spiritual leader of Frostgate, High Priest Orlaith presides over religious ceremonies and offers guidance to the city's residents. She is highly respected for her wisdom and devotion.

7. **Councilor Reynard Ironhelm**: A member of the Council of Advisors, Councillor Reynard is an experienced diplomat and politician. He represents the interests of Frostgate in diplomatic affairs with neighboring regions.

8. **Master Engineer Eveline Frostforge**: The head engineer of Frostgate, Master Engineer Eveline is an expert in constructing and maintaining the city's structures. She is known for her innovative engineering solutions.

9. **Guildmaster Gideon Stormweaver**: The leader of the Frostgate Artisans' Guild, Guildmaster Gideon is a skilled craftsman and artist. He promotes the city's cultural development and supports local artists and artisans.

10. **Ranger Captain Bryn Wildwood**: A renowned ranger and tracker, Captain Bryn is responsible for patrolling the outskirts of Frostgate and protecting the city from potential threats.

These key figures in Frostgate wield considerable influence over the city's affairs, and their actions and decisions shape the destiny of Frostgate and its people. Their ambitions and rivalries create a dynamic political landscape that can provide intriguing opportunities for adventurers and a backdrop for gripping tales within the city walls.

Key figures in the lands of Frostfire

City Officials:

1. **Lady Freya Snowmantle**: The ruling Lady of Frostfall, known for her strong leadership and wise counsel.

2. **Lord Aric Ironhelm**: The Lord Chamberlain, responsible for overseeing the day-to-day affairs of Frostfall and advising Lady Freya.

Prominent Citizens:

1. **Lady Isolde Frostwood**: A skilled diplomat and Lady-in-Waiting to Lady Freya, entrusted with delicate negotiations and international relations.

2. **Sir Cedric Winterbourne**: The Captain of the Frostguard, an elite group of knights sworn to protect Frostfall and its people.

Guild Leaders:

1. **Mistress Evangeline Nightshade**: The head of the Whisperwind Society, a guild of bards and storytellers dedicated to preserving Frostfall's history and culture.

2. **Master Gunther Frostforge**: The leader of the Flameforgers Guild, responsible for crafting exceptional weapons and armour for Frostfall's defense.

Merchants:

1. **Lisette Silverbrook**: An ambitious businesswoman who runs Frostfall's bustling marketplace and manages various trade ventures.

2. **Erik Stormweaver**: A renowned trader and merchant, dealing in rare artifacts and magical curiosities.

Tavern Owners:

1. **Eliza Moonshadow**: The owner of the Moonlit Bazaar, a unique tavern and marketplace where rare magical items can be bought and sold.

2. **Gareth Whitewood**: The proprietor of the Frosty Tankard Inn, a popular establishment known for its hearty food and lively entertainment.

Cult Leaders:

1. **High Priest Bjorn Frostclaw**: The leader of the Cult of the Frost Mother, a powerful ancient cult that worships the Frost Mother and seeks her blessings for bountiful winters.

Adventurers and Heroes:

1. **Eldric Stormrider**: A fearless adventurer and captain of the Icewind Corsairs, a group of skilled sailors and explorers who brave the frozen seas.

2. **Aria Swiftarrow**: A master archer and protector of Frostfall's borders, known for her precision and unwavering dedication.

Scholars and Sages:

1. **Archmage Elowen Frostbloom**: The most renowned mage in Frostfall, responsible for the study of elemental magic and the protection of the realm from magical threats.

2. **Thalia Starfire**: A wise seer and scholar, well-versed in ancient prophecies and mysterious visions.

Commerce of Frostfire

Commerce in the lands of Frostfire is a tapestry woven from the contrasting beauty of its warm fertile plains and towering, ice-capped mountains. The combination of these diverse landscapes brings forth a unique blend of goods and trade opportunities that enrich the realm of Emberfrost.

The warm and fertile plains of Frostfire yield a bounty of agricultural products, including grains, fruits, and vegetables. The region's skilled farmers and cultivators tend to the fertile lands, ensuring a steady supply of food for both the local populace and neighbouring city-states. Frostfire's abundance of crops makes it a crucial breadbasket of the realm, and its traders play a pivotal role in distributing sustenance throughout Emberfrost. The city of Frostgate serves as the primary trading hub for these exquisite creations, attracting merchants and traders from all corners of the realm.

The Sunblaze Peaks mountainous terrain also brings forth opportunities for specialized industries in Frostfire. Craftsmen and artisans create cold weather survival gear and equipment, vital for traversing the treacherous frozen landscapes of the mountains. Frostfire's traders supply essential items like insulated clothing, ice cleats, and enchanted gear to travellers, explorers, and the Frostwardens who guard the mountain passes.

Frostfire's strategic location at the convergence of warm plains and icy mountains positions it as a key player in the trade of valuable furs and pelts from the region's colder climates. Traders eagerly seek these luxurious materials, which are crafted into garments and accessories prized for their warmth and elegance.

Moreover, the lush and temperate nature of Frostfire gives rise to a thriving market for fine wines and spirits. Grapes cultivated in the region's fertile vineyards produce exceptional wines, and skilled vintners take pride in creating unique blends that are highly sought after by nobles and connoisseurs across Emberfrost.

The combination of fertile plains, towering mountains, and skilled craftsmanship creates a vibrant and diverse commerce in the lands of Frostfire. The city of Frostgate stands at the heart of this economic activity, serving as a vital link between the warm and the frozen, and fostering trade and cultural exchange throughout the realm.

Local festivals of Frostfire

In the lands of Frostfire, where warm fertile plains meet the towering mountain range, the people celebrate a diverse array of festivals that blend the richness of both environments. Some of the local festivals celebrated in Frostfire include:

1. Winter's Embrace: As the winter season descends upon Frostfire, the Winter's Embrace festival marks the beginning of the snowfall. The festival welcomes the first snowflakes with joy and excitement. People gather around bonfires, drink warm beverages, and participate in snow games and activities like ice skating and snowball fights.

2. Mountain Peak Revelry: Celebrated during the warmer months, the Mountain Peak Revelry honours the majesty of the towering peaks surrounding Frostfire. The festival includes hiking expeditions to reach the highest points, where breathtaking vistas of the fertile plains and distant horizons await. There are storytelling sessions about legendary mountain adventures and a grand feast to celebrate conquering the heights.

3. Blossom Symphony: With the arrival of spring, the Blossom Symphony festival celebrates the blooming of vibrant wildflowers across the plains. The meadows come alive with a burst of colours, and people create intricate floral patterns and garlands. The festival includes music and dance performances in the midst of the blossoms, creating a harmonious symphony of nature and art.

4. Dragon's Ascendance: A festival inspired by ancient folklore that tells of a benevolent dragon residing in the mountains. The Dragon's Ascendance festival involves making offerings to the mythical creature for prosperity and protection. People release paper lanterns into the night sky, symbolizing the dragon's ascent into the heavens.

5. Hearth and Harvest: As autumn sets in, the Hearth and Harvest festival celebrates the final harvest of the year. The plains are covered in golden hues, and people come together to share the bounty of the land. The festival features hearty feasts, traditional music, and dances around bonfires, giving thanks for the abundance of the harvest season.

6. Starfall Spectacle: Celebrated during meteor showers, the Starfall Spectacle is a mesmerizing festival that honours the beauty of the night sky. People gather on elevated platforms to witness the shooting stars and make wishes upon them. The festival also includes stargazing sessions led by astronomers and sages.

7. Plains Rhythms: A festival dedicated to the vibrant cultural heritage of Frostfire's plains, Plains Rhythms showcases traditional music, dances, and art forms. Different communities come together to present their unique performances, creating a colourful tapestry of local talents.

8. Solstice Serenade: Held during the summer solstice, the Solstice Serenade celebrates the longest day of the year. The festival includes a grand gathering in the plains, with music, singing, and communal dances to embrace the sun's warmth and light.

These festivals in Frostfire reflect the harmonious coexistence of the warm plains and the icy peaks, blending nature's contrasts into joyous and meaningful celebrations for the people of the realm.

Fauna and Flora specific to Frostfire

In the lands of Frostfire, a realm of contrast and wonder, a diverse array of flora and fauna thrive, adapted to both the warm fertile plains and the cold, ice-capped mountains. Here are some notable examples of fauna and flora specific to Frostfire:

Fauna:

1. Frostfire Phoenix: A magnificent and rare creature that embodies the essence of the realm, the Frostfire Phoenix is a symbol of both fire and ice. Its wings shimmer with frost, while its feathers emit a warm, fiery glow.

2. Snowstrider Reindeer: These majestic creatures are well-adapted to the snowy terrain of the Frostfire mountains. Their large, powerful hooves allow them to navigate treacherous ice and deep snow with ease.

3. Frostfang Wolves: Resilient and ferocious, Frostfang Wolves are native to the colder regions of Frostfire. Their thick fur and sharp teeth make them formidable hunters in the icy landscapes.

4. Aurora Bats: During the nights of the Frostfire winter, the skies come alive with the graceful dance of Aurora Bats. These luminous creatures emit a soft, enchanting light as they soar through the sky.

5. Icewing Owls: Silent and wise, Icewing Owls are revered as symbols of wisdom and mystery. Their feathers are said to hold magical properties and are often sought after for crafting powerful artifacts.

Flora:

1. Icebloom Flowers: Delicate and enchanting, Icebloom Flowers are a rare sight in the frozen lands of Frostfire. They bloom only during the brief period of warmth in summer, adding vibrant colours to the icy landscape.

2. Frostwood Trees: These ancient trees are well-adapted to the cold climate of Frostfire. Their bark glistens like ice, and they provide shelter for many creatures that call the realm their home.

3. Glacier Roses: These hardy and resilient roses bloom even in the harshest winter conditions. Their petals shine like ice, and they are often used in herbal remedies for their healing properties.

4. Emberfern: An unusual plant that thrives in the warm plains of Frostfire. The Emberfern has leaves that emit a gentle warmth, providing a natural source of heat for small creatures during the chilly nights.

5. Frostfire Crystals: These exquisite crystals are found deep within the heart of the Frostfire mountains. They are highly valued for their beauty and are believed to hold magical energies.

The diverse fauna and flora of Frostfire add to the enchantment and mystery of the realm. As adventurers explore the lands, they will encounter these extraordinary creatures and plants, each adding to the uniqueness and allure of Frostfire's natural wonders.

Local laws of Frostfire

In the lands of Frostfire, where warm fertile plains meet towering ice-capped mountains, various local laws and regulations govern the conduct of its inhabitants and ensure the smooth functioning of society. Here are some specific local laws in Frostfire:

1. Preservation of the Natural Balance: Frostfire places great emphasis on maintaining the delicate balance between its warm plains and icy mountains. Strict regulations govern hunting and fishing to ensure the conservation of wildlife and protect the ecosystem.

2. Mountain Pass Safety: The mountain passes of Frostfire are essential routes for trade and travel. It is mandatory for travellers and merchants to follow designated paths and register their journeys with the local authorities to ensure their safety and avoid accidents.

3. Protection of the Fire Glades: The Fire Glades are revered as sacred lands in Frostfire, and it is strictly prohibited to disturb or damage these unique and beautiful regions. Anyone caught trespassing or harming the Fire Glades faces severe penalties.

4. Ice-Mining Safety Measures: Frostfire's mining industry focuses on harvesting ice from its mountains. Regulations are in place to maintain the safety of ice miners, and strict guidelines govern the extraction process to avoid avalanches and collapses.

5. Magical Ice Regulation: Frostfire acknowledges the presence of magical ice formations, some of which possess unique properties. The unauthorized or reckless use of these magical elements is restricted, and only trained individuals are allowed to handle them.

6. Agricultural Practices: Farming is a crucial part of Frostfire's economy. Farmers are required to adhere to guidelines regarding land usage, irrigation, and crop rotation to ensure sustainable agricultural practices.

7. Hospitality for Travelers: Frostfire takes pride in its reputation for warm hospitality. Local laws encourage citizens to extend kindness and assistance to travellers, offering shelter and provisions when needed.

8. Tolerance of Magical Diversity: Frostfire has a diverse population, including individuals with magical abilities. Discrimination based on magical affinity is strictly forbidden, and laws promote inclusivity and mutual respect among citizens.

These local laws contribute to the orderly functioning of Frostfire, fostering a balanced coexistence between its natural beauty and the vibrant communities that thrive within its borders. The observance of these regulations ensures the safety, prosperity, and well-being of its inhabitants in the face of the region's unique climate and magical influences.

In Frostfire, adherence to these local laws is not just a matter of governance; it's a reflection of the deep connection between the land and its people. The residents of Frostfire view these regulations as a sacred pact with the elements, a commitment to protect their homeland's delicate equilibrium. This profound sense of responsibility has led to a harmonious coexistence between the warm plains and icy mountains, fostering a unique culture of respect for both nature and each other. Violating these laws is not just a legal transgression but a breach of the unspoken trust that binds the inhabitants of Frostfire to their majestic and diverse landscape.

Cults and religions of Frostfire

In the lands of Frostfire, a realm characterized by its unique climate and formidable mountains, various cults and religions have emerged, each reflecting the harsh environment and spiritual beliefs of the inhabitants. Here are some of the specific cults and religions found in Frostfire:

1. The Frostheart Covenant: This ancient and revered cult worships the Frostheart, a legendary crystal said to have fallen from the heavens during a comet's passing. The Frostheart is believed to hold immense power and wisdom. The Covenant conducts sacred ceremonies to pay homage to the crystal and seek its guidance in times of need.

2. The Cult of the Frost Spirits: A shamanic cult that venerates the spirits of the frost and snow. They believe that the spirits of nature inhabit the snow-covered mountains and can bestow blessings or bring calamity to those who cross their paths. The cult's rituals include dance, drumming, and offerings to appease the frost spirits.

3. The Brotherhood of the Howling Wolves: This secretive cult reveres the wolves that roam the snowy wilderness of Frostfire. They believe that the wolves are emissaries of a greater celestial wolf deity. The Brotherhood performs moonlit rituals and ceremonies to invoke the spirit of the celestial wolf.

4. The Frostborn Clan: A tribal cult of nomadic people who revere the ancient Frostborn, said to be the ancestors of the clans. They follow sacred rituals and rites to honour their ancestors and seek their guidance in matters of the heart and soul.

These cults and religions add depth and richness to the cultural fabric of Frostfire, each offering a unique perspective on life, nature, and the spiritual realm. Some of these cults may be practiced openly and integrated into the everyday lives of the people, while others might remain secluded and reserved for those who are initiated into their mysteries.

Rumours and adventure hooks for Frostfire

1. The Frozen Heart: Rumours speak of an ancient artifact hidden deep within the ice-capped mountains of Frostfire. Said to be a crystallized heart of a powerful ice elemental, the artifact possesses the ability to control the weather and freeze entire regions. Adventurers are tasked with retrieving or safeguarding the artifact, leading them on a treacherous journey through blizzards and icy caverns.

2. The Icefall Cult: Whispers of a secretive cult that worships an ancient ice deity have spread across Frostfire. Villagers fear that the cult's dark rituals may be responsible for the unending winter that grips the land. The players are enlisted to infiltrate the cult, discover their intentions, and put an end to their malevolent practices.

3. The Thieves of Frostgate: A notorious group of thieves known as the "Icy Shadows" has been targeting wealthy merchants and nobles passing through Frostgate. The players are hired to apprehend or negotiate with the elusive thieves, and in doing so, they might uncover a plot that goes far beyond simple theft.

4. The Spirit of the Glacier: Legends tell of a mystical spirit that resides within the heart of a glacier in Frostfire. It is said that those who make contact with the spirit gain profound wisdom and insight. The players embark on a spiritual quest to seek out this ancient being, facing both physical and metaphysical challenges along the way.

5. The Frozen Expedition: A renowned explorer disappeared while leading an expedition into the unexplored frozen wilderness of Frostfire. The players are called upon to follow the explorer's footsteps, braving deadly avalanches, icy crevasses, and hostile creatures to uncover the truth behind the mysterious disappearance.

Adventure Hooks:

1. The Icebound Temple: An ancient temple, buried deep within a glacier, has been unearthed after a century of being lost to history. The players must navigate through a labyrinth of frozen chambers, solving puzzles and overcoming guardians to uncover the temple's secrets and the power it holds.

2. The Frozen Drake: Reports of a fearsome ice drake roaming the mountains of Frostfire have reached the city of Frostgate. The players are hired to track down and deal with the creature before it causes further devastation to the local wildlife and settlements.

3. The Crystal Harvest: A rare and valuable crystal is rumoured to grow in a hidden valley where the cold meets the warmth. The players must brave the harsh elements to locate and harvest these crystals, all while facing competition from rival treasure hunters and dealing with the magical properties of the crystals themselves.

4. The Frostfire Tournament: A grand tournament is being held in Frostfire to showcase the martial prowess and magical skills of warriors and mages from across the realm. The players are invited to participate, seeking glory and recognition, but they soon realize that the tournament is a cover for a more sinister plot unfolding behind the scenes.

5. The Frozen Feywild: A magical portal to the Frostfire Feywild has opened, allowing creatures from this icy realm to slip into the mortal world. The players must navigate this surreal and dangerous realm, confronting fey creatures and powerful beings that are not bound by the laws of reality.

These rumours and adventure hooks beckon adventurers to venture into the frozen expanse of Frostfire, where they will encounter mythical creatures, ancient artifacts, and magical phenomena. As they explore the chilling landscapes and face the challenges that lie ahead, they will unravel mysteries, gain fame or infamy, and shape the destiny of Frostfire and its inhabitants.

Sunfire Dominion

City State – Sunfire Dominion

In the city of Sunfire Dominion, nestled between high mountains, the sparkling coastline, and the proximity to the desert, areas of interest are:

1. **The Sun-Kissed Plaza**: A bustling square at the heart of the city, bathed in warm sunlight throughout the day. Here, traders, merchants, and entertainers gather to create a vibrant atmosphere of commerce and celebration.

2. **The Citadel of Radiance**: A majestic fortress that stands as a symbol of the city's strength and resilience. From its elevated position, it overlooks the coast and the vast desert beyond, providing strategic defence against potential threats.

3. **The Golden Harbor**: A busy port where ships from distant lands dock to trade exotic goods and treasures. The harbour serves as a crucial gateway connecting Sunfire Dominion to the wider world.

4. **The Duneswept Bazaar**: A lively marketplace where colourful stalls offer spices, fabrics, and unique trinkets from the nearby desert. The market is alive with the vibrant cultures of the desert nomads who come to trade.

5. **The Oasis Gardens**: A lush oasis tucked within the city's boundaries, created through ingenuity and careful water management. The gardens offer respite from the arid climate and showcase a variety of plants from both the desert and other regions.

6. **The Flameweaver's Guild**: An esteemed guild of skilled fire mages and pyromancers who harness the power of the sun and flames. They are sought after for their expertise in fire-based magic and the manipulation of heat.

7. **The Temple of Eternal Light**: A grand temple dedicated to worshipping the Eternal Sun, the source of life and energy in the Sunfire Dominion. It stands as a centre of faith and enlightenment, attracting pilgrims and devotees from all over Emberfrost.

8. **The Cliffside Caravanserai**: A unique structure perched on the edge of the cliffs, providing a resting place for desert travellers and caravans. Here, visitors can experience the desert lifestyle and partake in cultural exchanges.

9. **The Solarium**: An observatory perched atop a mountain, offering unobstructed views of both the celestial night sky and the sun-drenched coastline. Astronomers and stargazers gather here to study the cosmos and the dance of the stars.

10. **The Sandfire Arena**: An impressive amphitheatre where gladiatorial combats and captivating performances take place. The arena hosts tournaments and events, showcasing the combat prowess and artistic talents of the Sunfire Dominion's inhabitants.

Sunfire Dominion, situated at the crossroads of diverse landscapes, thrives as a vibrant fusion of coastal, desert, and mountain cultures. Its strategic location, abundant resources, and reverence for the Eternal Sun make it a centre of prosperity and cultural exchange in Emberfrost.

Other key towns and villages in Sunfire Dominion

In the radiant realm of Sunfire Dominion, where the lands are next to high mountains, on the coast, and near the desert, here are the main towns and villages:

1. **Sunholm**: The capital and heart of Sunfire Dominion, Sunholm stands tall at the base of the grand Sunpeak Mountains. It's a city of grand architecture and intricate mosaics, reflecting the kingdom's vibrant culture. The Royal Palace, adorned with golden domes, sits majestically at its center.

2. **Sandshore**: This coastal town is a bustling port that connects Sunfire Dominion to distant lands across the sea. The sun-kissed beaches attract travellers and traders alike, and the markets overflow with exotic goods from far-off lands.

3. **Emberbrook**: Nestled along the banks of a winding river, Emberbrook is a picturesque village known for its artisans and craftsmen. Skilled potters and weavers create beautiful pottery and textiles inspired by the warm colours of the setting sun.

4. **Dunesreach**: Perched on the edge of the vast desert, Dunesreach is a desert oasis surrounded by lush palm groves. The village's residents are skilled in water conservation and trade precious spices and rare herbs found only in the desert.

5. **Goldenshade**: Amidst sunflower fields and orchards of citrus trees, Goldenshade is a village renowned for its exquisite fruits and fragrant blooms. The villagers celebrate the harvest with lively festivals and dances under the shimmering sun.

6. **Mooncrest**: High in the mountains, where the sun sets, Mooncrest is a village with a mystical aura. It is said that during the full moon, the mountain glows with an ethereal light, and the villagers hold ceremonies to honour the celestial spirits.

7. **Sandsong**: Found on the outskirts of the desert, Sandsong is a lively town famous for its skilled musicians and dancers. The captivating melodies and vibrant performances honour the desert's beauty and the harmony between nature and its people.

8. **Silversand**: This coastal town, blessed with silver sandy beaches, is a favoured destination for relaxation and leisure. Visitors come to bask in the sun and enjoy the refreshing sea breeze.

9. **Cinderforge**: Situated amidst volcanic peaks, Cinderforge is a town built around ancient lava formations. The villagers are skilled blacksmiths who craft exquisite jewellery and artifacts inspired by the fiery heart of their home.

10. **Starfall**: Located in a valley surrounded by mountains, Starfall is renowned for its stargazers and astrologers. The village's residents are deeply connected to the celestial realms and believe that the stars hold secrets to the kingdom's destiny.

These towns and villages embody the vibrant spirit of Sunfire Dominion, where the majestic mountains, coastal beauty, and desert charm create a realm of diverse cultures and awe-inspiring landscapes.

Key figures in power and influence in the city of Sunfire Dominion

In the city of Sunfire Dominion, the key figures in power and influence are:

1. **Lady Arwala Ishulay**: Arwala, sister of Queen Imara, is a powerful and influential figure in her own right. She is known for her strategic acumen and plays an active role in the city states governance.

2. **Lord Raoul Sunstrider**: Lord Raoul, husband of Lady Arwala, is a charismatic and visionary leader. He is admired for his wisdom, diplomacy, and dedication to the prosperity of the city state.

3. **Grand Vizier Malik Sandborn**: As the chief advisor to the Lady Arwala, Grand Vizier Malik wields significant influence over the city states policies and decisions. He is a skilled diplomat and negotiator.

4. **Commander Talia Flameguard**: The head of the Sunfire Dominion's military forces, Commander Talia is a seasoned warrior and tactician. She is responsible for the kingdom's defence and military strategy.

5. **High Priestess Serena Sunweaver**: The spiritual leader of Sunfire Dominion, High Priestess Serena presides over religious ceremonies and provides guidance to the kingdom's citizens.

6. **Merchant Lord Tobias Goldsun**: The leader of the Sunfire Traders' Guild, Merchant Lord Tobias is a prominent figure in the kingdom's trade and economy. He is known for his business acumen and wealth.

7. **Councillor Alistair Stormwatch**: A member of the High King's Council of Advisors, Councillor Alistair represents the interests of the people and ensures their voices are heard in the kingdom's decision-making.

8. **Lady Selene Moonshadow**: An influential noble in Sunfire Dominion, Lady Selene is a patron of the arts and a prominent socialite. She hosts lavish events and supports cultural development within the kingdom.

9. **Arch mage Lucian Firestorm**: The head of the Sunfire Academy of Arcane Arts, Arch mage Lucian is a renowned spellcaster and scholar. He oversees magical education and research in the city.

10. **Ranger Captain Elara Swiftwind**: A skilled ranger and tracker, Captain Elara is responsible for patrolling the borders of Sunfire Dominion and protecting the kingdom from external threats.

11. **Lady Elowen Sunseer**: A prominent figure among the Sunfire Dominion's elite, Lady Elowen is known for her passion for the arts and patronage of local artisans. Her support for cultural endeavours enriches the kingdom's artistic landscape and fosters creativity.

12. **Captain Cedric Stormrider**: A daring naval officer, Captain Cedric commands the Sunfire Dominion's formidable fleet. His leadership ensures the security of the kingdom's coastal regions and facilitates maritime trade.

These key figures in Sunfire Dominion hold significant power and influence over the kingdom's governance, culture, and prosperity. Their interactions and decisions can shape the fate of the realm, creating opportunities for intrigue, adventure, and epic tales within the radiant city of Sunfire Dominion.

Key figures in the lands of Sunfire Dominion

City Officials:

1. **Lady Arwala Ishulay**: The reigning Lady of Sunfire Dominion, known for her strong leadership and dedication to her people.

2. **Lord Kaelen Sunstrider**: The High Chancellor and chief advisor to Lady Arwala, responsible for overseeing the governance of Sunfire Dominion.

Prominent Citizens:

1. **Lady Elara Emberheart**: A prominent noblewoman and Lady-in-Waiting to Lady Arwala, respected for her intelligence and grace.

2. **Sir Malik Fireblade**: The Captain of the Sunfire Knights, a skilled and honorable knightly order dedicated to protecting the realm from external threats.

Guild Leaders:

1. **Thalorin Goldentongue**: The head of the Illuminators' Guild, a society of scholars and sages dedicated to unravelling the mysteries of ancient texts and artifacts.

2. **Master Caelia Moonshadow**: The leader of the Moonlit Coven, a mysterious and powerful guild of witches and warlocks who draw power from the phases of the moon.

Merchants:

1. **Jareth Stormcaller**: A successful merchant and trader, known for his shrewd business acumen and vast network of connections.

2. **Lyra Emberweave**: An enterprising cloth merchant, renowned for her exquisite fabrics and elegant designs.

Tavern Owners:

1. **Gavin Firesong**: The proprietor of the Emberlight Tavern, a popular establishment known for its lively atmosphere and captivating performances.

2. **Isabella Sunflower**: The owner of the Sunfire Spice Bazaar, a vibrant tavern and marketplace where exotic spices and delicacies are traded.

Cult Leaders:

1. **High Priestess Selene Shadowsong**: The leader of the Cult of Eternal Sun, a devoted cult that venerates the mythical celestial body known as the Eternal Sun.

Adventurers and Heroes:

1. **Roran Blazeheart**: A fearless dragon rider and hero, renowned for his valour in protecting Sunfire Dominion from aerial threats.

2. **Elysia Dawnstrider**: A skilled ranger and guardian of Sunfire Dominion's borders, known for her connection with nature and her ability to track down elusive enemies.

Scholars and Sages:

1. **Arch mage Thaddeus Emberwing**: The foremost mage in Sunfire Dominion, responsible for the study of fire magic and the training of aspiring wizards.

2. **Lady Mariana Sunseeker**: A wise sage and historian, known for her extensive knowledge of Sunfire Dominion's past and its ancient artifacts.

Commerce of Sunfire Dominion

Commerce in the lands of Sunfire Dominion is as diverse and vibrant as the varied landscapes that grace the realm. Situated near high mountains, on the coast, and close to the desert, Sunfire Dominion boasts a unique blend of trade opportunities that cater to both local needs and the demands of distant city-states.

The coastal regions of Sunfire Dominion provide ample opportunities for maritime commerce. The well-protected harbours and bustling ports facilitate the trade of goods, passengers, and cultural influences between different regions and city-states. Ships from all corners of Emberfrost and beyond dock at the harbours, fostering economic ties and cultural exchange.

The mountains of Sunfire Dominion are rich in precious stones and minerals. Granite, marble and quartz are among the valuable treasures found within the depths of the mountains. Expert craftspeople in the region skilfully make exquisite building finishes, statues and decorative features attracting wealthy buyers and traders seeking these rare and hardwearing items.

With the desert lying at its borders, Sunfire Dominion also plays a significant role in the trade of spices, herbs, and exotic goods from distant lands. Trader's journey through the desert's scorching sands to bring unique products from far-off realms, filling the markets of Sunfire Dominion with a vibrant array of foreign wares.

Agriculture thrives in the northern temperate regions of Sunfire Dominion. The fertile lands yield an abundance of crops, such as grains, fruits, and vegetables, which are essential for sustaining the local population and for trade with neighbouring regions.

Sunfire Dominion is also home to skilled artisans and craftsmen who create fine pottery, intricate tapestries, and other artisanal goods. These products are highly sought after for their beauty and craftsmanship, attracting merchants and traders looking to enrich their offerings with unique items.

Furthermore, Sunfire Dominion's proximity to the desert opens up opportunities for the trade of valuable spices and dyes. Merchants from the city of Sunfire Dominion venture into the arid lands to acquire these coveted commodities, which are then distributed throughout Emberfrost and beyond.

Amidst the bustling markets and thriving trade routes of Sunfire Dominion, there exists a group of resilient and daring individuals known as the Desert Traders. These intrepid merchants embark on arduous journeys across the scorching sands of the neighbouring desert, venturing into the heart of the arid wilderness to source exotic goods from far-off realms.

The Desert Traders are a vital link between Sunfire Dominion and the distant lands beyond the desert's horizon. They navigate the unforgiving terrain, braving sandstorms and extreme temperatures, to acquire precious commodities like rare spices, aromatic herbs, and vibrant dyes. These prized treasures, not found within the borders of the dominion, add a touch of the exotic to the local markets.

Their caravans, adorned with colourful fabrics and laden with treasures, make their way through treacherous desert oases, establishing trade connections with nomadic tribes and distant trading partners. Upon their return to Sunfire Dominion, these intrepid traders enrich the local markets with a vibrant array of foreign wares, drawing the awe and admiration of residents and traders alike.

The commerce in the lands of Sunfire Dominion is a reflection of the realm's diversity and resources. Its strategic location near the coast, mountains, and desert has established the city as a key player in the economic prosperity and cultural exchange that flourishes across Emberfrost.

Local festivals of Sunfire Dominion

In the lands of Sunfire Dominion, where the high mountains meet the coast and the desert, the people celebrate a vibrant array of festivals that draw inspiration from their unique surroundings. Some of the local festivals celebrated in Sunfire Dominion include:

1. Sunfire Festival: The grand Sunfire Festival marks the beginning of the summer season and celebrates the power of the sun. The festival takes place on the coast, where people gather to witness the sunrise over the horizon. They engage in various water sports, including swimming, sailing, and surfing, to cool off from the summer heat. The festival culminates in a spectacular display of fire dancing and fireworks as the sun sets.

2. Sand Dunes Symphony: Celebrated in the desert regions, the Sand Dunes Symphony honours the beauty of the shifting sand dunes. People participate in camel races, desert safaris, and sandboarding competitions. Musicians and storytellers gather in desert camps to create a symphony of traditional tunes and tales.

3. Mountain Song Festival: As autumn sets in, the Mountain Song Festival takes place in the high mountain villages of Sunfire Dominion. The festival celebrates the changing colours of the leaves and the tranquil beauty of the mountains. Musicians and singers from different communities come together to perform folk songs and ballads, connecting the mountain dwellers through music and shared stories.

4. Seafoam Spectacle: Celebrated during the monsoon season, the Seafoam Spectacle is held on the coast as the stormy waves bring forth foam. People engage in boat races, fishing competitions, and water-related festivities. The festival is also dedicated to honouring sea deities for safe voyages and abundant catches.

5. Eternal Ember Eve: Held during the winter solstice, the Eternal Ember Eve festival celebrates the warmth and light of the ever-burning embers that keep the mountain villages cozy during the cold season. People light bonfires and exchange gifts, and the festival is marked by singing, dancing, and a feast of traditional winter delicacies.

6. Desert Starlit Nights: A festival that coincides with meteor showers, Desert Starlit Nights is celebrated in the desert, where the night sky shines bright with stars. People gather in open spaces for stargazing, storytelling, and making wishes upon shooting stars.

7. Harvest Harmony: Celebrated during the harvest season, Harvest Harmony brings together farmers, artisans, and communities to celebrate the bountiful yields of the land. The festival includes colourful processions, folk dances, and a grand market where people trade their produce and crafts.

8. Flameheart Revelry: A festival that pays homage to the legendary Flameheart dynasty, Flameheart Revelry commemorates the deeds of past rulers and their contributions to Sunfire Dominion. The festival includes historical reenactments, parades, and a grand banquet in honour of the Flameheart legacy.

These festivals in Sunfire Dominion capture the spirit of its diverse landscapes and cultural heritage, creating joyous occasions for the people to come together, celebrate life, and strengthen the bonds of their communities.

Fauna and Flora specific to Sunfire Dominion

In the lands of Sunfire Dominion, a realm nestled between high mountains, the coast, and the desert, a vibrant array of fauna and flora thrives, adapted to the diverse landscapes and climates. Here are some notable examples of fauna and flora specific to Sunfire Dominion:

Fauna:

1. Desertwind Gryphons: Majestic creatures with the body of a lion and the wings of an eagle, Desertwind Gryphons soar the skies above the desert plains. Their golden feathers shimmer in the sunlight, and they are believed to be emissaries of the sun god.

2. Sandstrider Camels: These hardy and stoic creatures are the primary means of transportation in the desert regions of Sunfire Dominion. With their humped backs and wide, padded feet, they navigate the sandy dunes with ease.

3. Flame-tailed Lizards: Tiny reptiles with bright red tails, Flame-tailed Lizards are known for their unique ability to withstand intense heat. They often seek shelter in rocky crevices during the scorching days.

4. Sunfire Phoenixes: Rare and revered, Sunfire Phoenixes are fiery beings that are said to be born from the heart of the sun itself. They radiate intense heat and are protectors of the realm.

5. Sand Serpents: Elusive and mysterious, Sand Serpents are giant snakes that burrow beneath the desert sands. Their iridescent scales reflect the colours of the desert, making them nearly invisible.

Flora:

1. Sunbloom Cacti: Resilient and beautiful, Sunbloom Cacti dot the arid landscape with their vibrant flowers that bloom in shades of orange, red, and yellow. They store water to survive the long periods of drought.

2. Oasis Palms: Tall and graceful palms that line the oases and provide valuable shade and nourishment to the desert inhabitants. The sweet fruit of the Oasis Palms is a cherished delicacy.

3. Emberthorn Bushes: These thorny bushes are native to the warmer regions of Sunfire Dominion. Their bright red berries are both a source of sustenance and a key ingredient in medicinal potions.

4. Solaris Vines: Climbing up the rocky cliffs and mountainsides, Solaris Vines bear golden flowers that seem to shimmer in the sunlight. Their nectar is a favourite of the hummingbirds in the region.

5. Moonlit Lilies: These ethereal lilies bloom during the cooler nights, and their petals emit a soft, soothing glow. They are often associated with moonlit rituals and nocturnal creatures.

The diverse fauna and flora of Sunfire Dominion add to the enchantment and splendour of the realm. As adventurers explore the lands, they will encounter these extraordinary creatures and plants, each contributing to the richness and allure of Sunfire Dominion's natural wonders.

Local laws of Sunfire Dominion

In the lands of Sunfire Dominion, where high mountains, coastal regions, and deserts converge, various local laws and regulations govern the conduct of its people and ensure a harmonious society. Here are some specific local laws in Sunfire Dominion:

1. Trade Regulations: Sunfire Dominion has a bustling coastal trade network. Laws are in place to monitor and regulate trade activities, ensuring fair practices and preventing smuggling or illegal transactions.

2. Sand Dunes Protection: The vast sand dunes of the desert are a dangerous place, and fear of further encroachment is ever present in the minds of Sunfire Dominions inhabitants. They are acutely aware of the ecosystem's balance. Laws prohibit any activities that may cause expansion of the natural dunes.

3. Water Usage Control: In the arid desert regions, water is a precious resource. Strict regulations govern water usage to ensure equitable distribution and prevent wastage.

4. Fire Safety Measures: Sunfire Dominion's coastal regions are vulnerable to wildfires. Laws mandate precautionary measures to prevent and control fires, particularly during the dry seasons.

5. Magic Usage Guidelines: The use of magic in Sunfire Dominion is prevalent. Laws regulate the practice of magic to ensure public safety and prevent misuse or unauthorized use of magical abilities.

6. Religious Freedom: Sunfire Dominion is home to a variety of religious beliefs. Laws protect the right to practice one's religion freely and promote religious tolerance among its diverse population.

These local laws contribute to the prosperity and stability of Sunfire Dominion, fostering a harmonious coexistence between its natural beauty and the cultural diversity of its inhabitants.

Cults and religions of Sunfire Dominion

In the radiant lands of Sunfire Dominion, a realm blessed by the warmth of the sun and the mystical desert winds, various cults and religions have blossomed, reflecting the unique environment and spiritual beliefs of the people. Here are some of the specific cults and religions found in Sunfire Dominion:

1. The Order of the Blazing Sun: This prestigious and revered religious order venerates the sun as the ultimate source of life and energy. They believe that the sun bestows blessings upon the land and its people, and they conduct elaborate ceremonies at sunrise and sunset to pay homage to the solar deity.

2. The Order of the Silent Sands: A nomadic religious group that reveres the vast desert and its ever-changing dunes. They believe that the shifting sands hold ancient wisdom and are a source of spiritual guidance. The Order practices meditation and desert treks to connect with the raw power of the desert.

3. The Order of Oasis Keepers: A sect of druids who protect and venerate the life-giving oases scattered throughout the desert. They believe that the oases hold a deep connection to the spirit of the land, and they conduct rituals to ensure the oases' prosperity and purity.

4. The Children of the Phoenix: A small and secretive group that worships the mythical phoenix, a legendary bird associated with rebirth and immortality. They believe that the phoenix will rise from the ashes of destruction to herald a new era of prosperity.

5. The Sunseekers: A group of wandering pilgrims who travel across the vast desert to seek ancient and sacred landmarks. They believe that such journeys grant them spiritual insights to the ancient civilisations, long since lost to the mists of time.

These diverse cults and religions form an intricate tapestry of beliefs and practices within Sunfire Dominion, shaping the spiritual and cultural lives of its people. Some of these faiths may be embraced by the general populace, while others remain esoteric and known only to a select few. The rich spiritual tapestry of Sunfire Dominion adds depth to the realm, making it a land of enchantment, fervour, and divine wonder.

Rumours and adventure hooks for Sunfire Dominion

1. The Phoenix Prophecy: Whispers abound of an ancient prophecy foretelling the rebirth of a legendary phoenix in the heart of Sunfire Dominion. The phoenix is said to bring a new era of prosperity and power to the realm. Adventurers are sought to protect or exploit this prophecy, navigating through desert oases, forgotten ruins, and treacherous sandstorms in their quest for the mythical creature.

2. The Lost Tomb of Ra'Sul: Legends speak of a hidden tomb deep within the scorching sands of Sunfire Dominion, said to be the final resting place of the powerful and enigmatic sorcerer, Ra'Sul. The players are hired to find and explore the tomb, encountering ancient traps, guardian spirits, and the allure of powerful arcane artifacts.

3. The Sandstorm Raiders: Rumours abound of a group of desert raiders known as the "Sandstorm Marauders" who mercilessly plunder caravans and settlements across Sunfire Dominion. The players are tasked with tracking down and dealing with this notorious band of thieves, uncovering their motives and unravelling the mysterious leader behind their operations.

4. The Oasis of Healing: Tales of a mystical oasis with miraculous healing powers have spread through Sunfire Dominion. People from far and wide seek the oasis to cure ailments and injuries. The players must navigate through the perilous desert, overcoming natural dangers and rival groups, to reach the oasis and learn the truth behind its magical properties.

5. The Nomad's Legacy: The sudden appearance of ancient artifacts in the possession of nomadic tribes, hints at a long-forgotten legacy from the realm's past. The players are tasked with unravelling the mystery behind these artifacts, leading them on a journey through shifting sand dunes, hidden canyons, and encounters with the enigmatic nomad tribes.

Adventure Hooks:

1. The Sunfire Tournament: A grand tournament is held in the capital city of Sunfire Dominion, showcasing the martial prowess and magical abilities of its contestants. The players are invited to participate, seeking honour, fame, and potential alliances. However, they soon discover that political intrigue and rivalries among the contestants add another layer of complexity to the tournament.

2. The Scorching Sands Expedition: An esteemed scholar has hired the players to accompany an expedition into the uncharted desert regions, in search of ancient ruins and lost civilizations. The journey will test their survival skills as they face extreme temperatures, sandstorms, and encounters with the desert's mystical denizens.

3. The Cursed Sceptre: An artifact, known as the "Sceptre of Burning Sands," has been stolen from the Sunfire Dominion's royal treasury. The players are tasked with retrieving the sceptre, following leads through bustling markets, secretive cults, and shadowy underworld connections.

4. The Firewalkers' Ritual: The enigmatic Firewalkers, a group of fire-worshipping zealots, have invited the players to undergo a sacred initiation ritual. To earn the Firewalkers' trust and knowledge of their ancient rituals, the players must prove their dedication by braving a perilous walk through a raging bonfire.

5. The Djinn's Whisper: Rumours speak of a djinn who roams the deserts, granting wishes to those who can find and summon it. The players embark on a journey to locate the elusive djinn, but they must be wary of the djinn's tricks and the potential consequences of their wishes.

These rumours and adventure hooks beckon adventurers to venture into the scorching landscapes of Sunfire Dominion, where they will encounter ancient secrets, magical artifacts, and mystical beings. As they explore the desert realms and face the challenges that lie ahead, they will shape the destiny of Sunfire Dominion and leave their mark on the history of this sun-blessed land.

Well done, fellow adventurer!

You have made your way through the third volume of fantasy role-playing game aids and the lands of adventure. But fear not, for the journey is far from over.

With each page, I hope to have sparked your imagination and helped you to create more memorable moments for your players. But there are always more tales to be told, and I am already hard at work on the next volume of adventure to help you on your way. There will be an Atlas of Emberfrost, with full colour maps and more information about the lands.

Remember, sharing the joy of a well-crafted plot is the best way to build a community of gamers who share your passion for adventure.

Thank you for your continued support. Where will your next adventure take you?

Printed in Great Britain
by Amazon

32348745R00112